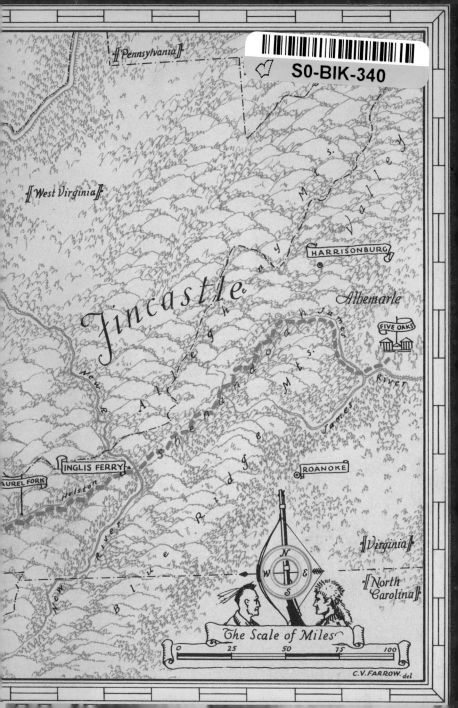

Pennsylvania

West Virginia

Harrisonburg

Tincastle

Albemarle

Allegheny Mts. Valley

Shenandoah Mts.

James

James River

Blue Ridge

New River

FIVE OAKS

INGLIS FERRY

LAUREL FORK

Holston

ROANOKE

Virginia

North Carolina

The Scale of Miles

0   25   50   75   100

N
W   E
S

C.V. FARROW. del

Charles J. Reeve

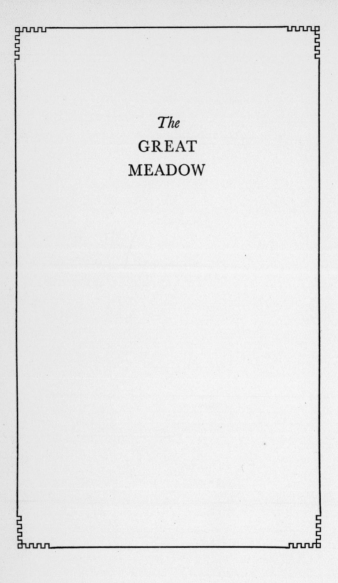

The
GREAT
MEADOW

Elizabeth Madox Roberts

is the author of

UNDER THE TREE

Poems, 1922

THE TIME OF MAN

A Novel, 1926

MY HEART AND MY FLESH

A Novel, 1927

JINGLING IN THE WIND

A Novel, 1928

The
GREAT
MEADOW

BY

Elizabeth Madox Roberts

New York
THE LITERARY GUILD
1930

TO

GLENWAY WESCOTT

THE GREAT MEADOW

1774, and Diony, in the spring, hearing Sam, her brother, scratching at a tune on the fiddle, hearing him break a song over the taut wires and fling out with his voice to supply all that the tune lacked, placed herself momentarily in life, calling mentally her name, Diony Hall. "I, Diony Hall," her thought said, gathering herself close, subtracting herself from the diffused life of the house that closed about her. Sam was singing, flinging the song free of the worried strings, making a very good tune of it:

There was a ship sailed for the North Amer-i-kee—
Crying, O the lonesome lowlands low—
There was a ship sailed for the North Amer-i-kee,
And she went by the name of the Golden Van-i-tee,
And she sailed from the lowlands low. . . .

"I, Diony Hall," her hands said back to her thought, her fingers knitting wool. Beyond her spread the floor which was of hard smooth wood, and beyond again arose the walls of the house, and outside reached the clearings of the plantation, Five Oaks the name her father called it by. Then came the trees and the rolling hills of Albemarle County and the

3

upper waters of the James—Rockfish Creek, the Tye,
Fluvanna, Rivanna. The world reached straight
then, into infinity, laid out beyond the level of herself in a far-going horizontal, although report said
of it that it bent to a round and made a globe. She
was aware of infinity outward going and never returning. "I, Diony," she said, throwing the little
strand of wool over her needle and making a web.
Back then from infinity, having recovered herself, and
the house stood close, intimately sensed. Sam's music:

> There was a ship sailed for the North Amer-i-kee—
> Crying, O the lonesome lowlands low . . .

The house was of two log parts standing near
together, a covered passage lying between which the
boys of the family had named the dog alley because
the dogs lay there to sleep. One of the buildings was
called the "old house" and this was used now for the
kitchen and for the weaving. There was a loft above
this room, reached by a corner stairway, and above
in the loft were two rooms where the boys and their
visitors slept. The dog alley was closed overhead and
floored beneath. Beyond it lay the "new house," a
building of equal size with the old and flanked by a
great chimney at the front as the other was flanked
by a similar chimney at the rear. Below in the new
house was the great room where the heads of the

family slept, where the elegant life of the plantation was enacted, where Thomas Hall, the father of the house, kept his books on a shelf. A corner stairway led to rooms above, two chambers. When the dogs, hearing a wildcat or a fox, would run through the dog alley on their way to the edge of the clearing, the boards of the puncheoned floor of the passage would rattle with a great clatter and then lie still. Thus the house stood about Diony.

1774, a blustering evening in the spring, and they sat together by the fire in the new room, Thomas Hall, Polly, his wife, and Reuben, Sam, Diony, and Betty, their children. Sam teased the fiddle to make it yield a song, but Reuben sat in idleness, resting from a hard day in the field where he had driven the plow among stumpy furrows. Diony and Betty knitted stockings of woolen yarn, and Thomas would settle himself to his book when he had trimmed the candle flame and over his face would flow a weariness that he must endure this slight interruption.

Diony leaped swiftly into the outer margins of each being and back then, thinking with the return, "I, Diony. I am one, myself." Polly found wool for the girls to knit, winding strands into balls. Diony looked at her as she sat slightly bent above the yarns in her lap and she saw that she was beautiful although she had passed the first of youth by and had become large and hearty. Her back touched the chair lightly and her body moved from moment to moment with the minute sway of the wool as it mounted on the ball, as it flowed through her fingers, but if one spoke to her or if two spoke together her subtle response was more infinite than speech. By the light of the fire as Sam had replenished it, Diony looked down at her own limbs as she sat swiftly knitting, at her moving fingers, at the roundness of her growing frame. She was like her mother, as had always been said in the house. "Diony favors her mother, Polly," had been said, or again, "She's the liven image of her mammy." Betty was a small shadow at the end of the bench, knitting half-heartedly, favoring nobody but herself. "I, Diony, myself," thought said, recovering. Thomas Hall was reading his philosopher, Berkeley, *The Principles of Human Knowledge* being spread now in his hands, or his right hand would be faintly lifted and stayed in its act, as if the inner reader would share the thought with some other but refrained, being lonely and discreet.

"Somebody comes here," Sam said. "My thumb has got an itch on the knuckle place."

Diony had heard a distant coming of horses along the creek way and she knew that Sam had heard. But Reuben spoke before she had formed her taunt.

"Your thumb, it's a scholar," Reuben began his

"Oh, why wouldn't we go there, Pap?" Reuben turned toward his father, but he turned quickly back to let the speaker continue.

"And this cane country spreads out past miles, a great content of land, but between here and there are a power of rough mountains."

"How are these mountains named, these you tell of?"

"He said they were the Ou-as-i-o-tos."

"Ou-as-i-o-tos," all saying it, trying the syllables on their lips, breaking them apart and fitting them together again, each time with a different music.

"There's a river through the land, he told us, a deep river with banks that make a sharp cliff in the white limestone, trees and growth over the hills. He said it was one of the wonders of the world, a river you might travel halfway over the earth to see, a wonder. He said it was called Chenoa, or Cho-na-no-no. Or some called it Millewakane."

These words were tried on all their tongues, chanted apart and together as all or one after another spoke them in all their possible ways. "Chenoa, Cho-na-no-no, Millewakane," as a chant went over the fireside. Then Nathan spoke through the chant.

"Some call it Louisa and call the land the same, and some call it Kentuck. It's said the rivers run together and flow apart again. It's a wonder how the rivers flow there."

"Chenoa. I like best Chenoa," Sam said. His eyes were bright and his bright red hair had broken from its binding string.

"He said he saw ten thousand buffaloes at the lower Blue Licks at one time, and they tramped one another under foot, mad to get at the salt," Nathan speaking.

"Do you, Sam, keep a flyen coach drawn by two horses, and do you take passengers to Kentuck every Monday and Wednesday? I've heard it said there's such a coach in Philadelphia." Reuben was teasing Sam's bright eyes and his falling hair. Nathan lifted quickly his hand as if he caught a new wonder out of the air and the other voices before the hearth were stilled.

"He told more. He told about a man, Dan'l Boone, a master hand to hunt and discover new countries. Boone has been over the whole of Kentuck and he lived there one winter season through, with his brother. Spring-o'-the-year, and Squire Boone, brother to Dan'l, went back to the settlements to get what was needed, powder and lead and some more horses, and Dan'l stayed. All by his lone self, he was, three months, and never once saw a white face. Not even a dog for company. Nights, and he lay in the cane or in a thicket, hid. Not even a fire, so the Indians wouldn't find out where he stayed."

"There was ne'er another soul but himself, ne'er

another white man nohow, in the whole country of Kentuck." A voice made a summary of this new wonder.

"I reckon Dan'l Boon is right well seasoned with Kentuck now," Polly said, speaking sadly, "by the time he stayed there three months withouten company. I reckon he's Kentuck-made to the bone marrow by now."

"Tell more about this Boone," Thomas Hall spoke then, speaking anxiously over Polly's sadness and hushing it away. "Did your surveyor hold speech with the discoverer?"

The talk sank and flowed about strong men who made brave journeys into the country beyond the barrier, or it lifted and sparkled with the rise of Nathan's hand that set forth a more bold hunter or a more daring exploit with one sharp gesture. The bright yellow smallclothes of the tidewater stranger were a mere ornament in the scene. "Such a country would breed up a race of heroes, men built and knitted together to endure . . ." and another voice, "A new race for the earth." Betty became weary and she fell asleep. She was but thirteen years old and not even the wonders of Kentuck could hold her against the powers of rest. The phrase, "great immense quantity of buffaloes . . ." stood under the power of Nathan's hand, or again, "To call up a buck

he made a bleat like the cry of a doe . . ." Or,
"Made the long journey around through the French
cities to the south. . . ." Somewhere beyond the
rich canelands lay other rivers running down into a
region beyond, running down into other seas. Tall
grass waved in the winds that blew in half-mythical,
half-reported caverns, an underground country. The
men who had gone there for this long hazard, Boone
and his company, had been called the Long Hunters.
It was all far apart from her now, behind unwieldy
mountains.

✧   ✧

Diony knew what name she bore, knew that Dione
was a great goddess, taking rank with Rhea, and that
she was the mother of Venus by Jupiter, in the lore
of Homer, an older report than that of the legendary
birth through the foam of the sea. She knew that
Dione was one of the Titan sisters, the Titans being
earth-men, children of Uranus and Terra. She had
a scattered account of this as it came from between
her father's ragged teeth as he bit at his quid and spat
into the ashes, an elegant blending of tobacco and
lore and the scattered dust of burnt wood, the man
who limped about before the hearth arising superior
to his decay. She could scarcely piece the truths together to make them yield a thread of a story, but
she held all in a chaotic sense of grandeur, being

grateful for a name of such dignity. Her brothers called her Diny, and they were indeed earth-men, delving in the soil to make it yield bread and ridding the fields of stumps, plowing and burning the brush. Thomas had been wounded by the falling of a tree so that the muscles of one of his legs were drawn and the limb shortened. This mishap had given the burden of the farm to Reuben, and with the burden of the labor had gone the burden of management.

A friendless woman named Sallie Tolliver helped their mother prepare the food at the kitchen fireplace, a woman who had come to them, walking back from the frontier of Fincastle County where her husband and her children had been killed in some Indian raid. She went silently about the work, but sometimes she was heard to mutter as she passed, asking a question, as if she questioned invisibles. Released from service at the kitchen fire, Diony milked the cows at the gap in the fence beside the barn. Betty would mind the gap, keeping back the calves, attending on her, and when the milk-taking was done, Diony walked away with the pails while Betty closed the gap with the wooden bars. She made nothing of the milk pails; she was tall and strong, being past sixteen. She strained the milk in the cool stone milk-house toward the creek and to the left of the kitchen. Here a spring ran out of a ledge of rock and made a pool in the hard floor. She would pour the fluid into brown earthen bowls, pouring it through a fine linen cloth, Betty attending her.

Diony could remember the building of the new house, but the old house had been built before she was born. Beyond the creek the land rose to a hill, and from this high place she could see the Blue Ridge as a wall across the west. Sam and Reuben had hunted through the mountain ridges and they knew the valley that stretched out beyond, where the Shenandoah took its beginning and flowed north. Diony went with the memories of this hunt, into the range of mountains and down into the valley. Her mother's people had come out of this valley, and thus she had two memories of it from which to borrow. Polly Brook with her parents had washed back over the Blue Ledge, as she called the barrier, in some movement of people. Earlier they had come out of England into Pennsylvania. They were a lonely people, being Methodists, given to simple living and humility. They were but a few in Albemarle. Their preacher came after long intervals from beyond the Ledge, and when he came there was a loud chanting of humility and holiness in the house.

Near at hand, the land touching their own, lying along the creek, was surveyed and owned, but no house was built there and no one came to claim it. A clearing five miles away down the stream made the plantation of the Jarvis men and their mother, Mistress Elvira Jarvis. Out along the river and the larger watercourses there were other families, the plantations better advanced and the clearings larger, the work done by black slaves. Thus the tilled land and the unbroken forests touched their parts about Diony. She came and went through the spring, milking, spinning at the large wheel. Sam would cry out some song he had learned from their mother, an ancient song that carried a strange monotonous tune:

> He found her in a ditch and he thought he had her
> there,
> And by and by I'll tell you how Moss caught his
> mare.

❖   ❖

Sam was making Betty a swing. He was hanging a long rope from a limb of the largest oak tree. Reuben stood by smoking his midday pipe.

"I'll cut this old tree when the saplen by the far milk-house gets a growth," Reuben said. "Five trees I'll still have then, and in a broader reach. And this one here will be in a manner dead with old age against ten years more. . . . There's rot already at the root." He spoke of what he would do when Five Oaks, the place, came to him. It was well known that it would be his because he was the eldest and a son.

"Where will my land be, for my house?" Diony asked. It came to her now, as a sudden disaster, that Five Oaks would not be her place. Other land higher up toward the Ledge would belong to Sam. "Where mought be my place?"

"You'd have to marry to get a place," Reuben answered her.

"But suppose I mought not," she said.

"Then God help you! Iffen a woman isn't married she has a poor make-out of a life," Sam said. He was bending over the rope, his hands making a knot, his face earnest in what he said.

"But God's sake! I never knew a woman that wasn't married," Reuben said, as if his saying were final, half muttering, as if it were no matter. "Come to think, I never knew one."

"Crazy Abbie, over at the court-house," Sam spoke after a moment of careful search. "She carries out slops in the ordinary, the tavern place. I never heard it said she ever had anybody marry with her."

"But iffen Diony turns out biddable we'll likely be able to find her a husband. There's a sign already on her . . ." Reuben was speaking.

"What sign?"

"Hit's on her mouth. She's got the marryen mouth."

"She must be careful not to get scarred with a pox or scalded with lye soap."

"And I'll make her a dower," Reuben said. "Iffen crops are good. Five hundred pounds of prime good baccer."

Diony walked in anger toward the creek, pressing her light feet hard against the ground at each step. She crossed on the stepping stones and went up the hill beyond, and presently Betty had overtaken her, ready to share whatever it was that troubled her spirit. From the hilltop she could look down over the cleared acres of Five Oaks and see the house spreading its two parts to each side of the dog alley, could see the shop and the barns behind it and see the farther woods that reached back into the running hills.

The pattern of the place beneath made a form that was marked as eternal in her mind. The five oaks stood in a placid fraternity about the log walls and gave shelter to the roof. The little stream lay as a ribbon of silver curling lightly through its stony banks. In mind she went down the slope and passed swiftly, like a wraith, across the ribbon of the creek, being weary now of the indefinite flowing of the farther earth, and she rested under the shade of the oaks and went then within the house and up the stair to her own sleeping place, where she lay down on her own soft bed and drew the coverlet over her,

as one goes acutely home to his own. There, surrounded, she passed more inwardly, wrapped in the
warm throb of her blood, her brown hair drawn over
her face. Shut securely within, wrapped in a garment
of sense, she went within again and yet again, a
hushed voice farther within saying some mute word,
as "come," or "here you will find me."

❖   ❖

Sam and Reuben sheared the sheep in April, working in the barn-shed beyond the milking place,
ripping the coats from the backs of the sheep with
great shears. Diony helped wash the fleeces at the
wash place, making a rich hot lye suds in the great
iron washing pot, and each fleece was beaten about
in the hot foam with battling sticks of wood. Then
the wool was drained of the water and rinsed once
and hung to dry on scaffolds. Her thought penetrated
the wool and went with the fleece through the hot
foamy bath and lay stretched with it on the scaffolds
in the shade of the greatest oak. In the night she
dreamed of planes of white frothy matter which the
sheep had shed and of the sheep going back to their
pasture, their yield gone beyond their power to recall. When the wool was dry Polly called her to help
pick it free of sticks and burrs, and if one of the fleeces
was of a richer whiteness and softness than the rest

she had a peculiar pride in it, as if she shared of some right with the flock. Sam would be singing a song, his falsetto voice that he used among the barns and cow-pens:

Many hist'ries have been read and many stories told
How Moss caught his mare. It was in the days of old . . .

In summer the cloth-making was of the wool, making garments for winter wear; in winter it was of the linen, the wear of the summer. Now, soon after the first meal of the day, Diony would be busy with the wool, and Polly's plans for it would run forward even while they sat at breakfast in the great kitchen room where Sallie Tolliver had put a trencher of ham and a fine wheat loaf on the board. Spinning the wool, she would work in the west end of the room, running back and forth to the rhythms of the great wheel. Out the small window she could see the garden patch along the creek, the flowing water beyond, and the hill. Stepping back and forth in the dance of spinning, she would recall words from her father's books, from one book: "It is evident to anyone who takes a survey of the objects of human knowledge, that they are either ideas actually imprinted on the senses or else such as are perceived by attending to the passions and operations of the mind. . . ." This would blend anew with the flow of the wool in her hands until the words and the wool were spun together and all stood neatly placed in her thought ready to be woven into some newer sort. . . . "It is evident to anyone who takes a survey . . ." She would hear Betty and Sam in a rough frolic in the dog alley, Sam's voice:

"I'm a torn-down Virginian. I'm a Long Knife. And iffen Virginia goes to war on Pennsylvania I'll offer Lord Dunmore my sword. . . ."

"Don't be so antic with that-there cut-tool," Betty cried out in defense. "I'm not Pennsylvany. Keep off, keep offen my head. . . ."

The wool was soft in her fingers, but heavy in bulk, being great in quantity and requiring much service of her. She would return to the words of the book and heed what they said, in substance: that all knowledge is of three sorts, that derived by way of the senses, that by way of the passions, and lastly, quoting now the words of the text, "ideas formed by help of memory and imagination." She could easily see the truth of this since she had discussed all fitfully with her father and had turned again to the book for renewal of faith when the words grew dim in memory. The whirr of the wheel came into her thought of the book as she fitfully remembered. "And beside all that, there is likewise something which knows or perceives them and exercises divers operations, as

willing, imagining, remembering. . . . This per-
ceiving, active being is what I call mind, spirit, soul,
MYSELF. . . . Some truths there are so near and
obvious to the mind that man need only open his
eyes to see them. Such I take this important one to
be, namely, that all the choir of heaven and furniture
of the earth, in a word, all those bodies that compose
the mighty frame of the world, have not any substance without a mind, that their being is to be perceived or known . . . that, consequently, as long as
they are not actually perceived by me, or do not exist
in my mind, or that of any other created spirit, they
must either have no existence at all, or else subsist in
the mind of some Eternal Spirit."

She could hear her mother walking in the room
above where she had gone to search out the dye pots
to make ready for coloring the yarn, and she heard
her calling to Sallie Tolliver down the stairway to
ask after the logwood, Sallie Tolliver going mutely
up the steps by way of reply. In the smith-shop behind
the house some strong hand hammered, blow after
blow, her father mending a plow. She clung rather
to the words of the book, letting the iron shriek pass,
Sam outside singing:

Many hist'ries have been read and many stories told
How Moss caught his mare. It was in the days of
old.

He got up early one morning thinking he'd find her
  asleep,
And all about the barnyard so slyly he did creep . . .

She turned the thought of the words that the book
used over and over with a pleasure in knowledge,
restating all for her own delight. "They, these things,
or any small part of the whole mighty frame of the
world, are withouten any kind or sort or shape until
somebody's mind is there to know. Consequently, all
the ways you wouldn't know, all you forgot or never
yet remembered, mought have a place to be in Mind,
in some Mind far off, and he calls this Eternal
Spirit." Her thought leaped then beyond articulation
and settled to a vast passion of mental desire. Oh, to
create rivers by knowing rivers, to move outward
through the extended infinite plane until it assumed
roundness. Oh, to make a world out of chaos. The
passion spread widely through her and departed and
her hands were still contriving the creamy fibers of a
fleece.

❖   ❖

Polly moved about among the dye pots, stirring
mixtures, or she cooked dyes over the open fire in the
yard, dipping the wool in and out, making bright
reds or dull blues of the spun yarn. She stirred mad-
der for yellow, or mixed a brown, standing beside

the kitchen press. Betty came in from the yard and sat dejectedly by the fireplace.

"Did you see was the old hen on the nest, like I told you?" Polly asked.

"That old door to the hen-house, set hit's head not to open and ne'er a thing could I do to budge hit. Stuck fast against the door jamb, and looks like the more I pulled the tighter she got a grip on the jamb, just to spite me."

"You're in too big a hurry," Polly said. "Push down on hit, a gentle push, and hit comes right open. You have to be gentle with hit."

"Do I have to spend my time to humor the old hen-house door?" Betty asked. "So spoiled hit's rotten."

Betty went to see after the hen as her mother required, and presently she returned to sit near Diony and she softened to the wool and yielded to it, offering help. "Talk to me, Diony," she begged, making a pretty light come to her eyes. Then Diony's heart swelled to a great size and seemed of a fullness that would burst, and a pity for Betty closed her eyes until the tears washed backward over her mind and eased her heart of its power, for Betty loved her with idolatry and clung to her. Betty lived in her words from hour to hour and came back to her again and again for renewing of life. To amuse her she had built imagined visits to the cities of the tidewater, preparing imagined welcomes at the homes of their cousins and uncles, the Montfords, down in the valleys below.

"Tell again what a city would be," Betty said. "Tell what would come to me iffen I went there, and all how hit would be."

"I never see cities," Diony answered. "I reckon I mought be a right outland person to my cousin Isobel and to Rufus and Anne. Isobel mought be right shamed to see me come that way. I never saw a city and you know it."

"Tell what would be, Diny. You can make all seem so . . . in your talk, and you said we could go, maybe, some day. We must go. You could take me there. Hit seems so likely!"

"Then we mought begin to go right now, to get the dresses ready. That would be first. A long scarlet cloak with a cape doubled over, for you, Betty Hall. Capes would become you right well because you are a small-built lady. Then a gown outen print cotton, brocade print, the ground dark with big red roses, a little blue inside some of the flowers for a shadow, and yellow for sunlight on the buds. A fine sight this gown would make when you took off the cape in a fine company, gentlemen and ladies. Then to tell the rest of your clothes, a pair of stays covered with white tabby before and dove-colored tabby behind. Some bibs and ruffles, some flounces and graduated falbalas of silk, pinked maybe. Some kid mitts and some silk shoes. A lead-colored habit, open, with a lilac lutestring skirt. A beautiful cushion to go on your head to hold out your hair. A taffety apron and some handkerchiefs . . ."

"For yourself, Diny. Now name your new linens and clothes."

"A blue cloak, dark sky-blue, like the sky in spring when you see it above trees . . ."

"A mantua coat, maybe."

"A fashionable calico gown, the ground dark like your gown, but little flowers pieded over it. Ribbon knots here and yon. Then some thread hose and a pair of silk shoes laced up, and three undercoats and a hoop coat and a powdered pompadour with a string of pearls to hang down off it, curls on my neck in the back."

"A fan to go in your hand," Betty cried out. "A golden chain for your neck."

"The things in a box on the back of a horse. Then we climb on our horses, a weather-skirt around us to save us from the dust."

"And then . . . ?" Betty asked, unable to wait.

"Down the creek through the water, past Jarvis's and on past the mill, night and day and on again. Smooth farms, roads to go, people to meet up and down the way, black slave-men on the road. We meet one with a budget on his back. Rivers to cross at ferries, and there are more black men to haul the boat across, budgets and pokes and parcels. At last it would be hard dark and we mought stay with our cousins that live in King and Queen County. We would come to the York River where it is broad, like a bay. There would be a wharf where ships land, and the house of our cousin William back from the river, a big smooth house, the wharf his wharf. We would be let in at the door and our cousin Anne would kiss us on the cheek and make us welcome. In the house would be fine mahogany chairs and tables and chairs covered with fine leather. Carpets on the floors, and the ladies would be dressed in dimity and silk."

Betty cried out with delight, but Diony carried forward the telling of the journey, being far away now from Albemarle. She could feel the soft carpet under her, and feel the cushion on her head and the silken shoes on her feet, the fine cool dimity over her body and the pinked falbalas flowing off her frothy skirts.

"This would be the great house where William lives. It would stand up on a rise of ground above the wharf, under some fine trees that came from France. From the porch we could look down on the York River, so wide it would be blue, and we could see the boats moored to the wharf, some with white sails and some barges. In the house there would be glass in all the windows, and shutters outside to open and shut to shade the windows from the sun and shelter from the rain. There would be a great hall, a dining hall, and all the other rooms with beds a-plenty. A long table would go down the middle of the floor in the great hall, chairs at the sides. Silver spoons to eat with and fine napkins to wipe your fingers on after you dip in your plate. Fine wine to drink, from Italy. Chinaware and silver and salt cellars. Rows of books in the wall, on shelves. Candles made outen myrtle berries, not tallow. To eat, there would be fish caught in the bay, bass and shad, and oysters maybe.

"When this visit is done we take a ship in the river and go out in the bay and sail to Baltimore. It's hard to say just what this would be, but maybe the sea would be a good-deal stormy and we'd have a sea-sickness come over us . . ."

"Wouldn't that be fine!" Betty cried out.

"When we'd come to land there would be our cousins on the wharf to fetch us home to their houses. We'd ride in a chariot maybe, a black man to drive and one to ride outside to open the gates. The town would have houses up and down the way and people would come and go in the streets. It's mighty hard to see all that mought be there. It's a far piece from here. We would put on our fashionable calicoes and go to church a Sunday, at our father's church. It would be a church with a name, like St. Anne's, but it would be some other name such as St. Stephen's or St. Luke's. Music would sound and the choir would chant a hymn. Chapel service, and we would hear a great scholar preach, and sit in a fine pew. Or maybe it's our cousin Isobel who takes us, then we mought go to St. Peter's, a saint's day, and a fine service in Latin, all in honor of St. Anthony or St. John or St. Augustine . . ."

"Hit makes me have cold shivers down my skin, to think about prayers to St. Anthony," Betty murmured. "I'd be afeared, and afeared of so much Latin, but I'd go. Any chance I got."

"Or back at the house, and you'd want to bridle when you go in a door if there's company inside. You'd hold up your head in a grand style. You'd curtsey at the door and then march across the floor and up to the grandest person in the room and make a bow to whoever 'tis. You'd have on a stomacher of lace held in, as like as not, with a ribbon tied in a bow. Or maybe there'd be a dance. Or maybe we'd drink tea on a wide grassy place under a beautiful clipped tree out of little silver pitchers and drink with pretty little sups. And read pretty novels. A chariot always stands by the door to take whoever has a mind to go somewheres."

"Oh, we'll go there," Betty cried out again. "Diny,

would you take me? Mought we go some day? Say and tell me, will you take me there, to see Isobel?"

"Iffen ever I can I will. I mought some day, for a fact."

"You can, Diny. Say you'll take me there. Say you will. Hit's a great scope of country to cross to go there. I could never go unlessen you could take me. Would you, Diny?"

"If ever I can I'll do so. Whenever I can find a way to go 'twould pleasure me as much as you," Diony said. "We'll go to the tidewater iffen it's in human power."

❖   ❖

Thomas Hall came to the weaving end of the kitchen, limping forward from the opened door. He took his surveying instruments down from the shelf and moved away as if he would work with them outside. Then Betty made her wheel purr prettily for him, turning it fast and setting the wool off in a swiftly running strand, stepping daintily back and forth and winding the reed with a great show, a crescendo in each measure.

"You're a right pretty spinner," he said. "You could almost hold a candle to Diony. But you lack enlightenment. Your head, it's not apace with your hand. I wish, Diony, you would teach this big ignorant wench here, your sister Betty, to read in a book."

"I tried to make her want to be learned, but she would not. I tried fifty times."

"Mammy, she won't read inside of books and Mammy, she makes out right well," Betty said. "I mought probably want to be like Mammy."

"Your mammy is a beauty," Thomas said. "And she don't have to read in books if she's not a mind to. Whenever you see the day you'd be half the beauty your mother Polly Brook is, you'd be free to let letters go by, Betty Hall. Teach her the letters, Diony."

"I read her a part of every book on the shelf and desired her to name which one she would like best to read, and she said not one suited her taste."

"Who wants to read in a book that goes, 'Secondly substance combination weight hardness subsisting, thirdly delight in the beholder, degree degree degree. Several simple ideas, modes, relishes.'" Betty made a little flutter as if she would spin again, but she enjoyed her situation, and she bent her head in a mock shame.

"You are a pretty case, on my honor," Thomas said. "I'd be right frighted to have you read. You'd out-do the Matchless Dorinda before a year is out. God's own sake!"

"Another book reads such a way as this," Betty continued. "'We are nowhere out of the reach of

Providence either to punish or protect us. An elk having accidentally gored a lion, the monarch was so exasperated . . .' "

"You liked the piece about the butterfly," Diony said. "She almost gave consent to learn to read it."

"Hit did well enough," Betty admitted. " 'A butter-fly proudly perched on the gaudy leaves of a French marigold . . .' Hit wasn't worth the pains to learn to read in books just to have that one piece. Diny read hit to me a many is the time. Hit says, 'I have wandered into regions of Eglantine and Honey-suckle. I have reveled in kisses on beds of Violets and Cowslips and I have enjoyed the delicious fragrance of Roses and Carnations.' "

"I might box your years," Thomas said.

"I liked better, unknown to Diny, one that goes, 'A tuberose in a bow-window on the north side of a stately villa, addressed a sunflower . . .' "

"I might box your years," Thomas said. He went away laughing. "Teach her to read, Diny," he called back from the door, "and I'll give you a pretty present, and tend her with copies until she learns how to write. Egad, the outland wench is my own blood. Could read pretty in a week if she would get her consent, but her head is set contrary and what, God's own sake, 's to do?"

❖   ❖

Diony would find her father's letters in the desk beneath his bookshelf in the new house, would search them out and read them again. He had come to the wilderness to survey a great tract of land for a company of men in Maryland, and he had taken his pay in land. He had brought the letters when he came, for they went back into some earlier life. The books on the shelf were above her head as she sat to read, the light falling from the high window that was like a port-hole, falling over her hands and over the opened letters, lighting the fading inks that had been put upon the page in pride and youthful daring. The letters were from Rufus Montford, their cousin. A young mind spoke out of the written pages, and she would read the proud words and turn the paper about, searching it for tokens of the cities of the world.

"You never had a letter, and little are you likely ever to have one," Thomas would say to her, had said to her, finding her there. "Read the letters of a gentleman. Wild manners she hath, this Diony, born in the back-country, but who's to teach her wantonness the manners of gentlefolk? Read then the letters of a gentleman till you know what 'tis to touch minds with his kind. Very remarkable! Thomas Hall, son of Luce Montford, has fathered a whole brood of back-country bumpkins!"

Left with the letters, Diony would imagine leisure

and letter-writing, a courier waiting at the door, his horse tied to a post but impatient to be off. Often the letters flowed lightly over remembered visits, cities, trinkets, a new dance figure, smallclothes, vests, silk stockings, bows for the knees, the buying of riding horses. Having imagined leisure, she would imagine cities where were houses close along a traveled way, but the trees would not evacuate, the forest would not utterly yield, so that back of each house stood the timber, a girl in linsey, her strong light body unstayed, her face unmasked from the sun, herself going down to take the milk from the cows. The people of the cities would be earnest, and they would meet one another with some deeply serious speech that entered into the searchings of the mind and penetrated the mysteries that lay beyond it, unafraid. They would greet one another with some beautiful words of welcome she could never name, or they would stop to take counsel together of this or that high purpose, or if they laughed together their wit was as rich as the sparkle of sunlight on frost. She would dream thus, under the high casement. Or she would turn again to the letters, asking assistance of them. Sometimes they were openly mocking. Rufus had married a wife. He wrote then:

"Came back from Philadelphia April. God Almighty! I wish you might have seen the baggage

I brought here. I was schooled in the how of a woman's gear before I had been two weeks married. Pack-thread stays, two stiff coats of silk, three caps, two bonnets, a pair of ruffles and a brace of necklaces and two fans. Remarkable! I contented myself with a new pea-green coat and a pot of pomatum. The rest of the wagons were loaded with kitchen gear, ironware for the wenches. I looked not twice at the collection after it was assembled by the merchant. My obedience to your mother, my aunt, honored sir." This letter, signed Rufus Montford, mocked in a gay manner, for the two men had been boys together.

Diony would search this and the other epistles, turning to them in mind as she went about among the cattle or as she sat to weave at the loom, or she would, the task being slow and forever of one kind, slip from the kitchen part of the house and sit at the desk to read the precious parcel again. Out of the faded ink would leap now and then some brightness as of such value as to engender motion in the mind, so that her thought would leap forward and her whole being awake one instant as if it had transcended its bounds, but in the end her desire was the more far-reaching and unsatisfied. She learned to place the letters by their tone, the first being wistful and earnest, being full of the most intimate confidences that pass between young beings, full of high hopes and great esteem and affection. Sometimes in a quick out-flash of imagination she would join this intercourse and would make herself, in secret, another party to the friendship that was now, for her father and her cousin, a mere ghost, twenty years spent. She embraced their youth and gave herself to be another in their group which she restored, building upon the letters, until she would sit momentarily in a warmth of intercourse where young men and young women planned and speculated daringly and interchanged love and quick looks of devotion and understanding—the high serious purposes belonging to the whole way of man on the earth. The letters, thus:

"We rode three days past Mr. Bradley's settlement. The weather was hot past comfort and we was bit cruelly by the gnatts. A very long and dangerous water then, flood out of season. Wellington prayed all the way, calling on his Maker and making a mighty discomfort for everybody. We came to the Quaker settlements then and rode on past Moore's and came to the end of all settlements. I expected every hour to be fired on by the redskins, but Judson, quick to see everything, pointed out improvements and kept to the trace. We ate bear meat five days, but one day Judson killed a fawn and I pigeons. We deadened trees and marked boundaries and entered all in proper writing. Coming back I fell into communion with myself as to the meaning of life, and the nature of substance and the nature of knowledge as it appears in the mind, and the originals of all things. For if unthought matter cannot have existence, I thought, how rich a substance we might have if we would set-to to make all more worthy and more rich in qualities by the mere process of thinking a greater degree of qualities into each, as if red might be more red by thinking, or blue more blue, or goodness more good, or justice more just, or whatnot, or some other which I cannot yet think. Until my mind was like to burst with cogitating ideas never before printed there and for the writing down of which I have but meager words. . . ."

"Schoolboy pulings!" Thomas Hall said, his voice coming upon her as a crash of thunder breaking loud over her contemplations. "Schoolboy drivel!"

He was looking over her shoulder with a laugh that lowered his nether lip and put a square line in his cheek. His mood was now mocking at his other mood. She knew what disaster he would now remember.

"He stole my mother's patrimony," he thundered at her from the door. "Nine thousand acres he got by the testament, and he was directed to pay a sum to his aunt, my mother, Luce Montford, married to Roger Hall. In the name of God amen! Fine words and justice ought to keep company."

"He didn't have the money," Diony whispered. "He spent all before it came to his hands, likely. Or he mought pay yet. . . . He mought pay yet. . . ."

❖   ❖

The young men from the neighboring plantation often came on Sundays to try their strength in lifting and wrestling matches, but these tests were made back in the woods, far from the house, for Polly required all about the place to keep the Sabbath. The smith-shop was closed and the forge was still. The tools were rested in the shed and the beasts were let stand idle, observing their Sabbath. The cows were milked of necessity, but Diony and Betty were given a Sabbath release from this task and Sam was required to perform it. Polly and Sallie Tolliver prepared a quantity of food on Saturday. The young men would break the Sabbath in a cleared place behind the first woods, wrestling and boxing there throughout a swift afternoon, returning in torn shirts and trampled leggings toward the time of sunset.

Or, on Saturdays, the boys would race their horses in the old field where the beaten way made a racecourse through the turf, or Jack Jarvis would bring his fighting cocks and set them against Sam's fowls, all the boys standing in a ring to see the chickens leap and spur each other, the young men betting their pence. Berk Jarvis, older than Jack, and Eli, older again, would take a quiet pride in the fringed hunting shirts which their mother had woven for them, and they would come when they had fresh new shirts to wear. Sometimes when their wrestling matches were done the young men would sit on the ground under one of the oaks, and Thomas would bring a great measure of beer from the cellar where he kept his brew. Then all would eat the apple pie Polly had made, spooning it out from earthen bowls or small platters.

The boys would tease one another about the girls who lived near the court-house town, and in their teasing they would name some remote Molly and Kitty. They teased Berk the more because he seemed shy of the banter.

"Molly said if a girl burns the bread she's a-baken she'll never marry. Said she burned up a whole pan-ful." The young men would laugh at this prediction and eat a great deal of the apple pie, spooning it fast.

"Kitty said to me, said if you cut your hair in the dark of the moon you'll go bald. Said it was a fact.

Said I took a risk when I let Jude, the blacksmith, cut my hair Saturday."

"Kitty ever was one to make jokes about serious matters. Some people's hair calls for a blacksmith to cut it."

"I'm more uneasy about Molly. Burned up a whole panful of bread. I can see Molly in a chimney corner! Molly's luck will go right hard against nature. Nature, she's not prepared for it."

"Kitty said if a girl finds a crooked feather in her hair she'll marry a hunchback. Said it was a true sign, never failed." The boys would look over Berk's head when they told of the crooked feather, or Reuben would run a careful finger down Berk's spine. Sam would be singing his song, making the fiddle cry out the strong note of each measure:

Many hist'ries have been read and many stories told
How Moss caught his mare.   It was in the days of
old.

He got up early one morning thinking he'd find
her asleep,
And all about the barnyard so slyly he did creep.

He found her in a ditch and he thought he had her
there,
And by and by I'll tell you how Moss caught his
mare.

He slipped a noose about her neck.   "Rise up, Old
Kip," said he,

But Oh, good Lord, the mare was dead, not one
  word would she say.

Tho' it's many a stroke he gave her but none would
  make her stir,
And now I think I've told you how Moss caught his
  mare.

Diony would sit beside Polly and Betty on the
bench at the side of the wall, or she would bring
another pie from the kitchen. The boys would attack the new helpings eagerly and begin their sport
anew.

"And what kind of feather did Kitty find inside
her hair?" Sam asked. "A tall straight one, I bet a
pretty penny."

"She never told me what kind she found. All is,
she said if it's crooked he's a hunchback, sure."

"Iffen she found a crooked one, you better, Berk,
walk mighty careful and take care not to get your
back hurted much. I'm oneasy about Berk Jarvis's
back. . . ."

Thus the Sundays would come to an end under the
oak trees. At the time of the harvest all the boys were
back again to the labor, cutting and threshing the
wheat, beating out the chaff on the threshing floor.
The cockerel waited without an adversary, but he
was not allowed to fatten and thus to fog his fine skill.
While the men sickled the wheat and beat it free of

the straw, Diony and Betty wove the cloth for the winter, making warm woolsey.

✧   ✧

Autumn brought the leaves down from the trees and the swine for winter meat were killed. The lard was boiled in a great iron kettle under the largest oak and Diony and Betty helped with the work, moving carelessly, not caring whether there was lard or not, but taking forward all that was required of them. Diony stirred the boiling lard with well-trimmed wooden sticks and she dipped the finished grease out of the cracklings when Polly told her it had boiled enough. The curing of the meat filled the late autumn, work going forward all day in the frosty air, and the wind washed over their bodies in a fine subtle spray. For many weeks none had come from the outside. The dusk would fall early and the nights were long. There were long evenings by the fireside in the new house.

One day, at nightfall, while Diony milked the cows at the gap, she knew by some slight uneasiness in the herd that a stranger had come to the plantation. Betty ran toward the house to learn who had walked in from the creek road, but presently she came running back to tell, for she would not leave Diony unknowing. Berk Jarvis had come bringing a stranger.

"What manner of kind is he?" Diony asked, taking forward the business of milking, her hands getting milk.

"A hunter," Betty said. "I never in all my time saw such a man as he is. I was beside myself as soon as I saw such a kind."

"A hunter is no monstrous sight to see. A hunter wouldn't fright me outen my wits now."

"This-here hunter is a different kind from e'er other ever you laid eyes on. Hit's outside my power to describe what sort he is."

Diony turned the stream of milk into the piggin with a swift free hand, thinking of hunters, and remembering that Berk Jarvis was such. He had a delight in his skill with his rifle and in his long journeys, for he had been back into Fincastle more than once. Each young man wanted to go farther than the rest. Now Diony was impatient to see this indescribable hunter Betty reported of, but the milk stream must flow in its accustomed flood. Betty moved lightly before the gap, minding away the calves.

"Do Berk Jarvis and this hunter that is a wonder to tell of, do they aim to take a night with us?" Diony asked.

Betty thought that they did. She lingered over her words, modifying all that she said with her continual astonishment. "He looks like nobody you ever before saw in life," she said.

"Tell me what he is. Say more about how he looks," Diony begged of her. The milk flowed slowly. The stream could not be slighted. Diony had a fine pride in her milking.

"I never had talk with him myself," Betty said. "But I think, apter than not, he looks what he does because he's been all the way into the wilderness. He's been all the way to Kentuck. I never in my time saw e'er other that's got the look he's got."

When the milk had ceased its flow, Diony put it swiftly in the dairy-house and went to the table where the evening meal was set. The two guests were in their places when, with Betty, she slipped lightly into her place. The stranger was past description strange. The supper moved swiftly, food taking the first place in the minds of all, but presently she was aware that the stranger Berk had brought had been into far regions beyond the mountains, had been to the country of Kentuck. He made no offer to speak, but when he was addressed he gave a courteous reply. Sallie Tolliver sat at the farther end of the table eating her bit of food, making herself blank and dull before the dull wall, scarcely making a shape when she arose to find more bread for the platter. She had been far into the wilderness of Fincastle. She would not speak of what she had seen there, and Polly, who knew her story, was as unwilling to speak of it. Diony turned from her dull shadow and viewed the stranger again, for he gathered a brightness about himself. His body was thin and his face was gaunt and clean-shaven. He would snatch quick glances at one or another of those at the board without moving his head, sending his eyes about on quick missions. His clothes were of fresh woolsey from some farmhouse. Diony thought that he might be old, but she could gather no more of him.

Thomas Hall brought his guests to the new house with ceremony as soon as the meal was done. All crossed the dog alley slowly, Betty staying her steps, suppressed and faintly amused, wanting Diony to share her put-by mirth. The old guest was given a chair near the center of the hearth circle, and Thomas Hall sat in his accustomed place with Polly at his right hand. Diony sat beside Betty and Reuben on the bench which was fitted along the wall to the left of the fireplace, and Sam walked about the room or sat, as his eagerness would allow. The young guest, Berk Jarvis, sat on a stool near to the bench, and he took a pride in the stranger as in one he had brought from a far place who would tell stories of strange wonders, for he gave a hint of what would follow.

Diony could see the old man more clearly now, the fog of surprise being gone a little way from her sight. He was far past middle age. His face was quick but ghostly under its weather marks and stains. He spread his lean strong hands along his thighs and looked from one face to another as if he scarcely knew the ways of houses and the uses of hearthsides although these had once been his knowledge, as if he slightly feared now the gentleness of women. Presently he was talking, slowly at first, Diony scarcely able to attend the meaning of what he said, being as yet surprised with the meanings his person yielded. He weighed each speech with care, making each phrase with pains, as is the way with men who have lived alone and have made decisions without the use of words or speeches. His voice was a sharp cutting-tool, placed guardedly to fall beneath a roof, carefully brought to lie low beneath rafters.

He bowed with courtesy whenever Polly spoke, or whenever Diony. His words were given with dignity, as if the silence of the unbroken forest and the cane had purged some ancient speech and refurnished its repose. Thomas took a delight in this speech regardless of what it reported of the wilderness, as if the words were more to him than the substance they conveyed, but the young men gave more heed to the cargo than to the conveyance. Diony saw her father's pleasure in the old hunter's words with a rush of love and pity, and her mind went swiftly to the letters in the desk under the shelf of books, to the books then. Only a little while had passed since the ceremonious entry from the supper room. The old hunter was clarified now, had stood forth, clearly seen and comprehended.

"Recruit the fire, Diony. Fling on another piece. We'll hear more of the Ken-tuck-ee. More, sir, more," Thomas called out.

Diony and Sam set the sticks together in the embers and moved swiftly back. The old man laid one thin hand along his thigh and spoke.

"Yea, it is a good land, the most extraordinary that ever I knew. Meadow and woodland as far as eye can behold. Beauteous tracts in a great scope, miles. A fine river makes a bound to it on the north, and another fine river flows far to the west, another boundary. To the east is a boundary of rugged mountains. And set above the mountains is a great cliff wall that stands across the way. Yea, you would know you had come to the country of Caintuck when you saw that place. A clift wall makes a steep barrier across your path beyond any man's strength to climb. But high up in the mountains, cut in the cliff, is a gate. I was in and out of it for years to peer out the land and to spy its wonders. I walked far there. All the fore part of one year and on until summer came I hunted beyond the Chenoa River."

"The Author of Nature has point-blank made a promise land," Thomas said. "A place fitted to nurture a fine race, a land of promise."

"The undergrowth pea-vine, cane, nettle, all mingled with every rich weed. Its timber a fair sight to see. Honey-locust, black walnut, sugar tree, hickory, ironwood, hoopwood, mulberry, ash, elm. Oak a-plenty. I saw ash trees fifty feet high. There's a bird there, yea, a marvel. A woodcock that's a wonder to hear of."

"Hear what he tells about the trees. Pea-vine under foot. Ash trees fifty feet high. Hit's a wonder," Sam's voice cried out and another voice joined him, one flowing after another.

"If it's wonders you desire I'll name a great wonder. At Big Bone Creek by the upper salt licks I saw a greater marvel. There you'd see the bones of some monstrous beasts on the ground. The joints of the spine bone make camp stools to rest a man, and a tooth weighs five pounds to lift. It's a wonder of the earth."

"Are these beasts all dead now?"

"All dead that I saw, but it would be a most fearful thing to meet one alive. I saw a jaw tooth over four pounds in weight. I saw a rib bone eleven feet long, or such a matter. A skull bone six feet across the forehead. Tusks or horns five feet in measure."

"Such a beast to walk the earth! I'd be afeared to meet one in the dark of a night."

"And all might not be dead. The live ones might come down through the cane."

"Hear what he says. He's a mind to speak again."

"In another place are the caves, if it's wonders you crave to hear. There's a country under the earth. Men live there, it's said, under the ground, under limestone rock. Miles, you can go, and keep yourself darkling, always under the earth. It's said there are races of men there, houses and cities, citizens of the caves, dwellers of the cave lands to the west. I never saw this marvel for myself, but I had report of it."

"Oh, I'd want to go there."

"And game everywhere in plenty, he says."

"Let him tell about the game. He's about to speak. Listen."

"Buffalo, bears, elk, pigeon, deer, waterfowls, beavers, otters, turkeys. You could never hunt your fill. Around the salt licks the beasts trample one another under and you can kill as fast as you can load your weapon and fire. The pigeons black the air with their wings and their flights are like a thunder in the sky."

"A man could live off the beasts. Could kill his food with his rifle."

"But a land of blood, the redmen say. No redman can live there. He would hear the footsteps of his fathers of a night, bones that walk in the dark. It's a fearful land to a redman, a forfended place. He would hear the ghosts of the Alleghewi, the old race that lived there before his time, a lost race, gone, the redmen say, now all out of the earth."

"Oh, I wouldn't go there. I wouldn't," a frightened voice cried, Betty crying with it, "I wouldn't go."

"Harken now. Let him tell. Harken."

"A redskin told me this, and told me the words that make the meaning of the name, Kentuck. Ken-tak-ee—Meadow Lands, he said. I recollect we talked a night beside a fire not far from the Big Bone Lick. Ken-tak-ee, he said, was the name of the whole place, Meadow Lands. A fearful country. Every rood a place where a battle has been. The land there is thick with broken battle-axes and under the ground run the bones of many men. A dark country. No redman lives there."

"I wouldn't go. I wouldn't."

"I aim to go, myself. Ne'er a thing could hold me," Sam said. "I'll explore the caves and see the bones of the beasts."

"I'd want a fine farm in the open country,"

Reuben said. "Six hundred acres would content me there."

"A safe place, though. A block-house near at hand."

"Quiet, boys. Harken. He's a mind to speak again."

"In the past summer season of the year, in June, a mighty man of valor, James Harrod, and thirty men, made a town in the caneland, the beginnings of a nation. I came to this place and I saw men felling trees and building houses. James Harrod and his thirty. Then Boone comes by to tell all Lord Dunmore is about to make a war on the redskins in the upper Ohio Valley, and all come back across the mountains to help fight Lord Dunmore's battles. But Harrod and his men will go back to the town they have begun in the cane."

"A new world has begun then, in that place. Hit's hard to see what mought come there."

"Tell more, sir, about the old race, those gone and forgotten out of the earth, that once lived there, and what relics they left." Diony asked this, wondering what it would be to belong to such a nation.

"I saw a great stone wall, a fortified place, built, I surmise, by the Alleghewi, upwards of three hundred feet long. Sixty feet high, it was, some of the stones five hundred pounds' weight. On the top of the wall you could see the stones the warriors carried there for weapons, stones to throw down on the enemy, piled high."

"I'd aim to go there, to that place," Sam said.

Diony looked across the hearth from one to another, but her quick look caught the look of Berk Jarvis, and they looked together, back and forth, his eyes bright and his head lifted as if he were about to speak. His long arms were bent, his wrists resting on his knees, his large hands loosely knotted together. Then some voice spoke.

"A long way to go," one said, "a long way."

"A long way, but the reward is more than the labor. Canelands the like never before seen on the map of the world. Or beyond the cane, tall trees, not too thick for beauty, a land of beauty, a garden place."

"But a weary road through the wilderness," Polly said then. "No path under foot, no trace to guide where you'd set your next step. Savages to kill you and get your skulp maybe. Hit may be a fair place . . . No way to send back for what you couldn't carry. Hit'll ever be the case for years to come."

"But the country is like paradise. Rich cane. Trees all in blowth in the spring-o'-the-year. Like paradise it is, so beautiful and good."

"Hit's said there's a woodcock there. Tell, please, about the bird you named a while ago, sir."

"A wonder, this is. Let him tell now."

"A woodcock there and its beak is pure ivory. I saw this witness for myself. Yea, I saw a woodcock with a beak that is like a jewel stone."

Diony looked across toward Berk Jarvis, her head suddenly lifted, her eyes bright, and all her inner part leaping. He smiled a delayed smile and looked happily back, and the look said to her, "I would go there, any chance I had, I Berk Jarvis," and her look replied, "I would go, I, Diony, would go to see the ivory-beaked woodcock."

"Could you name the seven rivers that flow there?" Reuben asked.

The old man sat quiet while he searched his mind for all seven of the fair rivers of this wilderness before he replied. When he had gathered all these strands of water into a thread of memory he answered, speaking softly, putting his speech with care.

"There is first the Tenn-ess-ee, the farthest water. Then, moving hitherward, you would come to the Shawnee River, and this has been called—it is a pity—has been sometimes called the Cumberland. There is one next called the Muddy River. I saw its mouth where it pours into the Ohio but I never explored its whole course. It is a fine stream, its yellow silt to show what a great scope of land it washes. Next comes the Pigeon River, not so great in size as the Shawnee, but a fine water with many meanders and many creeks to drain a great content of land. A wonder of pigeons come to roost along its course, until they dark the sky with their flights. . . . I recall then the most lovely river of all . . ."

He sank into a reverie as he contemplated this stream, letting his thought slip with its winding course among high cliffs and tree-grown hills, and Diony, having heard report of it, knew what name he would say when he took back his dreaming mind from its curving course and consented to speak again. He looked quietly into the embers and presently he spoke, naming the river softly as one might name a lover.

"Chenoa. It's called Chenoa, or some say Cuttawa, or Millewakane. Among all the rivers of the world there is no river it would give you greater content to see. I saw it in the spring-o'-the-year when the redbud brush was in flower, a blowth over the whole face of the rock-cliff, and wild plum. The river runs through a gorge gouted out through the rock, and the walls of the river stand like walls of laid stone to wind with the flow of the stream. Beyond on the level above, is a rolling land like a garden, cane-lands and groves of woodland . . ."

"The other rivers," Reuben said, drawing him back to the task of naming all. "Could you name the rest, sir? "

"Oh, wait," Diony cried out, "wait. Don't name another yet. This river, tell more of how it was, please, tell more."

"The Chenoa. Wild plum in flower in the spring-o'-the-year. Mile after mile, and a high cliff on both sides like set stones in the wall of a fine ruin. Chenoa. You'd read about the Rhine as a fair stream, high stones and shaped cliffs the like you might never see again on the earth. . . . But the Chenoa is a fine stream, lovely to see, the shapes on the stones to make a power on the mind. . . ."

"It must be a great content to a man to go into a new country and name there the rivers with names he would fancy. . . ." "To name a river and write it on a map." Sam and Berk spoke these fancies, echoing the one upon the other. They made an interval in which the old man dreamed quietly of the far-off water he had named with affection. He spoke at last, beginning softly, passing to the remaining of the seven streams.

"The Great Salt Lick comes next and it has a wonder of salt licks in its valleys. Close to its course are spread the bones of the great beasts. Then last, nearest the mountains, is the Chatteraway, running down from above."

The old narrator fell into a reverie then, having given report of his travels, having spent his vigor in recounting, and he made as if he would gladly rest now. But he arose to bow with a strange grace, a deep slow courtesy which belonged to some remote life he had known beyond his knowledge of the wilderness, when Polly arose from her chair. He stood as one offering homage until she moved away from the fireside.

"I'll lay me down to sleep now," Thomas Hall said. "We'll go all." Being requested, he gave the old narrator a pile of skins by the kitchen fire, and left him to sleep there. All went quickly to their places.

II

THE clock of the season had run around the year and the herbs were growing, even under the frost. Polly was searching out the garden seeds, turning out drawers and cupboards, putting a plague on the mice if they had destroyed any. Diony felt the coming of the spring as she flung the shuttle through the web to weave the tow linen for the summer wear. "Not one of the heavenly bodies nor any part of the furniture of the earth can have being without mind to think it. Mind," the shuttle said, beating time against the pound of the reeds as she whipped the threads into cloth, and now the Thinking Part turned slowly to prepare a spring for the world.

Warm days eased slowly out of the south. The boys went to the creek with a handful of soft soap for each put into an old stoneware mug, and they carried a towel of coarse tow. They were swimming behind the screen of willow bushes and the sun was falling down warm on the surface of the pool. They had flung their clothes on the bank and leaped bravely into the pool, laughing and shivering and plunging about, the pool being shallow and the water dim-

58

pling here and there over stones. Then they came to
the sand and rubbed their bodies over with the soft
soap that Diony had made, a fine cleansing jelly of a
soft gray texture, and it ran as a salve or an ointment
over their flesh and was worked into a soft lather
with the smooth water of the creek. Back then to the
pool, their heads plunged under and the soap washed
free, the plovers flying about overhead and filling
the air with plaintive cries. At mid-afternoon the
boys came from the water, flinging their discarded
clothes in a high-spirited return, telling of the joy of
the bath, retelling their exhilaration, winter put by
and spring being come.

Then Diony carried water above to her room in a
wooden keeler in a fine anticipation, soft soap in the
same little earthen mug the boys had used, and a
smooth strong towel. The breeze came in at the open
window, spring. A house bird out on the ridge of the
roof, a starling, made a pleasant bird-clatter, and
another and another, following or calling all together. A soft delicate lather of foamy content was
spread over her strong full body, her round slender
limbs and her small round trunk, and she saw the
whole of herself at one time, a revelation. She washed
then away the spongy coat of foam that the soap
made, dipping one foot and then the other in the
keeler and letting the drops fly off into the cool mov-

ing air. The bath has come near an end and she
stands free in a fine chill and a drunken afterglow, a
token of spring. She rubbed her flesh into a rich
flame and her mind leaped and started with the
drunkenness of excessive health and a fine day.

❖   ❖

The year was going around, like the hands of the
clock in the new house, leaving themselves, the
people, as still as the dial, making seasons and hours
over them. Diony felt the year go past and once, for
a moment, she heard the great ticking. There was
war in Boston, the colony fighting the King's men.
Some said that all the colonies would snatch themselves free.

Diony's dress was made now like a woman's dress,
but smaller, for she was past sixteen. In one of the
upper rooms alone she put on her mother's dress and
it swallowed her into its folds. The drooping roundness of the dress made her afraid to know that she
would come to a stature that would fill it. She was
fearful of the dress, and she turned herself about in
the upper room, looking down on the large limp
masses of printed cloth which had come long before
from the tidewater. It was her mother's one fine
garment; it was the one fine garment of the whole
plantation. When Polly wore it, it covered her ample

roundness and buttoned down across her round bosom and fitted smoothly over her fine arms. Diony stared at herself within the mold of the cloth and she shuddered and snatched the dress from her body, flinging it on Sallie Tolliver's bed. But when she had stood a moment beside the bed, a change spread over her knowledge of the dress, and she took up the garment with a sweet loathing that turned all to joy as she put it on anew. She brushed the folds of the cloth with her hands, slowly, accepting her new self and being ready to run to meet all that would come to her. Standing in the garment, she felt herself burgeon slowly to a roundness and firmness that satisfied it, that lifted its limp folds and swelled the shoulders and arms, that poised the skirt to a fine point of grace. Then she took the dress gravely from her body and hung it on its peg in the corner beside Betty's childish little frock, and she took her own garment to her body again, buttoning the front opening gravely, and she went gravely down the stair, being no longer in awe of adult being. Her mind sank into a maze, both ways, Betty's way and Polly's way, being equally known to her, and the year continued to make seasons over her.

Then several from down the stream came to look at Thomas's horses and to buy. "Horses will be needed in the army," one said. Four men came to

buy from first to last, among them a young man,
known to Thomas, a man who came in a fine style.
"We live humbly here," Thomas said, bringing the
young man over the threshold to the large common
room in the new house, where the visitor talked
gayly of the life in Williamsburg and Richmond.
Diony walked demurely before the stranger, as a
young woman should. He was a man of dignity,
coated and combed in the tidewater manner, wearing settlement finery everyday. A black groom rode
with him to tend his horses. Polly gave the groom a
bed in one of the out-buildings beside the smith's
shop, a little fearful of his dark skin, and Betty kept
apart, but she listened well to all the dressed-up
young man said and repeated much of it after he
was gone. While he stayed Diony was not let milk
the cows, but she and Betty stayed indoors and
occupied themselves with the nice tasks of gentle-
women.

Again a visitor, a girl from a plantation down the
river, brought by Thomas when he came back from
one of his journeys. Her name was Nancy Webb; she
was the daughter of one of Thomas's friends. On her
first day at Five Oaks she taught Diony and Betty
new ways to try fortunes to find out who would be
their lovers and to discover if they would have hus-
bands. She was a quick little black-eyed girl, and

presently she was teasing with Sam, who liked to push and pull a girl's words about. In secret she put a four-leafed clover in her shoe, known only to Diony, so that whatever young man she met thereafter would be her future husband. It was summer. Diony slighted the weaving while Nancy stayed, but no one minded, for there were bolts of cloth put by.

The year had spun round; war on the coast; Nancy Webb with a clover leaf in her shoe, meeting Sam in a path. All had danced in the kitchen room, the men taking turns at the fiddle. Autumn had come then, the fire popping snow and snow following. Nancy Webb had been a long time gone, but she had caused new ideas to be imprinted on the mind. She was full of little secret ways of knowing. "You are pretty," she had said to Diony, a new learning, a new way of thinking of oneself.

"How am I pretty?" Diony asked.

"You'll find out against a man comes along that's got a tongue to tell you with. They're a tongue-tied set, not to 'a' told you sooner. Those boys down the creek, the Jarvises, they'll tell you, only they are a slow-spoken lot, little to say."

Nathaniel Barlow came again to look at horses, bringing his groom as before, and there was bright

talk before the fire. Diony sang three songs to Sam's
fiddling, two ballad songs and a hymn, singing:

> Come, all ye fair and tender ladies,
> Take warning how you court young men.
> They're like a star in the summer morning.
> They first appear and then they're gone.

Barlow seemed to care little for the war, now he was
far from it, but pressed to speak of it he told of the
flight of Dunmore, the governor, and made a ram-
bling story of gunpowder and a new legislative body
sitting. He talked with Thomas about the families
living in New Kent and gave news of recent marriages there. He was a lover of music and must needs
have Sam play again and Diony sing:

> Lord Beichan was a noble lord,
> He thought himself of high degree;
> He could not rest nor be content
> Until he had voyaged across the sea.

"She could play on the spinet," he said. "Mistress
Diony could make tunes on the harpsichord in no
time. She'd learn off fine."

Diony had a picture of herself sitting at a piece of
musical furniture and she felt her fingers tripping
lightly over the little white keys, making a tinkle to
accompany her song. The tunes tingled in her arms
and in her shoulders, wanting an outlet by way of
her hands, and she went swiftly in mind down into

the lower country with this Nathaniel Barlow to sit there on elegant chairs and bow and curtsey at strange doorways, herself settled, at home there, on land she owned for her own home. But she let him pass finally, and let the low countries be diffused, taking their spinets into fogs of unknown ways. But she smiled no less and went on with her singing:

> She has got rings on every finger,
> And on one hand she has got three;
> And she's as much gold around her middle,
> As would buy Northumberland of thee. . . .

❖   ❖

They were back at their home-ways again, Barlow being gone. Sam pounded hominy in the mortar, working in the sheltered sunny place beside the house wall through a bright afternoon. The corn had been soaked until the husks were pliable and they fell away when they were broken by the maul. The water in the creek lay as a sheet of brass in the bright afternoon sun, and beyond this the hillside arose rich in brown or dull green. Sam lifted and dropped the maul, and Diony took away the finished hominy and dipped more of the soaked corn out of the piggin, she his handmaiden. While they worked two came up the creek road, scattering the geese until they flew over the bright brass of the water in a white

curve of mellow noise. Then Berk Jarvis and Nathan
Jones, having tied their horses beside the stream,
came toward the house and lingered about the hominy trencher, their coming bringing Reuben from
the mending shop.

The talk was of the news from the seaboard country, of the congress that was sitting in Philadelphia.
The newcomers had been to mill; the miller had
given report and gossip while the wheel broke their
corn. Thomas Jefferson, John Hancock, Peyton
Randolph, George Washington—these names were
called again in their excited surmises. Soon all that
any of them knew had been reported, but opinions
doubled back and forth in the bright warm sunshine
before the house wall. A bench beside the door made
a seat for Diony and Betty when they cared to sit.

"I'd like to see the King's men flusterated before
summer sets in," Reuben said. "Men are a-goen to
be needed down around the coast. If Wallace and
Campbell go out with the militia I mought go too."

Nathan began to talk about the country on the
upper waters of the Holston where the rivers from
the mountains drain down into the Tennessee country, his hand making a sharp upward stroke as he
brought this new country into their thought. A man
from Carolina named Henderson, a rich man, had
gone there, and had made a great treaty with the

Cherokee Indians, he said. A hundred wagon-loads of goods were gone out to pay the Indians for the land beyond the farther mountains, for a strip of Kentuck. Henderson called the country "Transylvania." A settlement had already been made, under this treaty, in the fine canelands, for Boone had gone into the country with a party of men. Nathan had seen a man who had been there and back, and he had report of the other settlement of Kentuck—Harrodstown. Both of these towns arose now in the heart of the fine cane country.

These stood for a moment dimly revealed as two small cabin towns in a vast waste of forest and tall reeds. Having seen them clearly in their fog of distance, Diony let them slip back into a vague fact, indifferently seen, and she asked:

"How far would you say it is to that place now? How far from this place where we now are?"

"Every bit of five hundred miles and over," Jones answered. "Five hundred the way you'd have to travel." He began to add miles together, reporting what his informer had told him.

The ways reached outward from the sunny wall, from the brightness of the winter day, going east and west. Betty denied any grace to this new country that lay five hundred miles beyond mountain ranges and rivers, and she laughed with Sam over the hominy maul, teasing, unamazed at Indian treaties and distances. The ways reached beyond, calling all that fed their ears now on Nathan's voice, but calling Betty to the cities of the coast, calling Reuben to an army, calling Diony. Nathan talked again of the Watauga country where the Indians had met the whites to sell their share of Kentuck.

"The Watauga country is halfway to the canelands," he said, "just about halfway, they say."

Narrow fertile valleys between mountains, these were his report of the halfway place. It was a good country of itself, he said, and well worth a man's consideration. Many had gone there and made settlements.

"Berk here aims to go there before spring sets in, before winter breaks," Nathan said slyly, as if he revealed a half-confidence. "I heard Berk say he'd aim to go to the Holston country and have a look about, and maybe take a look at how the road goes on to Kentuck. Halfway is a good start on the way. Did I hear you say you'd aim to go, or did I dream whilst I had a nap of sleep today?"

Berk nodded a shy acquiescence. He would go to the Holston country, to Watauga, and have a look around among the creeks there. Reuben brought a noggin of ale in honor of this departure and all drank of it from two cups or from the main vessel, passing the drink from hand to hand, waiting to hear Berk tell more of Watauga, and presently he told all he had heard of it. Countries stood forth then in Diony's mind as having presence, there being many countries to be inhabited, each one different from the others. Berk talked of this land eagerly, once he let himself speak. Diony looked at him, attending to his speaking mouth, to his person, putting his departure upon all that he said.

She looked at him, having a new knowledge of him now in her mind, knowing that he would go. He was a quiet man, vaguely freckled about the eyes. She thought of him as belonging to the girls who lived down near the court-house town. Often he would sit still for many moments together while some other talked, but when he moved at last he obliterated his stillness with swift nervous motion. His gaze would bend to the ground, or he would smile a belated smile that came to his face after some amused thought had crossed his mind, and over his late smile would pass a minute ripple so that his lips had a small crook run over them. Sometimes he would smile just before speaking as if he paid for his spoken word with a bright coin. As he sat now beside the house wall he drank from the same noggin from which she and Betty drank, reaching for it when he had ceased speaking and giving it gravely back. He talked of the country lying out into the southwest.

The way there was not overly steep or rugged, he said. He would follow the horse trails, and his talk brought to light now the Watauga forts, lately built to shelter the settlers. The shadows of the afternoon began to spread outward toward the east as if the day were passing, and Diony remembered what Nancy Webb had told her of herself. "You're pretty," Nancy Webb's voice said. "These boys down the creek, they'll tell you, but they are a slow-spoken lot not to 'a' told you sooner. . . ." Into this knowledge of Berk Jarvis, as told by Nancy, came the newer knowledge of Berk as one who would go far into the country of the Southwest, would go halfway to Kentuck to look at the way. A deep wish arose within her on the instant, a wish to know more of the structure of his being, to know all that he remembered and all that he saw as he looked outward, and to touch all with her own knowledge, and to know what it would be to him to go.

He drank from the noggin, smiled a part of his slow smile, and handed the vessel gravely back to her. His fringed hunting shirt was decorated with bright colors, the work his mother, Elvira Jarvis, had put upon it. His winter cap, made of furry skin, lay on the ground beside the butt of his rifle. He was a hunter and he took a pride in wearing the dress of such, but over his hunting shirt he wore a coarse coatee of heavy homespun cloth. His woolsey trousers were as those worn by the other man, close-fitted and banded at the knees, and his stockings were of Elvira's knitting. His fine hob-nailed shoes had been made by the cobbler at Charlottesville. He was strongly made and strongly put together for the long journey, his clothes new and fit, and Diony knew that his hunting shirt was but newly made, that his mother had just stitched it, preparing him for going. His hair seemed a fair brown when he leaned to take up his cap, and it blew in the winter sunlight. It was braided at the back and clubbed behind his head, tied up with a leathern strand.

Diony saw his hunting suit clearly then, all of it together, and she knew that he would go a long way and perhaps never come back. She heard Nancy Webb's voice lilting in her ear, saying an up-and-down phrase, "These Jarvises ought to 'a' told you, but they are a slow-spoken set. But they'll see it against another year . . ." The voice died out and arose and fell, mingling with the soft wind that blew at her hair.

The young men began to talk of their height, disputing and standing up together to measure. "I'm six foot," Berk said, but Reuben claimed this measure: "I'm six myself, and I'm short of you by a trifle." Sam brought a measuring rod and they measured themselves by the house, Nathan acting as judge. Reuben was found to be six feet and Berk six and a hand's breadth over. Diony saw Berk's blue eyes leap together and take an inward look, and he said there was more of him than he had supposed. His mouth, being wide and thin, was quick with its smile, once it was let, but his eyes restrained its pride now and made it wait on their pleasure. His measured height stayed on the house wall, the mark seeming high now that he had moved away from it.

"You better stay all night. You better pass a night here," Thomas Hall said.

"No, I said I'd get back afore sundown," Nathan made his reply. This speech brought Sookie, his wife, forth, a bright little chatterer whom Polly liked to have for a neighbor, brought her as expecting Nathan back, looking for him now perhaps. Sookie was immanent, pervading the going of the men, as one having a power over the going of Nathan. It came to light then that Berk would go any day, that he would go south with a returning pack train that had gone down the river a month earlier. All shook his hand and wished him good-bye, and at once the horses were clattering on the stones of the creek, taking the two men away, and Diony knew suddenly that Berk would go a long way before he came there again.

❖   ❖

Diony and Betty were spinning threads of flax, each at a wheel, making ready to weave the coverlet. There was a flavor of Nancy Webb in all that was done on the wheel, for Sam had been down the river to a wharf and he had seen her in her father's house. A renewed image of her leaped into Diony's mind out of Sam's talk now, Sam's cautious admiration guarding under his careless report of her. Nancy Webb would move swiftly, Diony thought, predicting, and Sam would never overtake her. She would be a married woman before Sam got the whole of his growth. Diony spun the flax, hearing the hogs scream in the December cold and knowing the sign, for if they scream for anything but their fodder they are crying at the coming cold. If a hog is seen staring toward the north the sign is that there will be cold weather, and again and again during the morning she had seen the sow staring outward toward a northerly way. Visitors seldom came to the plantation during the cold of a winter. The people of the house were shut together by the intimacies of the cold.

"Winter season makes me call to mind all ever I heard said of the tidewater places," Betty said, speaking softly. "We could talk now about the low cities, now whilst we spin, Diny. Could you take me there?"

"It's little I know to tell," Diony answered. "Tidewater people are curious, many ways. We wouldn't fancy to be there with folks that use all day inside of parlors and flower gardens and streets and such-like places, Betty."

"Oh, I would, I would," Betty cried out then. "I'd content myself with tidewater life. Hit would pleasure me mightily to be there, but not unlessen you come too. I couldn't content me there withouten you, Diny. I couldn't go except you mought go too."

"It's unlikely I'll ever go. We best put tidewater places outside our thought and content ourselves here, Betty."

Betty was still then for a space of time, so still that Diony glanced once toward her as she spun the flax, as she made the little wheel purr and wait attending on the needs of the spun thread. When Betty spoke her voice was half hushed away, as if she brought it under discipline and divided it from a flow of tears.

"I would always content me to be wherever you stay, Diony. I always set my heart on you, since I was a little tinsy tad, and I always loved you best and looked up to you."

"But afterwhile, any time now, a young fellow mought come along, and then you'd forget you ever took such a fancy to me. Past fourteen you are now, and by and by you'll look back and laugh to see you ever set store by your sister so mightily. You'll forget me against you get a husband and it's right you ought to. 'What a fool girl I was,' you'll say, against you get a young man to love you."

"Don't say hit," Betty said, speaking starkly, "don't say hit. No man-person could ever stand beside you, Diony, in my thinken. I mought have a husband of my own, and as like as not I will. Every woman has got to, seems. But I'd never look up to e'er a human man or woman like I look to you."

Diony pondered this for some time before she spoke, spinning quietly at the flax, making no sound but those that came from the softly creaking treadle and the whirring wheel. Her eyes followed the flaxen web which was a yellowish gray like some woman's hair, and as such it clung to her thought and twined gray spirals about any words her throat contrived but left unsaid. Her mind slipped then to her father's books and tried to bring this idolatrous devotion into relation with what she had read, and she divided the several processes of willing, imagining, and remembering, and placed the supreme act in one governing Spirit where all unimagined and unwilled and unremembered acts are kept before they are called into being. Having come then to the inner thought, the inmost realization, she held it one brief instant before it slipped swiftly beyond her most penetrating reach, and she turned then to think of Betty and her worshipful regard for herself, until she fell into a dream and lived only in the flowing of the flax and the soft singing of the wheel, her eyes fastened on the moving thread. She spoke out of her dream, her voice scarcely heard:

"Why is this so, as you tell it, Betty?"

"Hit's so because you're the most . . . to me. I couldn't name the reasons."

Diony continued to dream, her senses a web of unknowing fibers that reached into and among the fibers of the flax. She waited until the high tide of emotion had passed from herself and Betty, until quiet had come. When she spoke her voice came as if it arrived quietly from some casual hour, two sisters chattering idly over their spinning.

"If a chance e'er came for you to go to some city in the tidewater, the first thing would be for you to know how to read books and how to write down letters, how to cipher numbers, or how would you know what went on there?"

"I could learn how to read in books in a little time," Betty said. "I'll begin today. I always aimed to let you learn me some day, Diny. I'll take down any book you think fitten and learn off in no time, you'll see. Whe'r I ever go to the tidewater or not. I'll learn, just to pleasure you."

"It would pleasure me right considerable to have you learn to read. It mought not be any use to you and you mought go all your days and nobody care whe'r you read in books or not. Heaps of people never read in books, and they know how to do as soon as the kind that read and handle print." Diony spun for some moments, letting whatever quiet the room held fold about her, a pity and a great love for Betty in her whole being so that she spun the flax gently and with greater care, making a thread of exceeding smoothness, such a thread as she had never made before with the filaments, as if a newer care were born into her fingers. Finally she spoke again:

"Some day we mought go down the river, past Richmond. When Reuben gets his new field made and grows crops there he would likely help us go. It would take a sight of money. Three fields in harvest would scarcely buy for us what we'd need, money along the way and pack horses and gowns and linens. If we took the boldness to go to see our cousin Isobel we would have to have three dresses apiece. We could go withouten the dresses for a little money, maybe, but with the gowns and linens three fields would hardly buy for us all we'd require to have. If

we work hard and help Reuben with whatever is to
do, and when we come back help again when he
wants to make a crop to buy iron for wagon wheels
and bolts, and to buy iron for the new forge or glass
for all the windows, maybe he'll let us go. We
wouldn't go to see Isobel withouten the linens and
clothes, and it wouldn't content you very much to go
down to some tidewater place in your old homespun
and hide behind some door to look out on what
passed, to come back home like a thief. If it's in my
mortal power to take you, Betty, we'll go."

Betty played over her web, bending herself to it
and flowing with the sway of the wheel, her pleasure
put insecurely under the labor of her hands, her
pleasure breaking forth from moment to moment in
the smile that rippled about her mouth. The little
wheels purred lightly, making fine threads of flax.

Coley Linkhorn, a Methodist, came from over in
the valley beyond the Blue Ridge, from the Valley of
the Shenandoah, coming riding into the plantation
one sundown. Polly was pleased to have news of her
relatives in the upper valley toward Harrisonburg
and she was pleased again to have Methodist thought
and prayers in the house. Linkhorn slept in one of the
upper rooms, beyond the room where Diony and

Betty slept, and Diony heard him praying late into the night and again early in the day.

Then Polly asked Sam to mount his riding horse and go over the countryside, into the waters of the Rockfish and the Tye, and to tell the Methodist families there that Coley Linkhorn had come, and to invite them to the plantation for two days of worship. Polly, with some of her neighbor women to help, prepared a quantity of food before the guests arrived, but Saturday was given to preparations as well as to prayers and hymns.

The men and women came early, sixteen or seventeen people coming up the creek road on horses or on drag slides. The women laid aside their shawls or foot-mantles in the new house and lingered there a little beside the fire, some of them smoking their pipes. Polly worked in the kitchen, making the meat pies or setting a great apple pie to bake near the coals. Long tables had been set in the kitchen room reaching well back toward the weaving place. Some of the women helped Polly inside, but others worked in the yard where a sheep was being roasted on a spit over the fire. In the bright warmth of the winter forenoon Linkhorn assembled all under the tree before the door and offered prayers or read from the Bible.

Nineteen men had come now, their women at

work helping prepare the feast. Mistress Elvira, the mother of the Jarvis men, of Will and Berk and Jack Jarvis, was at hand. She worked outside at the spit, a tall woman who bent and stooped now and then among the pots and ovens, deferring with quiet dignity to Polly Hall because Polly was the mistress of the house, proposing each plan to her before she put it into use. She walked quietly about before the outer fire, and two or three girls were at hand to serve her. Diony went back and forth between the women in the kitchen and those outside, carrying messages or utensils, went between Polly and Elvira to fetch for both of them. Seeing Elvira's face, the first that she had seen of her for many months, she saw how much Berk's face was like to it and was startled at this appearance of his image.

Diony watched in secret while the tall woman came and went, or she watched more minutely when she passed near. Elvira's hair was dark, but she carried one white lock, a birthmark, well back from her forehead. As her hair was bound the white line wove a continual strand through the dark mass, a sharply defined stripe of gray in the brown of her tight coil. The planes of her face were large and her smile would wait upon some inner thought. Diony saw her taking care of the roast that steamed over the fire and saw her turn it about with the crank.

Requested, she brought a long wooden spoon from the house and her hands quietly questioned the woman's hands as they gave the tool across before the fire, although her mind did not know what thing her hands were asking. When she turned away from the fire and started back across the open space her apron became untied and fell to the ground in a crumpled pool of soft linen which she trod over.

"Your sweetheart's a-thinken about you," Sookie said, pointing to the fallen apron. "When that trick happens your lover-person is a-thinken . . ."

"Who's a-thinken?" Diony asked.

She was shy to pick up the apron with all the women watching what she did, all repeating it, "Diony's sweetheart is a-thinken of her," but she tied the garment about her waist again. Elvira turned back to the roasting flesh and arranged the dripping pans, but in the instant she smiled and a crooked ripple passed over her lips, a shadow of the real, scarcely there on the older mouth that had grown strong and heavy with much living.

On Sunday there was food enough for all laid by and the day was given to prayers and singing and the interpretation of the scriptures. Worship lasted well into the afternoon and none broke the Sabbath with cock-fighting or wrestling. The great hymns arising in the large room of the new house seemed of a

strength to raise the walls to a more lofty height, and
as Diony fitted her voice into the great flowing din
she felt the leaping inner pleasure of shared moral
desires, wanting goodness for herself then, wanting
goodness for all men.

❖   ❖

In late spring, 1776, Reuben yoked two steers together under a wooden collar and made them plow
his new field. The stumps, burned to charred ruins,
dotted the cleared spaces, but the soil rolled up nevertheless under the tough plow of stout wood that was
beaked with a shard of iron, and Sam walked beside
the oxen to guide them. Betty had learned to read
some of the words in the books, catching at them
gayly. The war seemed very far away, far from
Virginia. From the mouth of the dog alley Diony
could look down on the creek and the garden patch
and the field where the oxen plodded all day in the
furrows to make a harvest of bread. Knowing what
went forward in the field she sat at the loom weaving,
throwing the shuttle through the web of fine linen to
make her coverlet, setting the Whig Rose design over
the white web in soft blue yarn. The light from the
high window came in a square that lit the loom and
her hands as they played swiftly over the fiber, and
she watched the power of the cloth as it grew, scarcely

heeding the treadling which her feet had learned to follow with skill.

While she was weaving thus Jack Jarvis came hallooing along the creek and Sam was heard answering. They were shouting back and forth from the creek to the field, flinging carelessness and boy-defiance. Jack had not come to see Sam, he shouted, he would have none of him. He had come to see Diony; he wanted private speech with her. She heard her name called thus in their talk and she passed the bobbin through the web, waiting until Jack came to her, thinking that he had come to pass the time away.

He stood beside the loom and half whispered to her. His brother Will was going outward toward the west, together with others, and their mother, Elvira, would go also. All were going southwest into the valley of the Holston, into the headwaters of the Tenn-ess-ee. Half the Jarvis household would then be gone, but he and Preston and Eli would remain in the James country awhile longer. He lowered his voice then and spoke as if of another matter.

He had had a message from Berk and he had a word from Berk to her, Diony. A man had come back from the Southwest where Berk had gone. A trader had come along the trail, on his way down the river with five horse-loads of pelts he had got back in Fincastle among the mountains. He had stopped a night and he had delivered the message. Diony stayed her bobbin to hear, her feet stilled on the treadles, waiting to know what message Berk would send to her by a man who had traveled two hundred miles since he had seen him. The words came clear and sharp across the stilled loom, given only by way of the mouth. Berk had said that he was safe, that he had planted a crop of corn. The words seemed powerful as coming two hundred miles through the mouth of a stranger. Jack repeated, adding the message that was for her:

"Tell Diony Hall Berk Jarvis is well and safe. Tell Jack Jarvis, my brother, to go to see Diony Hall and to say to her that Berk Jarvis is well, to say to her that Berk will come back and that he would be right proud if she will wait for him."

Diony pondered this message carefully and then she said, beginning to weave again:

"Berk Jarvis can write. Why wouldn't he write a letter? Why wouldn't he say this to me by way of his own written words? I couldn't scarcely get my consent to accept it iffen it comes to me in any such way. I couldn't scarcely."

Jack stood embarrassed for a short time and Diony passed the shuttle through the web, weaving cloth.

"Iffen you could see Like Graves, the man Berk gave the message to carry, you wouldn't wonder

Berk, he wouldn't trust anything so puny as a letter in his hands. He is a right big giant and a big coarse sort, can't read himself and got mighty little patience with anything so triflen and weakly as a piece of paper writ over with words. Sakes bless us! Berk would know he couldn't trust Like Graves to keep a hold onto anything so little and lady-like as a letter. As apt as not Berk did write it down and Like, he lost it afore he got outside Berk's sight. I wish you could see Like Graves and see what a big coarse sort he is and see what a power of curses can fall out of his mouth when he whoops up his pack horses, and see his buckskin shirt that's all grease and bear oil and filth, so dirty iffen he brought you a letter inside his pouch he's got sewed onto the front side of his shirt you'd be right put-to to know which way to hold it to see clear of the lice a-crawlen over it. Now a word outen his mouth, comen to you in this way, is cleaned and combed by the wind afore it reaches you, and comes hearty enough too. It's seasoned with Like's heftiness, but it's a sight cleaner. And so I lay it humbly at your feet, Mistress Diony Hall, and you're right welcome."

Diony laughed then and she felt that she blushed for an instant, but she wove at the cloth while she accepted Berk's vows. Jack leaned against the beam of the loom, watching her hands as they tossed the shuttle back and forth in a swift sleight. Presently he said:

"Will and our mother are a-goen there now in two days or three, and they would carry intelligence of any word you might want to send Berk. I judge Berk, he'd be right pleased to have some answer to his letter, this big hefty letter I tell you about. Will Jarvis can read and he sets store by learnen, and he would carry a written letter back and engage to take it all the way. And Mammy, Elvira Jarvis, is a woman-person and sets a right smart store by messages and letters and such-like dainties. Iffen you want to send word back to Berk you got a heap better chance 'n he had to get it carried safe. I'll engage Will Jarvis, he'll carry your love-letter safe and give it over right-away he got there to the proper party."

Diony wove this into her cloth, but she said nothing, giving only a smile for comment. She began to see that Jack was unlike Berk and to feel a different person, not Berk, as standing near. He was not so tall and he carried a broadness about himself as if he settled squarely into the ground. His hunting shirt was plucked by the briars and small threads raveled out from it, as if he had walked straight forward through brush. His eyes, bent down to follow the shuttle, were of some dark sort, and Diony was thinking that they did not have to be blue, and thinking of the strangeness of eyes bent downward as if they did not see. Then he was talking again:

"Berk, he'd be proud to get some word from you, that I know. It's near two hundred miles to the place where he is and over three mountains, and more rivers 'n I can name. Halfway to Kentuck, he is. I hope you got his token he sent by Like Graves and could see past the lice I aimed to bresh away afore I set it in front of you, and see Berk Jarvis himself is behind the token a-waiten for some word. Maybe it wasn't a good way to send, but Berk, I know, did the best he could with what he had at hand and any token Like Graves brought would be right hefty a token. As I say, Like, he's a rough sort, strong-fisted and all, and anything light would 'a' lost off long afore he got here. It to come here at all shows what a hefty thing it was he carried."

"What makes it come to Berk Jarvis's mind to say such to me now?" she asked. "Six months and over it is since he went away, and it comes to his mind to say what he says. It's a wonder of the earth."

Jack was troubled at this comment, and he had no answer ready at once. But he found words at last:

"You're pretty as a picture, whilst you sit there to make trouble for me and Berk, and all times. Berk, he knows. One time I heard him say . . . But I won't engage to name all he said."

Diony wove while this speech floated away into the air, putting a blue thread or a white one, as the pattern needed, into the web. "No," she said. "I will send my word to Berk Jarvis too by word-of-mouth. I won't write back a letter. You can tell him by Will and Mistress Elvira I got his token and I am right pleased to know he is well and safe. Tell him I still live on the creek and it's likely I'll be here when he comes back, that I've got no handy plan to take me away right now and no wish to be taken."

"He'll be proud to get word from you, that I know. I'll tell Mammy and Will all you say in your own words, but I'll tell too what way you look whilst you piece the words together and what kind of smile is around your mouth. They can take it all back to Berk for a token. I expect he'll come back here by October, and then he'll give you his own token, first-hand."

"I always heard it said the Jarvis men are a slow-spoken lot," Diony said, "little to say. Seems now you make out a right handy talker. Since you came and stood beside the loom you said a right long discourse. Have you got more to say, Mister Jack Jarvis?"

"Yes, I got more, for it's my belief Berk, when he comes again, will be maken steps towards Kentuck. Many is the time I've heard him say he was more 'n half of a mind to go there and settle down. He's gone now to the Holston country more to spy out the way to Kentuck and try the road a piece of the way. He's planted a crop of corn there on the Holston to have grain when he sets out on the long travel. It's my belief when he finishes what he set out to do there he'll come back here and have a word with you on the matter."

Diony made no comment on this surmise or prophecy although it startled her into some new relation with the Jarvis men, first with Berk, but with Jack too, for he leaned near and was the speaker. His surmise and report, being given as true, spread outward through the threads of her nerves to the last fine web of sense. By the time she had passed three shuttles across the warp before her, the disclosure seemed to be an ancient story, already known and true to all her members, Berk being immanent, present in her own mind, as if he had not gone away.

"Did Berk send any more word by way of Like Graves?" she asked. "Did he hint at all this by way of the letter you told about a while ago?"

He had not sent more. "Egad, Diony, I know Berk Jarvis well enough to make talk for him." Jack was retelling and giving proof. "He means every last word I say." Diony let the matter go as stated, and she led Jack to talk of the southwest country as he had got report of it from Graves and the hunters.

Will Jarvis and his family would live there hereafter, and their mother would go. Diony recalled then that her father had said that the Jarvis men were a roving set, never satisfied. Berk had planted himself a field of corn to make grain for the farther journey, and her sight went far into the Southwest to see Berk plowing strange lands, making a long slow field that would grow into a harvest to feed him on the long march.

❖   ❖

Betty leaped into the books and out, her quick mind snatching at the words, and presently she was reading the fables. The oxen plodded up and down the new field, dragging the rich new soil, Sam walking beside them to keep them in the way. News came from Philadelphia in July: Congress had declared the colonies free. A new feeling came from the land, from the field and the oxen, all being free now. The war was far away, never clearly brought before the plantation, for it was beyond Virginia. The men were fighting about New York and along the Hudson River, but presently a rumor came of war in the Southwest among the forts along the Holston. "There's war in the southwest part," Sam said, flinging the truth at her as he came in from the creek, "war where Berk's gone." The new field was giving an abundant growth. It was a free field, no longer belonging to a

sovereign king, but the plow went over it as before
and the corn grew in the accustomed way. "When
men go from here I'll go," Reuben said, thinking of
the war on the seaboard. George Washington was
moving his army about New York, report of this
coming up the river and thence up the creek to
settle into the mill, to be doled out with the turns of
their wheat. There was a newer rumor of fierce war
in the Southwest, the Indians and the King's men
driving the settlers to the forts. Diony wove at her
coverlet, war being a bird of two great wings, one
spread east among the sea-cities, the other west
among the forts. It was a phantom fowl in which she
could scarcely believe, but it flew over the land. She
trusted the little that lay between herself and Berk
to keep itself secure.

A letter came to Thomas from Nathaniel Barlow.
It was brought by a black servant and given cere-
moniously. When Thomas had read it silently, his lips
moving lightly over the words, he called Polly and
Diony to listen and read it slowly in the privacy of
the new room. The letter: "Honored sir:—Business
keeps me at the seat of government and forbids my
attending on you in person to make known to you
my desire by word of mouth . . ." The words
played through Diony's mind, fine words cloaking
a simple wish. . . . "Either banish the idol if I

must or admire the fair with open expressions of esteem . . ." Her mind remembered the long flowing strains of the words, but her senses forgot their import, they being useless to her. . . . "I have had sufficient witness of her amiable character and her beauty . . . she the most worthy of her sex . . . Would deem it an honor should Miss Diony accept my hand . . . in the holy bond . . ."

Thomas had made an answer to the document, writing carefully at his desk the half of a morning and clothing Diony's refusal in elegant words of delay, calling her a child and saying that such matters had not yet entered her consideration. While the letter was being prepared Diony had a clear sharp image of Berk in her mind's eye, seeing him stand before a house, before all the objects of thought, before the labor of the farm.

The Whig Rose grew into the coverlet, blue flowers and threaded designs upon a field of shadowy white. When Sam went to the mill again a better news was astir, for the fight in the Southwest was said to be spent of its force and to have settled vaguely back into some farther country, the Indians being defeated.

❖   ❖

Diony and Betty were digging a few sweet potatoes for Sallie Tolliver's cooking, the boys being busy with the harvest. Betty gathered the potatoes into a hickory basket after Diony had broken apart the shallow earth and brought them up with the hoe. The soil fell into crumbs of damp red mold, and out of the clods came odors of sweet decay. As her hoe severed the earth to let the fruit out, her thought spread widely to grasp some other way of the earth where would be soil of some other kind, and she wondered of the mold where Berk had gone and what soil he plowed.

"Ouch! Sakes bless us!" Betty cried out, stepping out of the row, drawing away from the labor.

"What part did you get hurted in?" Diony asked.

"I ruined my ankle on a briery weed. Diny, I'll ask Sam to make fast a little seat between the two button trees, a kind of bench seat for us to sit on, against another year goes by. Would you like that, Diny? A seat fixed out under a tree I always think is pleasant. Hit would be easy to make and a handy place to go to hem our hankerchers and such-like. Would you like that, Diny, a pretty seat down along the creekside to rest ourselves on?"

Diony knew in that instant that she would go with Berk wherever he went, and she felt a pain arise within her to know that she would hurt Betty, mingled with a wish to be gone. Her whole body swayed toward the wilderness, toward some further part of the world which was not yet known or sensed in any human mind, swayed outward toward whatever was kept apart in some eternal repository, so that she leaped within to meet this force halfway and share with it entirely. Her eyes followed the hoe and fixed themselves on the brown potatoes it uncovered as they nested in the brown of the earth. She moved a few paces along the row while she kept the high power of her fervid wish, and she glanced once at Betty and saw the brightness of her eyes and the free motions of her small body, her quick upturned face and sharp demands, her hostility to the back-country as if she held herself reserved from it, and she saw then that Betty was somehow fashioned for great love and that there was nothing at hand which was sufficient to share her need. On the instant the air seemed split apart and the day severed, the sunshine slashed open, she and Betty standing apart in the rent, alike but hostile, and she saw that she herself was fashioned likewise in some curious way, and that there was nothing between the hills of Albemarle which was enough to use all her strength, until it seemed that the whole of the wilderness beyond the mountains, the whole of Kentuck, would not appease her, that she would love it all and still have love to spare.

A cool air drifted up from the creek, but the sun fell steadily warm on the garden. Diony broke a

crust of the soil and turned it apart, making free
several potatoes before she spoke. Then she said, as
if she played a light game with her wayward self,
tapping the soil in a rhythm with her speech:

"A bench would be pleasant for us, and when
Nancy Webb comes . . . I don't know. I mought go
a long piece afore it's fastened to the button tree, if
Sam, he's not right peart about fixen it soon. I
mought go as far as the Chenoa River, the Millewakane. I mought be gone soon now."

Betty said nothing at once to this playful speech
and Diony moved down the row, opening the last
potato mound in the ridge. Then Betty said, as if
lightly, shielding the weight of her decision under
half-spoken phrases:

"You promised, Diny . . . I learned to read in
the books. I already learned." She took the last of
the potatoes into her basket, gathering them one by
one with her slim fingers, stooping easily over the
chopped soil. "You promised . . . A promise is like
a sworn testament. Hit's bonden and true. Lasty,
hit is."

November frosts were white over the burnt grass
when Berk came back, the leaves in a grand way
with color. Diony had begun to move softly about,
faintly subdued with waiting and stilled by the re-

ports of continual wars. Thomas Hall would read aloud the Declaration of Independence, the great words of Thomas Jefferson thundering through the house at evening. . . . "We hold these truths to be self-evident: That all men are created equal, that they are endowed by their Creator with certain unalienable Rights . . ." The chill settled out of the sky, falling upon the warm earth that was blanketed with rich leaves, autumn being a certainty that could not be dissuaded. Reuben said that when he could market his tobacco he would buy himself two black servants, men to labor for him in the fields. Diony heard the last crying of the crickets in the tawny grass, but she heard too a horse's step on the creek road and heard a step coming through the garden at nightfall. There was hurrying about through the dog alley and Sam crying out a war-whoop. "It's Berk!" he called through the house.

When he came into the kitchen room Diony lifted her eyes swiftly to see what he would be after a year in the new country of the Southwest, but her search told her little. A large strange man sat at their board that evening, but once when he smiled there was a sudden appearance of the one who had gone away. After supper, in the new house, he seemed willing enough to sit looking happily into the fire, or he would glance quickly toward Diony. The war in the

South was nearly over, he said, the Indians already defeated. When the evening was advancing he let their urgent need for report of it prevail over his reticence and he told a long story.

Early in the summer word had come that the Cherokees were preparing to march, that they were mending guns, making moccasins, and beating corn into flour, were pledging themselves to a course of war by painting their bodies with the tribal emblems. June, and word came that they had struck the settlers in Georgia. By July the whole south country was in war, every fort threatened. Seven hundred Otari Indians were on the way to attack the forts, and all through the mountains the Indians were on the march, roused and armed by the King in England, the seaboard war and this being the same. . . .

He told of bold fighting in the Island Flats of the Holston River, the settlers running to the forts, the cabins burned, the cattle and horses carried away, the sheep and hogs shot with arrows. All the roads and trails leading to the forts were filled with terrified settlers running for safety. He had gone with a company of riflemen, had marched out to meet the Indians at Island Flats. They were a hundred and seventy men strung out in two long lines with scouts at the flanks to save them from surprise. The Indians were led by a brave man, Dragging Canoe. Long files of whites were strung out over open country or retreated into the trees, the Indians practising their cunning, the lines running forward, attack and counter-thrust. The whites had thirteen scalps when the fight was over. While this fight went forward on the river the Watauga forts were assailed by another army. The fort was crowded with women and children, only forty men there to bear arms. The rush was discovered in time and the fort held without loss. . . .

Diony turned her mind back across the summer and remembered swiftly all that had come to her while Berk enacted these perils. She lost the design of the story and lost the intention of it in the myriad of details that rushed forward until the whole became a roar of war and a crash of rifles. One battle did not differ from another in danger. At night Berk slept continually on his arms, by day he marched more inwardly into the Indian country to deal the counter-blow. He had served under Colonel Anderson, and his narrative delayed now while he told of the leader, of the strained life in the fort where the people were forced to live on parched corn.

He told of continual war over the whole frontier, every man in mortal danger, farmland plundered, crops laid waste, women and children killed, houses burned. Then the settlers prepared a great counterattack to strike down the Cherokees in their own villages. He had gone out with a fighting companion, John Gowdy, in an army now of two thousand men under Christian. On the first day of October the army marched, mostly on foot, armed with rifles and with tomahawks and knives. His speech was rugged, never easy and free with the story, but the battles grew under his telling. The Indians fled, begging the Creeks for help, but there was no help to be had. The tribes were accepting the peace offered and Dragging Canoe had fled to the mountains. Peace would come now, the Indians being humbled. Berk had quit the army then and had come back. The questions that leaped about the fireside now directed the story and swayed it here and there.

Sallie Tolliver came tipping down the stair from the room above where Berk's voice had surely found her out, and she went, a tall bent apparition, across the floor toward the dog alley, going to the kitchen room to find silence there. She walked swiftly through the telling of the battles, scarcely clicking the latch as she passed the door.

Back then, Berk told of a succession of single combats, a man against a man or against two. Gowdy grappled with his man once and flung him over an embankment and emptied his rifle into his side while he lay. He himself, intent on Gowdy's danger, had neglected his own, and a redskin was upon him to lay hold of his rifle and wrench it from his hand. The crash of rifles was incessant, the cries of the dying, the shouts of the leaders, the war-cries of the savages, curses and groans and the stab of the knife. Diony heard this story now with a wish in her mind that this would be the end of war, that Berk Jarvis would find peace, that he would not go again with an army, that all battles would henceforth be done. She would not ask a question to bend the tale or to check it, but she let all pass over her as it would. It was Berk indeed who sat by the fire, the teller of the story. His strong hands were knotted together. He smiled once at some question Sam asked, yielding the query a slow mirth and an after-mirth that brought his former way of life back to him. Thomas was talking now and Diony glanced from mouth to mouth and saw these instruments distorted, mouths become some strange flutes or horns, shaped cunningly to play out war, to cry out battles. Thomas Hall's mouth bent and twisted now as a clattering bugle blowing the science of war, making philosophy out of stories of death.

Mouths were hungry instruments that bent about reports of killed men. Diony saw the shape of her father's word as it played on his mouth but she gave no heed to his sayings. Berk, sitting quietly now before the fire, beyond Reuben, stooped to take his ease, his body relaxed, would let his gaze dwell on the fire as if he went far into a reverie and as if he forgot herself and the house about him and all the company, as if he remembered then the nights of the march toward the South, the crash of rifles and the on-rush of savages, the cries and curses and war-whoops of battles, as if he remembered now gladly. Then her eyes would search his averted face and his drooping eyes, his unguarded mouth, and she would love him with a rush of passion that almost stilled her heart in its beat, would love him for the dangers he had passed and the cruel images that were pictured on his mind, and she would gather all into her for-giveness and forget it and shelter it there.

The father brought bedtime swiftly, and all dis-persed, turning hither and there without ceremony. Diony went with Betty above to the upper room where they slept. The candle guttered and dripped its oily tears that rolled in slow and useless grief down the candlestick and made an ugly pool on the slab of the bedside table.

"Hit's a sluttish light," Betty said, sadly. "I could blow out the flame and not grieve myself to lack hit."

Her tone wove a sadness through the shadowed air and Diony lay in the bed and covered herself, shrinking within the loneliness of her own thought. Betty distrusted Berk and grieved now that he had come. Diony withdrew toward the dark of the bed and sank into the blackness of the wall when Betty destroyed the feeble light. Betty's sadness and displeasure lay beside her as a stark bedfellow and she went apart into the oblivion of sleep.

❖   ❖

Out in the frosty cold of the early morning to milk the cow, leaving Betty asleep in their bed, Diony let the telling voice of the night before recede from her memory and let all that was told beside the fire become now a finished music, judged and settled into her knowledge, but not sounding now in her ears. A fog had rolled up from the river to lie over the white frost of the early night, and now the frost and the mist made a brilliant silver air that leaped and sparkled in the sun. The last of the leaves were falling and the ground was spread with gold. A golden leaf would drop through the bright air, and then another, a slow rain, and a flock of birds, going overhead, were a swift flow of flashing wings that beat across the shimmering welkin. The cow appeared in the mist and her tawny coat made bright color before the dust of white frost that lay over the cow-pen, her long vapory breath joining the body of the mist. The fowls moved quickly about, in search of corn, white geese and speckled guineas and dark hens that were colored like calico. Diony stood up in the sparkling frost, bringing the cow through the opened gap, her hand on the animal's back, feeling herself to be shut into the dazzling brightness of the morning, as taken apart into the great blinding whiteness of sunlit mist and the raining gold of the leaves. Berk came to her there and together they were secluded in the bright frost. They could scarcely see the smith-shop or the barn and could but dimly trace the outline of the dwelling where it lay as faint lines of darkness behind the radiant air. He took the piggin from her hand and put it by, and a few gold leaves fell, drifting past her shoulder. Then she saw his smile appearing, lighting first his eyes and coming then toward his mouth, and when they had smiled once together he kissed her, shut with her into the miracle of the air and the sun. There being then no need for words to pass between them, they milked the cow and carried the milk to the milk-house where they set it away in the earthen jars.

Breakfast was ready in the kitchen when Polly called them from the door. All were present, and Thomas Hall directed the talk to the country beyond the ranges, west and southwest, taking their thought back to the matter of the night before. Berk sat between Sam and Reuben on the long bench at the side of the table, and Diony sat apart, near to Betty and their mother. There was questioning as to what the land was in the southwest, as to how it appeared. High mountains stood up in the report of it, great peaks with fertile valleys, rivers dashing down past brown boulders, flats and high valleys where grew natural pasture. Diony saw the green of summer trees in the land where Berk had been, and she saw the land sloping down into the farther southwest dotted over with clearings, farms for the white man when he had taken them. Indian villages stood dimly in the pictures, bark houses gathered together about a fire, traders going there to sell the white man's goods for pelts. Far beyond, bent away from the southwest, lay Kentuck, the richest and most desired part.

"That land, hit belongs to the Indians," Polly said.

Her mouth drew into a fine hardness, a protest against the wilderness. "Hit belongs," she said again, grimly. Diony saw the reason of all Polly uttered as it smote Berk and Sam and Reuben until they sat stilled, their food neglected. Berk made a movement as if he would speak, but he was abashed before Polly's anger, seeing the right in what she said through the power of her skillful mouth that flowed from moment to moment into newer ways of loveliness. She did not yield, but sat in uncompromising beauty, erect in her chair, her head lifted when she spoke.

"Hit's Indian property. The white man has got no rights there. Hit's owned already, Kentuck is. Go, and you'll be killed and skulped by savages, your skulp to hang up in a dirty Indian house or hang on his belt. Hit's already owned. White men are outside their rights when they go there."

Indetermination settled over the board and distress visited the young men. Outrageous battle, fire, burning at the stake, rapine, plunder, the jackals eating the dead. They saw all these and right divided itself from wrong anew. Thomas Hall spoke then. Striking the table over which he leaned with a great blow, his fist clenched, bringing decision back to their thought.

"If the Indian is not man enough to hold it let him give it over then," he said. "It's a land that calls for brave men, a brave race. It's only a strong race can hold a good country. Let the brave have and hold there."

"Yes, sir, yes," Berk joined him then. "If he can't hold, if he's afeared and frighted to stay there, let him cry for't. If he sees ghosts there and hears noises and is frighted by the Alleghewi . . . Dead men's bones! If he can't keep it he can leave it alone.

Stronger men are bound to go in there, more enduren men."

The young men leaped to support the opening Thomas and Berk had made. Right settled to new ground and reared itself in new places. Their voices cracked sharply over the board, one after another.

"The most enduren will take . . ."

"You couldn't hold it safe for weak men until they think it safe to go there."

"The Long Knives are the strong men you named. The Long Knife is bound to win there."

"The Big Knife."

"Who is it calls the Virginians the Long Knives?"

"Hit's the Shawnees. They call all Virginia the Big Knife."

"I look to see the Long Knives take Kentuck."

"You couldn't hold a land safe for weak men."

"Strong men will go in and take."

"Strong men will win there."

❖   ❖

Berk told of the crop of corn that he had made on the Holston. It had escaped the ravages of the battles and was plucked and housed now, ready to make him grain for the farther march. Men and women had gone, he said, to the cabin towns, Harrodstown and Boonesborough, beyond the long wilderness through which Boone's Trace marked out the way, for Boone had marked out a way through the forest and had chosen places where the streams could be forded, a master-work. He would go, Berk said, when the spring came, when the rivers were safe for fording. He would take Boone's Trace to the canelands around Harrodstown. He had come back to get Diony's promise that she would go too. He talked slowly, finding his words with care, glancing toward Diony as if he asked assistance in the telling. He was not afraid of Indians, he said.

"They're a poor sort, under all their paint and war-noises. If you guard yourself against surprise he has got a mighty little advantage. I never yet in all my time saw one Indian keep his courage up when he begins to lose a fight. Run, he will then, and hide in the brush. I'm not afeared to set out on Boone's Trace and a company of fifteen or so goes too. . . ."

"But not Diony," Thomas Hall said, standing over the table and striking the board with a great blow. "Not my Diony to go there."

Quiet settled over the board. The food had been eaten or was set aside. Polly shifted in her chair and acquiesced by her movement to all that Thomas said. Diony bent her head and waited.

"Not Diony," he said again. "No, sir." He struck the table with a final blow of decision and pushed

his bent limb free of a chair, moving swiftly toward
the door. The company broke apart, scattering away
from the table, and Sallie Tolliver began to clear the
board. Thomas limped noisily out at the door and
went from the house. Sam and Reuben had gone
outside hurriedly. Betty began to spin at the wheel
where the wool yarn was made, stepping lightly back
and forth. All the acts of the plantation went forward
with decision and vigor.

Diony took her mantle about her shoulders and
went out with Berk and they walked toward the
creek. The morning had cleared and the bright mist
was gone, and the last of the leaves were falling.
Behind them the business of the plantation went
noisily on. Polly was hurrying about the house and
the meat-cabin, making ready for the butchering of
the swine, which labor would come with the first
hard freezing. Reuben and Sam were shucking the
corn, at work in the doorway of the barn, and
Thomas shouted orders from the stable or he limped
briskly about among the horses, bringing his young
filly out into the sun. It was a colt he was raising to
make himself a fine riding mare and he had a great
pride in it. As they walked toward the creek Diony
could see him briskly rubbing the animal's fine coat,
and he fitted a saddle to its back to teach it the feeling of a burden. The sunlight fell broadly, widely

dispersed after the brilliant mystery of the early
morning, and Diony knew that she would finally go
with Berk wherever he desired, the clear fine light
of the morning being spread over the whole ground
with equality and evenness.

They came back to the house and sat in the dim
half-light of the new room, letting the doors slam
without their assistance, letting Polly call from the
window, letting Thomas hammer out a shoe for the
mare colt on his smith's anvil. The fire in the chimney was a great bank of supine brands that had fallen
into a dark nest of hot embers, letting heat out
steadily. Diony was abashed at her father's words, at
his strong blow on the table, sickened by them until
her breath was slow in her throat and her head
bowed. The blows on the anvil made now a great
musical protest that rang through the whole plantation. Across in the kitchen room Betty was spinning
wool, her steps scarcely audible through the clamor
of the iron in the smithy.

They talked of the common things of the farm,
putting their deeper concern a little apart from themselves, and Diony gave bits of news of all that had
happened in the past year, of what had come to
Sam's fighting cocks, of Reuben's plans. Reuben
expected to buy two black servants, two men, to do
the work of the fields. Polly had never wanted black

slaves and Thomas had given way to her protest, but
Reuben made his plans and Polly would not deny
him. Coley Linkhorn, the Methodist from over in
the Valley of the Shenandoah, had come during the
summer and there had been singing and prayer in
the house. Whispering together they talked of Coley
Linkhorn, the great blows falling meanwhile on the
iron of the anvil where a shoe for the little mare colt
was being prepared, loud swift denials, in iron, making a continual protest to all that they held in mind.

Berk kissed her sadness then until it flowered into
a newer joy, and whispering together he told her his
plan, a device they would carry out as soon as her
father gave a willingness; but the iron voice outside
was still unrelenting, beating hard and fast through
his words. They would go to the country behind the
mountains and start a new world there, he said. He
would have horses to carry them and horses to carry
their packs, and there would be corn enough. The
price of land in the cane country was twenty or
thirty shillings for a hundred acres, and he told her
what gold he had saved and what silver he had
earned from the sale of pelts, all now secreted in his
money belt.

"How will we go and what way will we go there?"
she asked.

"Up the river and over the Blue Ledge, through

the Valley of the James, and then easy, the way down
into Augusta County. Then down in a south direction into the waters of the Kanawha, but you keep
southwest and go over a long ridge into the waters
of the Holston."

There would be stations along the way where
they could rest and get provisions when their sup-
plies ran low, he said. It would take three weeks to
bring them to the settlements where Will Jarvis had
gone, and they would rest there with their kin. Then
in a greater company they would set out on the real
journey, over mountains and up and down ridges
and over fords, and come at last to a lonely country,
the Wilderness, where the stations and forts came to
an end and where the mountains would stand as a
wall across the Trace. Beyond that he knew only a
little. There was a long journey after the Great Gap
was passed, through an uninhabited country where
one might travel a hundred miles and never meet a
human face. The great protesting blows were falling
on the anvil outside, ringing through the farm and
beating against Berk's words as he spoke softly of the
journey. His report grew dim and merged with the
trees, and sank into the maze of unthought travel,
sank into miles of untraveled paths and scarcely
marked trails, sank into the deeps of a caress that
blurred the thought of going and rested them in the

fog and mist of the lost way where the loud cries of the iron could no longer reach them. When this caress was done and they were vaguely satisfied again the path emerged beyond an unknown and gathered into a dim vista that led down into a land of high cane and rolling meadows and elegant woodlands, the place toward which they were set, Kentuck.

"Then the land is to claim and a house to build," Berk said. "A fort is at hand to shelter us until the cabin is covered. Harrod's Fort is the name of the place."

He said that he would go far into the southwest now on a long hunt, to get many horse-loads of pelts with which to fill his money belt. He would go back into the wilderness now and hunt until the end of the winter. The loud blows on the anvil fell more widely dispersed now, but they fell with a great strength, as if determination argued back-handed with reason and subdued it. Berk talked of the hunt he would make in the country to the southwest, saying that he would go with Evan Muir, a man of great experience in the woods, who knew a region where the game was still in plenty, of mountain fastnesses where the beasts hid themselves. The winter was fixed, the season of this hunt, arranged for them. After winter came the uncertain spring which they could not predict, and viewing it, they fell again into the certainty of their own endearments.

III

THE blows on the anvil had become little and thin, put there by a careful hand, and between each stroke there was a long pause while the hand waited on the reflective part of a man. Noon had passed and the odor of cooking foods floated through the room, the dinner being prepared in the kitchen. The day outside was warm in the sun, but within the coolness of the morning still lingered and the dull embers gave out a subdued warmth. Diony scarcely lifted her gaze above the globular billows her skirts made as they sank away to her feet, but Berk sat near, his chair touching her chair, and they continued to whisper together. The anvil had left off its outcry altogether, and presently her father's broken step came on the stones behind the house and he was heard asking for her at the kitchen door.

He came across the dog alley, his limp slow and his step halting at the stand where the water for drinking was kept. When he came through the door into the new house Diony and Berk arose, but he waved them back to their places, and he went toward his desk where he fumbled among the books

113

there, turning papers about. When he had found the book for which he had been looking he made as if he would go away again, but he smiled toward Diony, the smile running twice over his smooth, thin face, receding and then returning, and he began to talk of some vague thing which the books held, of the eternal aptitude of matter, which was, he said, peculiarly fitted to hold the properties that gathered to it, of the wholesomeness of the necessities inherent in things. He talked of Rhea who, he said, signified succession and who was the mother of six gods: Jupiter, Vesta, Neptune, Ceres, Juno, and Pluto; and these took their fitting places in the heavens or in the earth or in the underworld of the ground. The great Mover and Author of Nature, he said, makes himself plain continually to the eyes of mankind through these visible signs, and he told of how admirably iron is fitted to the work of the forge and how wood suits itself for burning on the hearth or in the furnaces, and how the bellows could increase a flame or the vat of water cool suddenly the red iron to a firm tough texture. He asked Berk when he had designed to go into the new country beyond the wilderness and Berk said that he would want to go late in the following spring, after the flood waters had run down from the streams.

He talked again, making unconnected sayings that

seemed to have no kinship. Men, he said, were the mouths of the earth, and through them the earth spoke in the general; but a man, in the particular instance, might understand and interpret and might see the signs put forth by the Author and Designer to reveal what lay under the outer show of properties and kinds. He told of one wonder after another, of deviations from the natural law, but he told again of how the kept law is a greater marvel than the deflected law, and how it, by its sufferance of the other, continually reveals a purpose beyond the knowledge of men. He would not stand in Diony's way, he said, smiling, although she had planned to take a long step and to go a long journey.

"It won't be said I hindered Diony," he said. He put the book back on his shelf, not having opened it, and he walked briskly toward the door, turning then to speak again.

"For such a length of time as it staggers the mind to contemplate, Man has been marching outward. . . ." He told of many movements of peoples. "Civilized Man is forever spreading more widely over the earth, historic Man bringing such men as have no history to humble themselves and learn their lesson. It's a strong mark of the hidden purposes of the Author of all things. . . . It will never be said of me I hindered Diony."

❖   ❖

When Berk was gone the winter settled over the land, a bright thin coldness that was often dispelled by the sun. Polly began to give good counsel and to speak more freely than was her wont, as if she spoke out of many lifetimes of solicitation. She had accepted Thomas's acceptance of the departure. Coming in at a doorway she would lay aside her utensil, whatever it was, having already given a sign by her act that speech would follow, the changes of her handsome face making a welcome for her speech. She spoke to no great length each time, but having eased her mind by the gift of it in speech she would resume her reverie. By midwinter she had told Diony many things, and they, as a woman and a woman, would listen together in silence to the after-wisdom that would gather about these utterances. Through the killing of the swine and the preparations of the meat, through the boiling of the soap and the making of the summer linen, she contemplated the departure, her care continual from speech to speech. But Betty took no recognition of Diony's going although she often frowned at Polly's words, or she would call her dog for a romp and go noisily away from them.

Polly brought the carded rolls of wool from the upper room, preparing for spinning, and she prepared a warp of fine linen to hold the weft of the wool. Turning back to the warping of the frames, having spoken once, she passed the threads about the pegs with a sweep of her arms, her body stooping and rising and her hand moving freely over the strands, and she said in summary:

"But hit mought be years before we'd ever know whe'r you got there or not and to what place you went. Hit mought be forever."

Betty was gone when these words were spoken, but at hand she gave cheerful help to the warping and spinning, and she spoke sometimes of what they would do next year or the year after, as if no change were contemplated. She would climb lightly to the seat in the loom and tread the harnesses into a quick shed, flinging the shuttle back and forth, or she would drat a knot gayly with her careless tongue. She was sitting thus, making cloth, when Polly said:

"And when the time comes . . . hit would ease my mind iffen I could know, and iffen I could know you had a woman-person to help you. . . ."

Sam gave her a gift. He gave her a dog he was rearing, a mongrel watchdog pup. He said that it would make her a fine hunter and that he had set great store by it, that he expected it to grow up to be a strong fighter and a good watchdog. He had named the dog Gyp, and he admonished Diony to begin to pet it so that it would go with her when she went, and he refrained from giving it any caress thereafter,

selling it utterly to her by this craft. Diony fed the
beast the meat offal and gave it pones of gritty
bread, and she took it with her when she went to the
woods, and after a little it owned her for mistress and
would come readily to her call, leaping about her
with a great rude delight.

"But you get Berk to help and don't be oneasy,"
Polly said. "Or maybe there mought be a woman not
too far away. But don't be afeared. The women-folks
on my side are all a strong race of women and you
have got the favorance of them in your body and
in the way your body is made. Now Betty, she's full
small and takes after some other kind."

Apathy settled into Diony's mind in the passing of
the days so that she could not visualize herself on the
way and she could not at any instant visualize Berk
although she had the measure of his height before her
eyes on the house wall. She would wonder how he
looked and she would try to see his form coming
through the door as an entire mass, or she would take
part by part and try to make these clear. One cold
day in February, walking in from the cow-pen, she
found a tuft of hair from the killed swine, and she took
up the bristles from the ground and put them into
the pocket of her dress. When she came to the kitchen
where Betty was spinning she sat beside the fire and
looked dizzily into the blaze, hearing Betty's voice:

"I don't know what's got into this wheel. Won't go, no matter what way you coax hit. Or iffen hit goes hit just stutters along, so mad hit can hardly turn. Hit ever was a contrarious wheel."

"Try the blue wool," Diony said after a little time for thought. "Try some blue. Maybe it's tired out on that white you had on all week. I wouldn't wonder if it's just plumb sick of so much all one kind."

The kitchen clock pecked dizzily at time and let it pass unhindered, and the spinning wheel was weary of white wool, wanting blue. Diony heated the shovel over the coals, and when it was of a burning hotness she named one of the hog bristles Diony and named another Berk, and she laid them parallel on the hot shovel. She watched them curl and bend toward each other, a sign that the two named ones loved together. In mind she denied herself knowledge of the trial of the hog bristles. She would take no account of this as a thing too intimate to be of real account. When the experiment was passed, well tried, she named a bristle Betty, and named another some supposed name, such as John, scarcely calling the name clearly, and she laid the two side by side on the hot iron, Betty watching the fortune of this from the distant corner. Denying any truth to the prophecy, making the hog bristles lie and making the hot shovel deceive, Betty spun at the contrary wheel.

Thomas Hall took a daily farewell of her, touching the books lingeringly as he stopped before them on his way to the field or the barns, but often he went stiffly out without speaking. Or he would begin to speak as they sat at the board and enkindle at his own words so that he would speak with more fluent phrases than ever he had before, as if he would borrow from his ultimate self or true essence, from his entire lifetime of groping words, to furnish her with some final saying, as if he would say all that he might say in a lifetime in some swift utterance. Polly dyed a fine brown yarn, and she told Diony that she must weave a foot-mantle, a cloth of a fine firm texture to be sewed into a great cape for her feet and limbs when she sat in the saddle on the journey. Diony made a plaid of black and brown, counting the threads with care to make a balanced design. Then she would know, as she wove, that this cloth would fold about her knees on the long march, and she would weave into it strands of farewells and a joyous wish to be off with Berk wherever he might take her, beating these desires into the fabric of the wool. Her father's voice:

> *Arma virumque cano, Trojæ qui primus ab oris*
> *Italiam, fato profugus, Lavinaque venit*
> *Litora, multum ille et terris jactatus et alto*
> *Vi superum . . .*

His voice breaking from the Latin chant would concede known meanings to all that he had sung, as "I sing of arms and the hero who, fate driven, first came from the shores of Troy to Italy and the Lavinian coast, he, *vi superum*, by the power of the gods, much tossed about, *multum jactatus*, much tossed about on land and sea . . ." Or Polly, the Latin subsiding, after she had quietly stitched at a seam of cloth for some time: "Don't make a practice to forget the Sabbath, Diony, whe'r you live in town or in your own homeplace, but remember to rest yourself and rest all your beastes and all your property, and don't give countenance to them that unthoughtedly waste the Lord's day. . . . Hit's not so much matter what the men-folks do that day iffen the women in the homeplace hold the Sabbath up for reverence, and seems like hit's the women has got insight and is natured to hold fast to the old customs."

Candles had been made from the berries of a tree that grew in the hills, a brittle wax from the tree being used, which would refine to a transparency and would yield a light fragrance as it gave forth its smoke in burning. During the evening these candles were burned without stint. Sitting before the fire, reading from his books, Thomas would share any delight with her, leaping into articulations at any moment, his finger lifted. Or Polly again:

"Here's some seed to plant I saved, to make you

sallet in your patch. You could pick out some good-
sized gourd seeds to take, to plant when you get
there. Gourds are about the usefulest kind that grows,
next after bread. You can do about almost anything
in a gourd."

She had tied the seeds in small squares of cloth,
each kind to itself. When the cloth for the foot-mantle
was woven a similar cloth was made for Betty, Diony
making the plaids identical with her own. Betty gave
but a negative interest to the matter. She was never
seen in conference with Sallie Tolliver, whom she
had never liked because the Tolliver woman was
thin and broken and covered over with sadness,
which was now of a stale nature but which was forever present in her abstracted and dull face. But
Diony placed these two together as if they were the
wings of some out-reaching fowl that pursued her.
They were equally silent as to her intended departure. Sallie, continually busy with the ovens, with the
fire, with the floors and the utensils, would fit herself
into the properties of dull objects, but sometimes
talk of her would haunt Diony, the voices whispering:

"Who speaks back to Sallie Tolliver when she
mutters on the stairs?"

"Leave Sallie be. Don't worry her now"—Polly's
voice.

"Who talks back when she stops to listen? I see her

ask a question and stop, and she'll nod her head."

"Spirits talk, ghosts maybe. I saw her once beside the ash tree . . ."

"Witches. You best be careful . . ."

"I saw her make a sign with her finger. To the witches. I saw her raise her hand and point forward. . . . On the stair."

"I heard her ask . . . and wait till she got the answer. I saw her soon of a morning, when she first comes down to open the doors."

"I see her when she sweeps with the brush-broom. Ask a question, the broom still in her hand."

"I heard her ask . . . and wait for some answer before she turned the bread in the pan."

"It's because she's been far into the wilderness."

"Hush. She's outside by the well-house. Don't name it out loud before her."

"She talks to some strange outsiders. You'll see her lift a hand and listen to what he says back again."

"She talks to demons, maybe."

"Hush, she's there, behind the chimney."

"She talks to Indians."

"She talks to scalps, maybe. Old scalps, dry and withered."

"To far-off places she remembers."

"She talks to the dead."

❖   ❖

The cold of the winter was passing and the weaving tasks were laid by, the foot-mantle well made and the bride's dress woven daintily of fine linen and wool, ready for sewing. Little remained in her mind of Berk now but the determined fact of her choosing, this moving her forward toward the completion of her apparel. The vivid moment of his coming stood before her as a bright point toward which she was faced, but himself she could not clearly picture. The voices arose and fell about her apathy, her mother's voice a refrain giving continual wisdom.

"And take care the least one always and don't let hit fall into the embers. A baby-child marked that way with a scar, hit's a shame to a mother and a sight hit shudders the heart to see. . . ."

Reuben gave her a cow he had saved, one of the finer animals of the herd. Diony fed her cow a warm mash of pounded corn and gave her the leaves of the fodder, all that Reuben would spare, to make her ready for the long journey, and she tried her little udders to fancy what would be when she and the cow were far away in the strange country she had chosen and when she would milk her there. She would look at the gentle beast intently, knowing that she would see her in a strange place surrounded by strange trees and canelands and such wonders as she could not then hold firmly in the picturing region of her mind. She would know that when she milked her there Berk would be actual and present, known to her flesh. She would explore the animal's back and her flanks, her horns and her dark muzzle, knowing each part of vague white as it broke through the red, knowing her darker feet, her bony hips and strong sinewy shanks, wondering that she should now know the cow better than she knew her lover. Word came from the court-house and from the mill: there was fighting with the British army around the mouth of the Hudson, George Washington retreating into the Jerseys; and Reuben rode out to drill with the militia at the court-house, saying that Virginia would have the war at her front door by the time of the harvest. Polly was saying:

"I hope, Diony," her hand stayed over her task, standing a moment beside the kitchen block where she chopped the meat to prepare it at last for the fire, "I hope the people about will be, all, a civil kind, and apter than not they will. But iffen they get in a quarrelsome way, rippets and ructions and tellen tales here and yon, don't you, Diony, make one in such a company. Keep yourself to yourself then."

Spring came swiftly after the intense cold and Diony listened to the first dove as it made its coo-singing, for she had been told that the direction of the first dove of the spring would indicate the direction of a girl's lover. The blackbirds were early, their coats as bright as brass. They came swaggering about in the cold and looking their best, caring nothing about the nest and yet not seeming to be able to leave off building it either. Diony saw herself woven into the firm texture of the spring, her hands hurrying their tasks now. Until evening the sash was raised and the damp air of the spring diffused itself through the warmth of the room and caught the throat with its bitterness, but the fire burned warm at night and the window was closed again. Thomas leaned near the light to read from a book, saying, "Harken," or "Attend now, Diony," and he would lift a hand to accentuate the beauty of a phrase; but Diony knew all that he read now, line after line, from many times hearing the words of the poet. The splendid words marched in dignity through the room and made pictures which she had only by some God-given report since she had never seen the matters there described. Her father's voice:

Save that from yonder ivy-mantled tower
The moping owl does to the moon complain . . .

She had never seen an ivy-grown tower, nor heard a curfew ring, nor seen a lettered tomb on which names or years were spelled by any muse. The fire burned lightly at the sycamore logs Sam had brought

to the hearth. Sallie Tolliver climbed the stair to the
room above, her going a part of the evening, her tall
spare body moving snake-like up the steps. Above
she would arrange herself to sleep on the farther bed,
effacing herself from all but the labor of the plantation. The psalm-like utterance of the poet lay in a
stratum over the room:

> Can storied urn or animated bust
> Back to its mansion call the fleeting breath? . . .

Betty sewed a seam for their mother, her thin face
bent over the cloth. All spring she had been unable
to eat her food, but she gave cheerful obedience.
Sam had walked outside into the dark where the
spring cries of the toads made a continual singing.
The reader's voice came to the end of the elegy, moving solemnly through the last aching, unfriended
lines of the epitaph with a mighty sonorous delight.
Then, when the stillness had set the verse apart, as it
receded in the soft crackling of the fire and the
rhythmic lash of the thread as it swept minutely
through the cloth, Polly spoke, a wistful pleasure in
her voice, a lyric desire up-welling out of her continual thought of the departure:

"And when you've named all the names you fancy
and when Berk is satisfied with names and's named
after all his folks he has a mind to, I wish you'd name

one, iffen hit's a girl-baby, Nancy Anne. I always had
a favorance to Nancy Anne to name a girl with."

❖   ❖

On a Sunday morning in April Thomas Hall
mounted his riding mare and went down the creek
road on an errand to the church of the parish, to St.
Anne's Church in the south of Albemarle County.
He left soon after dawn. Diony knew that he had
gone to publish the banns there between herself and
Berk Jarvis, and knew that her name and Berk's name
would be read out together in the church that day at
divine service, and likewise on two Sundays thereafter,
a preparation required by the laws of Virginia.

Berk coming back from the south brought the day
of the wedding to hand. He became large and firm in
her mind again, a shape that focused her departure.
In the opinions that were passed back and forth
Diony knew that the war had brought changes to the
minds of men, old laws falling away and new customs
taking their places. Preparations moved swiftly now
and the plantation was in a ferment. Coley Linkhorn
had come to the creek valley to marry her to Berk.

"Could a Methodist marry couples?" Sookie Jones
asked. She was sitting by the fire in Polly's room
stitching a seam in the wedding dress. "Would it be
lawful iffen a Methodist said the words over you?"

Polly spoke after a moment of thought, stitching
at her seam meanwhile. She said that in Pennsylvania there was marrying without the Church of
England to cry banns or make prayers over the man
and the woman. Diony's banns had already been
said at St. Anne's Church and put on the register
there for all to see. It was her wish that Coley Linkhorn should say a ceremony over Diony in his own
way. The matter was hushed then under their stitching needles, and their thoughts floated on the prick-
ing of the needle points that went in and out to fasten
the cloth together to make the gown. Remembering
Linkhorn's great power in matters of prayer it
seemed right to Diony that he should make the
marriage service over her.

❖　　　❖

Above stairs, the day of the wedding having come,
Diony put on the blue linsey gown which she had
woven and which Polly had made. For her head
there was a bonnet of stitched cloth which lay out on
the bed now, beside it her cape and her foot-mantle.
Sam had brought her shoes from Charlottesville and
she had woven her stockings with her fingers and her
knitting needles. About the dress were supreme farewells, for as she slipped the skirt over her head she
heard the people of the house running here and there

below, opening and closing the doors, voices calling to one or another, steps in the dog alley. All belonged to her by reason of her departure, the calling feet, the admonitions, the coming guests. Her mother's voice:

"The clock's outen humor again. I started the hands off myself to try to make hit want to go, but hit's set hits head . . . Behaves right o'nary this week."

There was a noise of weights falling together and then the slow loud ticking of the clock. The slow steps of Sallie Tolliver came almost silently, plodding in and out of life, unwilling to speak out anything she knew of the wilderness. Diony caught all into her fingers as she clasped the pin in her dress and drew the throat seams together, listening as she dressed herself. Polly's voice flaring again in a pretty throaty music over the passing hurry:

"I expect Sam's been in the clock again. Sam worries the clock a right smart on the sly. Looks like Sam has got a blight on himself, to love to tease and worry the clock the like he does. . . ."

Now she drew the dress together with the pin Thomas had given her, a pin which he had brought out from hiding on the morning of the wedding. It had belonged to his mother, he said, and it was of gold, curiously made in some place beyond the sea.

On it there was a delicate tracery of leaves and stems. It fastened with a clasp and set securely above her breast, and she was proud to be the owner of it, but she was saddened for an instant to know that there was not another pin for Betty. She accepted the pin at last without regret, taking it to herself completely because she was going far away from any report of her grandmother Luce and would henceforth have of her only what she then had in her being.

Sookie Jones came up the stair bringing Betty, and Anne Jones followed. There was much laughing and teasing. If a girl sews a lock of her hair in the hem of a bride's dress she will find her lover before the year is out, Sookie said, and she wanted Betty to try this omen, but Betty would not, shaking her head in refusal. There were men's voices calling below and then a great crash of noise that shook the house and flung powder through all the air, for the young men had fired their guns before the house door, a salute to the wedding. All the Jarvis men were at hand now, and Coley Linkhorn had come. The Jarvis men stood quietly together, talking but little or speaking in low voices, and over their talk fluttered the talk of Anne and Sookie Jones, who were afraid if too great a stillness settled over a wedding, and they made a light pretty noise with their voices, for a good omen. Giles Stafford and his wife had come, and the

Owens families from down the river. Berk's friend came, Evan Muir, riding from the Jarvis plantation where he had left his pack horses, for he would make one of the party going with Berk and Diony on the long journey.

Thomas Hall and Polly brought cups and a great tankard of ale, an offering to the event, and all assembled now in the new house, and the drink was quietly taken while the guests stood before the smoldering fire. Then Linkhorn prayed a deep prayer that searched their hearts and found there the mercy of God, a long prayer while all knelt together, and when this was done they relaxed and drank again from the cups.

Then Linkhorn drew Diony and Berk together and joined their hands and said the words of the binding part of the ceremony, and after this lengthy discourse all present took the wedded pair by the hands and wished them godspeed. Then Linkhorn prayed again with a great voice that had by this time become awake, as if it would call souls to repent, and he blessed the union and called upon God to watch the young man and the young woman in their long march over the Trace to the new world. He enumerated the dangers of the way with a great trembling voice that flung out a report of fire in the night, rapine, women and children snatched away by savages, burned at the stake, tortured slowly as long as life might last, thrown to the beasts, eaten of their flesh, their bones left to whiten under the sun and rain. Diony's hand lay firmly on Berk's arm while this recital of death poured over them, herself being acutely alive, her life touching Berk's life where her fingers rested on the muscles of his bent arm. Having made death appear with a great speech of terror, a swift speech of hurried, half-articulated words that leaped out of the dark of his great voice, the priest brought life back to the company, making it flow outward from the touching flesh of the man and the woman where it had not utterly expired. He gentled his speech to a whisper, told of the holiness of the marriage tie, of the goodness of God, the mercies of the Redeemer, the joy of sins forgiven, the comfort of the Spirit, the blessings of health and love and neighborly kindness. When his last amen had settled over the place all stood quietly as if they were spent by the grand thoughts that had rolled over them from some power beyond the world, and they drifted, one by one, to the outside, where the men gathered about the ponies Berk had brought to take himself and Diony away, or they walked to the hog-pens to look at some fine beasts Thomas had there.

Diony was aware that there was whispering. Giles Stafford and Lester Owens and some of their women

were standing together to whisper, disputing something with Evan Muir and with Jack Jarvis, but their
voices would be hushed if she came near, and Jack
drew apart from them in anger. Polly had rolled the
things she had given Diony into compact bundles,
the cuts of woven cloth, the blankets, seeds for a garden, a few vessels, knives and spoons. Thomas had
given her two books from those on the shelf. The
gifts had all been assembled and rolled into packets,
tied into the cloth, the bundles now lying on the
floor behind the house door ready to be set on the
backs of the pack horses whenever the time for the
departure came to hand. Diony knew that there was
a strange whispering among the guests, dissent, and
she knew that Jack spoke sharply to Stafford and left
him in anger and that Evan Muir had taken Berk
apart to whisper and that their eyes showed distrust
while they talked together. Presently she saw that
Thomas knew what troubled the wedding and she
saw that he walked swiftly away from their comment
and denial, hostile to all Stafford maintained.

All drank again from the cups of ale and tried
again to be merry, and the men kissed Diony, as was
their right, and the women shook her hand. Standing
with Berk and Evan Muir before the fireplace, Diony
knew what troubled the guests and why Stafford
and Owens whispered.

"They say it's not a lawful ceremony," Muir whispered. "They say only one kind can say legal marriages."

"Only rectors out of the state church, they say."

"It's a new world now, a new day. We don't have to live by a state church. It's a free country."

"Free or not, there's the law," Stafford said. All had come to the wide space before the hearth. "I wouldn't want to make trouble for anybody. All is, a ceremony ought to be legal or shame is bound to follow. In 1661 a law was passed. It's known to all. 'No marriage be solemnized nor reputed valid in law but such as is made by the ministers according to the law of England.' "

Thomas was reading aloud from the Declaration of Independence, finding confirmation of his idea. "Life, liberty, and the pursuit of happiness," he said, reading. There were many opinions spoken. Polly went briskly about her preparations for the feast. Her eyes were bright with denial of Stafford's criticism.

"I'm married now," Berk said. "This lady here is Mistress Diony Jarvis henceforth. Diony, did you marry me when you stood along beside me a while ago and listened to all Coley Linkhorn said?"

"I married Berk Jarvis," Diony said. "Coley

Linkhorn said a prayer over us and married us in a right way."

"Legal or not, hit's a marriage," Polly said. "My church can make as strong a marriage tie as e'er another."

"It's only Tories would hold what Stafford holds," a voice whispered.

"If any doubt has come to trouble any man in Albemarle, we'll go away now, this hour," Berk said. "Married we are and married we'll go away from here. We won't have to prove the law of the Tories against we get in the wilderness."

"Hit's a wilderness marriage. Let be." One or two spoke.

"Married for the wilderness."

"Don't trouble their souls with doubt."

"It's a miracle; the old law come back."

"Married fit for the wilderness."

"Without law, but no matter."

"Quiet! A new day. No matter."

"Amen, amen, amen."

❖   ❖

Peace settled over the throng, their amens a finality over the subject. Their eyes were bright, but none spoke harshly again. Berk made ready for a swift departure, and when the moment came there

were but few final admonitions, for the weeks of
farewell lay behind them through the winter and
spring. The packs being ready, the cow was brought
from the barn and the dog was called and induced
to follow. Diony, wearing her mantle and her flaring bonnet of stitched cloth, walked out of the house
and through the dog alley, seeing Sallie Tolliver
shrink into the dark of the kitchen doorway, knowing
that this relic of the wilderness had been where she
herself was going. She stepped from the entry and
walked away, touching the red soil of Albemarle
with her feet for the last time. She passed Betty by,
seeing her thin little face that was wasted with inner
grieving, but at the horse block she stopped and
kissed each one. She climbed to the horse block and
made ready to mount, her impatient horse pawing
at the ground. Sam helped her to the saddle, a
courtesy, for she could easily mount alone. Berk led
the pack beasts, and the cow had been taken forward
by the other Jarvis men.

The pack horses wore bells around their necks and
these were all unstopped in honor of the bride's
journey, which was thus begun with a dainty clatter
and tinkle. Thomas mounted his little mare to ride
a short way down the creek as an escort. Diony
gathered her bridle tight and spread her foot-mantle
over her knees, making it secure, Polly assisting her,

and in this instant she remembered all that she had ever promised Betty, and she saw cruel grief and remorse and pity as if they were set apart in some far place to be met with greater pity, but she chose Berk on the instant with a great desire and chose to go with him to Kentuck and to find out there a new country and a new way of being.

Her careless little horse took a step forward and then another, on the way now, the journey begun, and she passed the house door and passed the dairy, looking back the last time at her mother's face. She waved her hand then and her horse passed behind the screen of the corn where it grew in the left-hand field, on the creek road now, going.

Suddenly, in the tinkling of the bells, she knew herself as the daughter of many, going back through Polly Brook through the Shenandoah Valley and the Pennsylvania clearings and roadways to England, Methodists and Quakers, small farmers and weavers, going back through Thomas Hall to tidewater farmers and owners of land. In herself then an infinity of hopes welled up, vague desires and holy passions for some better place, infinite regrets and rending farewells mingled and lost in the blended inner tinkle and clatter. These remembrances were put into her own flesh as a passion, as if she remembered all her origins, and remembered every sensation her forebears had known, and in the front of all this mass arose her present need for Berk and her wish to move all the past outward now in conjunction with him. They went quickly along the road, the seven pack horses making a seven-keyed music that played about her choice and wrapped it in a fine pride. The air was pleasant, the hills vividly seen, the water in the creek being bright over the brown of the stones.

Five miles down the stream the Jarvis fields came into view. There were pack horses tied at the door of the house and all was ready. Eli had loaded Berk's horses with the powder and the lead, with the salt and grain, and now a larger pack train was arranged. Jack Jarvis and Evan Muir, with Diony and Berk, made the four who would go. The last good-byes were said. Diony leaned from her horse, her bonnet pushed back from her face, and kissed Thomas Hall for the last parting. He limped then toward his mare that flinched at the clatter of the bells.

The road went down the creek, following the water closely, making toward the south, but Diony knew that it would turn to the west and mount the Blue Ledge. From the lifted field before the Jarvis house she saw the distant ridge, a gray haze over it. The road ahead ran down the creek and was lost in indeterminate water. The familiar hills, the look, the gesture, the passing step of Thomas Hall—she looked on them for the last time, her thought confused with sadness and pleasure.

❖　　　❖

The flowing of the bell music made the journey seem more swift than the feet of the ponies declared. The road was narrow and but little beaten, but it was clearly defined. No one mentioned Stafford and Owens, nevertheless these with their comments filled the minds of all. The afternoon passed, mile after mile and hour after hour, and the hooves beat steadily on the way. There was a cabin inn, an ordinary, twelve miles up the river, and Berk had planned that the day should come to an end there, but as night began to fall the horses seemed unwilling, and the inn yet being several miles away, no one urged forward the journey. The summer evening was warm, and the ledges of stone, where they out-cropped, were firm and dry. There was talk of staying the night in the open.

"That-there ordinary, it's a lousy place," Jack said.

They made a feast of the cooked foods Polly had stored for them, and they took the milk from the cow. Then the men chopped tender boughs from the ever-green trees, Muir and Jack Jarvis working at this, and they made a bed for Diony, smiling at what they did, spreading the blankets over the twigs, Muir taking the greater care and testing all until it was of a fine softness. Then Jack made another bed like it close at hand for Berk, spreading blankets and skins, testing the quality of each and rearranging the twigs until a fine soft couch was made.

"And if you're not married, God help you," he said, finishing his labor.

The moon set early and the night became dark. When Jack and Muir had gone apart, Berk and Diony talked together, making their plans anew, or they built what lay between them to a more firm bond, passing beyond the province of speech in their communing, drawing each instant nearer together. Diony heard the wolves howl in the mountain hills. She slept heavily, drugged by the fatigue of the long ride, and through the deep of her sleeping she heard the tinkle of the bells the ponies wore. The howling of the wolves continued, entering her dreams, making her aware of Berk as near and aware of the country she had chosen to enter, for her trail lay ahead, pointing toward the way of the wolves. Her dream entered the cries of the beasts, Berk being near, being more near, and she was folded with him into the core of danger and blood-hunger and hate, being secure.

IV

DAY after day they went forward, rising with the road as it mounted the Blue Ridge and passing over the range at Blue Ridge Gap, meeting the road from the lower Shenandoah Valley at a place Berk called Big Flat Lick. Here they rested for a day and let the ponies graze, and the men repaired the pack saddles. The cabin inn was small but it was a shelter from the rain that fell. The food Polly had cooked was gone now, but at the inn or in the open they baked cakes of cornmeal over the fire and ate this with meat they had killed. There were three dogs, among them Gyp who ran at the heels of the horses, her tail curled over her back as a dark brown plume, running to Ken-tuck-ee.

"We've covered nearabout seventy miles," Berk said. The men disputed of the miles, but they agreed in summary. Strange soil was under their feet, and the waters ran swiftly over strange stones.

Creeks were forded, sometimes the way taking them into midstream for a mile or more. It was difficult to keep the pack horses in the trail, for they would wander away to nibble the grass among the trees. The little roan mare carrying a part of Diony's load would rub her saddle against low saplings and try to brush off the burden. Berk would bring her back to the path and give her a sound curse for her waywardness.

They followed an old trading path which had been used by the Indians before the coming of the white men. Now it was cut by faint ruts that wagons had made, for traders went over it now and then to carry goods to the cabins farther back or to the Indians in Tennessee. Diony went the way eagerly. Vistas never before viewed by her eyes unfolded, and she leaned her head forward at times to see through an opening of the trees. She entered each view, thrust forward from within, as if the mind of the Spirit beyond herself were unfolding itself to her continually, as if she went forward eagerly to meet each disclosure. Thus the road unwound before her gaze, coming into being well in time for her use.

They crossed the New River at Inglis Ferry and stopped there to rest four days at a cabin clearing, the men hunting. Diony sat to rest in the door of the cabin beside an old man who lived there with his sons. He was a talkative old man who had lost all of one leg, and when he arose he hobbled unevenly here and there on a crutch that was made of a crotched sapling. The cripple, old Bethel, leaned over a powder horn he was carving. She had an illusion of him as Thomas Hall cut farther away, a new philosophy coming out of his mouth and out of his hand.

He told ill-connected stories that finally fitted together into a merry, lewd recitative. He was an unforgiving old man who had lost his wife, his leg, and then his daughter. He had turned simple and cheated disaster by being continually merry and lewd. He sat on his one remaining leg, which was rheumatic and dry-withered, and he carved fine letters into the surface of the horn. When he knew that Diony was a bride he said that he would finish the horn for her. He had already decorated it with mythical trees. Now he wrote verses on it with his fine tool, carving the words with slow pains.

"I take a notice a heap to how names begin," he said. "Some years the people that go by the Trace are all spelled with a B. Other summers, and it's all P's or G's that go. I recollect one summer a man went by named Hannibal. I made up a song when he was gone on his way, to call to mind what manner of man he was."

When he rose to his foot it was as if he crawled up out of the earth. He confused Muir with Berk and called Muir the husband, and he would call out ribald sayings. When he leaned over the horn, his head low, he seemed very little and crumpled, like a withered bush beside the house door, and Diony could scarcely believe that the song of Hannibal, as it flowed about the cabin in disjointed inquiries and replies, came from the little withered half of a man that sat against the wall. His carving hand shook over the hard surface of the horn, but out of his tremulous skin there came some firmness that set letter after letter into the text he had devised. Or he would fling out a crumpled bony hand and touch Diony, feeling the flesh of her arm. He would look at her suddenly with sharp old eyes that were in no way dimmed.

"Hannibal Hane was the man's name," he said. "And when I look him right in his eye I see he'd as soon kill a man as rob 'im of a sixpence. As soon rob 'im as look 'im in the eye, and a little rather. Bound, he was, for the Indian country to waylay on the rivers for plunder, and come out on the Spanish cities towards the south. I made a song to recollect what kind he was:

> "Oh, Hannibal Hane of the northern sea,
> Where were you borned, in what countree?
>
> In a pirate ship there I was born,
> Me and my fathers all beforn.
>
> Hannibal Hane, where will you dwell?
> Wherever are men to plunder and fell.

Hannibal Hane, where will you die?
On the gallows limb when the law comes nigh."

Diony saw each letter as it was minutely cut into the dark pearl of the horn, and she saw the quivering hand that caught itself each moment into some straight sureness and made a line or wrote a curve. Or, to renew his vital part and make his carving clear, he would put out a cold bony hand and touch her warm flesh, fingering her arm or her thigh. She loathed his hand and pitied him as well, but she respected the work of his hand on the horn and loved all things with a sudden flood of passion, allowing his touch.

"Your horn is the best ever I did make," he said, muttering. "I made a fine horn when I lived on Yadkin . . . took time, took my time. . . . Mistress Jarvis, there's lawless men a-plenty scattered through the whole woods to the west. . . ."

He worked steadily, intent on having the horn finished by the time Berk moved forward. He would sit beside the wall, crumpled to a little pile of bones and worn buckskins, and he would call Diony back to sit beside him if she wandered away. She knew what words were written although he kept the flask continually in his hands or tied about his shoulder. On the third day while he wrote the last legend she knew the whole of it. It was written:

Berk Jarvis I am your powder horn
I am your friend since you were born
Fill me up with good black powder
I'll make your musket bark the prouder
If good lead balls you mold for me
I'll find the heart of your enemy.

It holds 2 pds good powder

He crawled up out of the earth and fetched himself another sharp tool from within the cabin. In a passion to preserve her he labored minutely over the fine lines of his legend. He called to Muir who worked among the ponies:

"Berk Jarvis, there's power in your horn. Indian law has not got enough power in it. It's time the law and the women went there."

When the carving was finished he gave the horn to Diony, handing it up to her with a sudden smile, and he sat embarrassed beside the house, looking down at the ground that was close under his eyes and turning his hard little withered head about while she examined the vessel and gave him her thanks. She turned it over and over, searching out each beauty that lay upon the dark pearl surface and each carved word. Its hard words cracked and snapped when she read them aloud.

Morning, soon after dawn, and the ponies were ready to take the trace. Diony mounted her beast and gathered her mantle about her. Old Bethel hobbled among the ponies, touching a rump here or a throat there, making a thin old clatter. Looking back, she saw an old worn-out half of a man, his eyes running tears, stumping about under the trees and waving her a farewell.

They passed over a rough mountain that wearied all, both the men and the beasts, but most it wearied Diony and Jack. They lodged themselves in a grove on the Laurel Fork of the Holston under the brow of a great mountain. Berk and Muir killed meat for their food and they made a lodge of boughs for Diony to rest in.

They followed the trail again and crossed another mountain that tried them less, and they came then to a cabin. Berk killed two wild turkeys here and these were eaten for breakfast. After a day of rest they were off early in the morning, the corn now being low and the cabin owner having none to spare them. Crossing the water at a ford of the Clinch, the little sorrel mare, the unwilling pack horse, dropped her load in midstream and spoiled much of the pack. Muir caught the beast in a thicket and brought her back, and when there was a convenient stop he cut a better saddle stick from a small tree and made a more secure load. They lodged that night in the open.

The way seemed endless. Diony stirred meal in a wooden bowl and mixed numberless journey cakes to bake on the board before the embers, stirring with a wooden stick trimmed from an ash pole. It was forever the same bowl and the same stick, the same journey cake eaten with the same appetite. The corn was diminished to a small measure that was carefully hoarded in the leather sack. Muir killed a wild turkey and he called the white meat his bread, the corn being now kept for Diony who could relish an unbroken diet of wild meat less than could the men.

Muir notched the days on a small stick he carried and all rested on the Sabbath. On that day the men shaved away the week's growth of hair from their faces and they washed themselves in the stream. Diony knew each beast, resting or on the way, and she knew how each set his hoof down into the soft turf or on the clattering stones, and the rhythm of their going was eaten into her mind and the sound of tramping pack horses into her ear places.

Her own horse walked daintily in spite of the irons that shod her feet. She set her little round feet to the wagon rut that ran through the grassy road and stepped lightly over the briars. Berk's horse was a

strong bay, the last beast to tire, the best to swim a
stream. Diony's eyes would float along on the heels of
the horses, riding on whatever feet passed before her,
as if feet were the measure of the earth. The men
took turns at leading the pack beasts and at keeping
the cow to the road. When a wide stream was crossed
a raft of logs was made, the trees felled, sometimes a
half day being required for this. Resting or on the
way, the men would ease themselves with their
tobacco. They put into their mouths large bites of
the dry twisted plant which they had prepared from
the Virginia growth. Berk would spit infrequently
into the grass.

"Smoken, it's a woman's work," Jack said.

"Hardly fitten to content a man," Berk, then.

"It's said tidewater men only smoke it. And I
wouldn't be surprised they do."

Viewing the heels of the horses as they swam
ahead of her against the green of the grassy road, she
saw themselves on the way, three men and a woman,
as if she saw all from some outside point, near but
apart. One man walked or rode continually to the
fore. Her powder horn was hung over his shoulder
on a strand of leather cut from an elk hide. This was
Berk Jarvis. Another, Jack, went more evenly, and
he cared for the supply of meat and corn. Evan
Muir brought the beasts back to the path and

watched the pack saddles. If there were sharp words, anger went off his shoulders as if it were chaff. He was thirty years old, he said. When he laughed there was a deep chuckle somewhere beneath his throat, as if it were quivering in his broad back. It was as if his laughter were a small thing inside himself, having a being of its own. Sometimes he would sing:

> There's a wild boar in these woods,
> Cut 'im down, cut 'im down.
> He grinds our bones and drinks our blood,
> Cut 'im down, cut 'im down . . .

She saw herself, Diony Jarvis, riding her nag, herself a strong girl with rounded limbs, a dim flush of red under her skin where her face rounded to make her cheeks. She saw dark eyes of some indetermined gray sort looking clearly out of their places and resting under curtains of skin that would lift up and down, her eyelids. Her hand, the woman's, was crumpled loosely over the bridle and it was covered with a knitted glove of soft cotton thread with a herring-bone design running over the knuckles. Under the riding mantle the woman's feet and limbs were crooked to the stirrups and the pommels of the saddle as she sat to the side with one foot crumpled over the other. Then the man, Berk Jarvis, left the head of the cavalcade and walked beside her, his hand on her horse's shoulder. He looked up to her face, saying nothing, his great hand moving with the rise and fall of the beast's step.

✧   ✧

For a week one day differed from another day only by its disasters. Jack's horse mired in a stream and sank to his neck in the water. He was dragged free of the mud after two hours of labor and rested on the bank until his breath was restored. Diony lost the count of how many times the Clinch River was crossed and whether the crossings were by raft or by ford. A rainstorm suddenly appearing, they were wet to the skin, but they kept the powder dry in the hollow of a great tree. They slept housed for the night in the hollows of trees, finding a little cramped ease, being glad to be out of the boggy out-of-doors. They had been on the way more than a month now, their slow-going timed to the slow-going of the cow and the burdened horses.

Beyond a ford, on a rise of ground to the left of the way, a great oak grew. Its stiff gnarled branches reached out to the brink of the water. Evan Muir stopped before the tree, drawing away to look. When he spoke he called the tree the Tory Tree, and he said that three Tories had been hanged there in the spring. He had passed north from the Clinch country and he had seen the bodies hanging long and gaunt from the great tree, the horses of the hanged men running away into the briars and their goods thrown under foot by the angry executioners. Muir rode under the Tory Tree and away from it, and his back stiffened in response to the dead men that had hung there.

"Lord, what a sight to see," he said, "three on one tree!"

Diony had never before thought of three men hanging on one tree, put there by other human hands. She was startled by this thought, so that her eyes left the plodding of the horses' feet as they beat over the grass.

When she had ridden beyond the tree she began to think of Bethel's words and to discover what he meant when he said that the whole forest to the west was scattered with lawless men gone there to plunder, and what his song of Hane foreboded. This troubled her while she rode a mile along the way. But presently the evenness of their own going, Berk to the fore, Muir, herself, and Jack, moving in the design already known to her by the way of the plodding horses, restored a design of evenness and order to her mind, and their going became of the order of law, as if they carried the pattern of law in their passage.

❖   ❖

They were drawing near the halfway place of which much had been told. Jack rode out from the cavalcade to make their coming known to the block-house and to his relatives in the cabins there. Toward nightfall Diony saw the cabins in a valley and saw the fort, the block-house, on a small rise of ground. Guns were fired to greet them and men shouted their names.

The mountains stood back, leaving a wide valley. The fort looked toward the east and commanded the small plain. Women were carrying water from the spring and children were running about. Smoke for evening cooking was arising from the cabins.

Will Jarvis took Berk's hand and he seemed scarcely able to speak for his pleasure. He rode beside Diony then, touching her shoulder with delight. He led them down the valley to his own cabin where his wife Susan and their mother, Mistress Elvira Jarvis, waited by the door. Elvira took Diony's hand in a smiling greeting, but she turned away to take up a child that whimpered and she stood uncertainly beside the house door, her movement a continual salute of pleasure and good-will. Presently she brought from some inner place a gift, a piece of woolen cloth ample to make a garment, and she gave this to Diony as a further token of greeting and welcome. Diony took the cloth half shyly for she

knew Mistress Elvira but a little. She looked across
then at the tall straight woman who had given her
the gift and she saw the massive planes of her face
and remembered then that Elvira was the mother of
five boys. She saw the brown folds of her hair and
knew that she had been forgetting the strange white
lock that grew out of the crown of her head and was
twisted among the tight coils of her hair.

It was pleasant to sit at the table for the food and
to eat the varied foods from wooden platters. Then
Elvira said that she would go with them to Kentuck
and she named another that would go, adding a
name again and again. A week of rest for the newcomers would pass and then the large party of fifteen
or more would take Boone's Road.

❖   ❖

They had come half way. Diony looked about at
the strange earth, at the mountains and the valleys,
at the beginnings of trails that led away. Will Jarvis
made the roads known to her, pointing them out.
One led back into the mountains, the way they had
come, the road to Virginia, to Prince Edward County
and to Albemarle and thence down to Williamsburg
and to the sea. Another curved up the Holston, east
and south, to the Yadkin country and into Carolina
and down again to the sea. The third would be her

way, that reaching north and west, over high mountains. A chill passed through her blood to know that
her way of the three would be the hard way.

All would sit about the cabin door on the trampled
earth or on the stools from the cabin, and there were
stories told of the war of the year before, Berk and
John Gowdy, his friend, recounting and remembering together. Black things, withered and dried, hung
over the fort on a pole, blowing now in the wind,
tossing as if they were old ribbons knotted together,
dangling together in a lax air. They were scalps from
the battles, put up as a warning and a sign if any
redmen were roving among the trees. Gowdy and
Berk told their stories together, scarcely speaking if
they could commune by half-coherent reminders.

"Tuesday, I recollect . . ." one would say.

"Then came a Wednesday. . . . At the ford . . .
by the big sycamore . . ."

Relaxed ease gave them long nights when they
slept securely indoors surrounded by other sleepers
in the cabin, other cabins being near. Caution and
danger gathered toward the end of the week. Several
had fled from the forts in Boone's country in April,
and scattered travelers came back now and then
along Boone's Trace in fear and despair. Thus it was
told about the cabins. Logan himself had lately come
to get powder for his fort, which was besieged when

he slipped out of it. Word of Logan was passed about, report of his bravery, his great brawn, his size, his goodness.

"He's the master of Logan's Fort," one said. "Boone's and Logan's and Harrod's, there's three forts in the cane country now."

"I hope I may see him myself," Diony cried out.

"I never saw such a man as Logan in all my born days."

"He came all the way here by himself, ne'er another in his company the whole enduren way."

A great man, a giant, a hero, walked out of a half-mythical land, striding down through an unbroken way to get ammunition for his people. Diony heard her father's voice reading from some book, his hand lifted in her sight as if he had said, "Harken!"

"Only two days he stopped here to rest," one was saying.

"Four kegs of powder and four horse-loads of lead. That's what he took back or engaged to follow. A week to come here, he took, only a week. Walked through the brush to keep off the Trace to miss any Indians that might be on the way. Said he'd be back in his fort in a week's time again. I saw him start off on the way."

❖   ❖

They rode forth in the morning of a fine day, set

now on the second half of the journey. A farewell salute was fired from the block-house and the cavalcade took the trail toward the ford of the Holston, toward the Clinch Mountain that stood high on the left, the first barrier.

They went at first without caution. The men were Berk Jarvis, Abram Perry, Martin Lucas, Sam Scruggs, Alex Harmon, John Gowdy, Evan Muir, Jack Jarvis, and Joe Tandy. The women were Diony Jarvis, Elvira Jarvis, Nancy Perry with an infant in her arms, and Hannah Lucas. The children were Anne Perry, Bob Perry, Levi Lucas, and two small Lucas children who rode in a crate on the back of a pack horse. They were nineteen people, nine carrying guns. A faint trace of wagon wheels showed where the road lay as it went among the trees and the stones. There were two or three pack horses for each person, and there were four cows in the train. One of Elvira's beasts was loaded with kettles and bedding, and there was a spinning wheel piled on the top. The steps of the horses made a continual beating and a clatter on the way. They crossed the ridge at Big Moccasin Gap, five miles beyond the ford, and camped there, weary of a day.

The journey became suddenly difficult beyond all that Diony had imagined. Powell Mountain was under their feet, hard to go and steep to climb. A storm in the sky, and there was rain and thunder, and they crouched under whatever ledges they could find. A pack horse carrying lead and salt leaped into a swollen creek and lost off the pack. Muir and Gowdy brought it back and recovered the load, but the salt was wasted. The mountain became an uneven stair and the boulders were harsh and difficult, the horses unwilling, so that each one must be led over the way. They camped on the mountain a day and waited for rest to renew their worn bodies. Jack would sing parts of a song:

> If I had known before I courted
>   That love had been so hard to gain,
> I'd lock my heart in a golden box
>   And fasten it up with a silver chain.

Berk swayed slightly as he walked, as if he beat time for the whole company. His horse was now carrying a part of the load. The march was difficult for the women and the children, and even the men were spent at the end of a day. Diony became strong under the strain of continual effort, and after a night of deep rest she could feel strength stored in her limbs and feel renewed life welling up in her vital part. Beyond Jack's song there was but little speaking from one to another.

"I clomb this mountain yesterday, seems," Hannah Lucas said as she went over the stones, leading the horse that carried her children. "And have I got to climb it again today?"

"I been a-climben it every day for four days," Elvira spoke this slowly, laboring. "Fast as you go over a ridge it doubles back for you to go it again. . . ."

"We mought go back yet. It's not too late. We mought."

"No, we won't go back." One after another spoke this. "We set out to go where we're a-goen . . . Go, we will."

Berk and Muir, climbing ahead, stood on the top of a small ridge and flung up their arms to shout. All went forward then with a quickened step, pressing the horses forward, and Jack sang again with a great whoop of pleasure. Diony was leaping within to know what it was that those on the ridge had found and why they continued to fling up their arms and point forward. When her horse rounded the stony rise and brought her to the top of the ridge, she saw, far to the west in a blue haze, dim above a succession of ridges, the great wall, the high ridge of white rock that stood up now in the clear morning, lit by the eastern sun. Over this wall their way would go. They stopped on the ridge to view the cliff, it being the wall that stood before Kentuck, and they wondered at their power and their determination, looking forward across many ridges and valleys, looking back into the way they had come, through dense stones.

"Oh, God knows!" one said. "Look where we've come from!"

"And look where we're a-goen!"

Powell Mountain. Wallen Ridge, one steep climb following another, difficult descents, stones, flinty uplands, boulders, hot suns, tired beasts and a scarcely marked trail. At length the high pitch of endurance was reached and thereafter the way eased down toward the west, hard to go even yet, but no longer a matter of intense suffering and despair. Berk and Muir killed a buffalo for food and all rested two days to feast, this being the first buffalo Diony had seen and a curious beast to her. One of the horses drooped visibly and a mule twisted his ankle and grew a great knotted tendon at the side of his leg so that he walked thereafter in a flinching gait, a new rhythm for Diony's mind to know and remember. They passed two graves at the side of the trail, piled over with stony earth. At a cabin station there were two lonely men who sold powder and lead, and Berk increased the load his horses carried. The wall to the west stood up continually now, a great cliff topping a mountain, white limestone set in an impenetrable cliff across the way, a wonder to dread.

"We'll go through that or over it, one," Diony said. "It's a wonder if we can . . ."

"Oh, God knows!"

Looking across the valley, it made the heart leap and lie down still in the breast for a space, to see this wall of stone and to know that it was set squarely before Kentuck. They came slowly down out of the mountains into the broad rolling expanse of Powell Valley, the wall, the barrier, now continually in their sight. They marched toward the cliffs each day now and yet it stood beyond. The respite was a delight, for Powell Valley eased away to a rolling reach of sheltered country, easy to go, but the cruelties of Powell Mountain and Wallen Ridge were not forgotten. The high rugged ridge of the Wall stood closer, the cliffs on the top an unbroken barrier now. They came to Martin's Station, a cabin in the forest. It was the last cabin they would see until the forts in the canelands beyond the long Wilderness should be reached. The faint wheel trace stopped here, for no wagon had ever gone beyond this place.

"How could we ever go over that rock cliff?" Diony asked.

"There's a gateway around to the south," the men told her. Muir bathed his scaled feet in a cool runlet and Alex Harmon and John Gowdy treated their swollen foot-joints with bruised herbs. "When we turn about to the south we'll see the pass high up in the ridge," they said.

She had taken off her shoes and was putting her feet into the cool water of the stream, sitting beyond a ragged willow. A watersnake left the sand under her feet and went away swiftly among the dark rocks, and her breath leaped at the sudden coolness of the water. The stream flowed lightly over her flesh, and, as Muir spoke, it seemed of a more intense reality, as if it were more of itself than formerly, as if the Gateway to be seen from the south were related to the wimpling flow of the creek, as if they were the same in some breath-getting, leaping inner part of herself.

On the next day, on the march, the men arranged a cautious formation. Berk with Martin Lucas, Harmon, Abram Perry, and Sam Scruggs, went to the fore. The larger children came next, driving the cattle, but Diony walked among the children to drive her cow, and she let her riding horse take the sick horse's load. Elvira rode, carrying the Perry infant in her arms, the Perry mother walking, for she had no horse. Hannah Lucas walked, or rode if there was an idle horse, and she led the horse carrying her small children. John Gowdy drove forward the pack horses; he was skilled at keeping these beasts in the trail. Jack Jarvis, Muir, and Joe Tandy came in the rear, walking, their rifles loaded. Thus they made a day's march of twelve miles and camped at night at the Big Spring. They could now see the Gateway, for all day they had been drawing near to the approach of it and rounding their path toward the south.

The cliff arose to a great height above them now, and there were dark indetermined recesses. Sheer cliffs stood six hundred or eight hundred feet above the pass, leaping up into the air with a great thrust and growing strange and dim with distance over their heads. They were on an old warriors' path, Gowdy said. "The north Indians and the south Indians go this way to war . . ."

They scarcely spoke together. Guardedly and half-heartedly they prepared the evening food. Diony saw fear on Nancy Perry's face, and fear and pride and caution on Elvira's. She knew that these were on her as well. They saw the day become veiled early when the sun went behind the ridges, and the night began. They had stopped to camp overshadowed by great masses of earth and stone.

"Hit's a fearful place. I wouldn't, oh, I wouldn't go into hit," Hannah said.

"You'd almost think monsters to be there. Some kind you couldn't name."

Disturbed, they prepared food, not daring to light a fire. They gathered in small family groups about the food, whispering: "Let's go back. I'm frighted of what's before. How did we ever think to set foot in such a place?" They were whispering as they took water from the spring.

"Hereabouts Boone's son James was killed. Here Boone lost his boy. They say he cried, Boone, a strong man, cried for the death of his boy. . . . Rebecca Boone . . . Here . . . in seventy-three, it was . . ."

"Iffen you go back you go without me to guard you," Gowdy called out. "No woman-person can make a terror to fright me. Woman-persons ought better to stay behind in the tidewater."

His talk of women angered Perry, for he had joined with the women in fright. Anger made him more bold and he went apart to glower. Hardness settled over the camp, hate and despair and fright. Elvira took the small Perry child into her lap and it slept on her large flat bosom.

They rested to sleep without the comfort of a fire. While she lay in this strange place, at the gateway to Kentuck, the great opening in the cliff standing high in the ridge above her head, Diony thought of Albemarle and of those there, but most of Betty. About her lay the men, each one sleeping on his rifle. She thought of Betty, living without danger, as a girl lives, and of how she came and went each day, going to the milk-house, taking the eggs from the nests when her mother reminded her of this task. As she pictured thus she heard the cry of an owl. It was a deep hooting sound that mingled with the herbs of the way over which she had passed as these were graven into her sight, and behind the veil of the herbs she brought an image of Betty as a more real and vivid object. The cry of the owl came again, scarcely nearer, but instantly, at its second coming, some unnatural quality in the cry called her to acute attention of it. There was an inflection of questioning in the call, as if a question were being asked by the way of an owl's cry. The answer came, an owl replying to an owl, but within it the reply to the questioned note, as if one said "Where?" and the other answered "Here." She touched Berk and asked him with her quick, startled hands to wake and listen. The ponies stirred and shifted uneasily, and then stamped the soft grass with their feet.

The owl called again, having moved farther away, and the reply came as if it were far, but Diony knew that these receding sounds might be a feint of a cunning approach. Berk waked Muir and Tandy, and presently all the men were awake. The cries moved to a greater distance and then ceased altogether.

"We'd best spell each other the balance of the night," the men said. "We'd best . . ." They made cautious whispered plans for guarding.

The moon rose after midnight and lit the trees with a strange dawn. The ponies stamped at the earth and snorted, being disturbed anew by the brightness, but the dogs knew danger and were still.

Diony lay down to sleep then, accepting all her perils. The owl was not heard again, although a true owl, overhead in a tree, cried three times and made her know how false the other cries had been. "We'd best keep a sharp lookout at daybreak," Muir said. She fell asleep hearing these whispers. "Break of day is their best hour for surprise."

❖   ❖

When she waked, the light of day had begun to spread over the trees. All the men were astir, being scattered about the camp as a guard. No fire was allowed, and so their breakfast was of parched corn which they had at hand, but in the brush there were a few ripe berries. Diony milked her cow although there was little left in the animal's body that was of the softness of milk. The women prepared the children for the march and the packs were given to the beasts. The order of their going was established, and all moved off slowly, taking the even pace of their habitual travel. They moved up the narrow canyon along the faint trace, Boone's Trace, over stones and brambles, but here and there logs had been thrown from the way or a tree felled to make the passage clear. Together, men and women, they went slowly forward, the men to the fore, the man's strength being in the thrust, the drive, in action, the woman's lateral, in the plane, enduring, inactive but constant. They marched forward, taking a new world for themselves, possessing themselves of it by the power of their courage, their order, and their endurance. They went forward without bigotry and without psalm-singing to hide what they did. They went through the Gateway into Kentuck. They walked quietly, being subdued by the greatness about them in the great cliffs and the fine mountain rises that lifted upward from the pass.

The feet of the horses made a slow uneven pattering on the stones as they went singly, for the way was narrow. A burdened horse piled with its pack seemed a minute creature in the great chasm. Laboring forward with her cow, Diony knew the whole company as it worked upward in a line, as it stretched far ahead through the canyon and back to the rear-guard that came, their eyes always on the trees. Berk went ahead of his men. He was cautious now, inquiring of every step. Diony saw him high up

in the pass, making the way, flinging a log from
the path or pushing away loose boulders. He was
strong-thewed and tireless, never satisfied with what
he had done. The whole line, Berk at the head, Muir
or Jack Jarvis at the rear, were small beings, contrived for endurance, and they crept through the
earth and burrowed through overgrown gulches.
They were small gaunt creatures, thrusting forward,
their sinews able to thrust again even after weariness
had settled over them. They walked all day among
canyons.

They passed to Pine Mountain Gap and crossed
the Cumberland River at an old Indian ford, and
they slept there, but they went forward again with
the same caution. At the end of this day they dared
make fires to roast the game they had killed.

The great natural barriers were now passed. There
were now the hills to go, the long untracked forest
marked only with Boone's Path. There was much
game on every hand. All night the dogs fought back
the jackals from the fresh meat that was hung in a
tree for safety. After a day of rest they were off on the
way again, Berk always forward, driving every man
beyond himself, relentless, lean as the wolf—man
assuming the wolf to overcome the wolf. Diony tried
to recall all the path she had come and all the mountains and rivers she had crossed, but the ways were

blurred and blended with dangers and fatigues, with lamed beasts and lost property, with hunger and wet and lightning striking fire among the trees, with owls hooting in the night, true and false, men running here and there, children running, to bring the cattle back to the path. Beyond all this lay some design she could not now state clearly. There was food and rest at a day's end. There were hours of dizzy going when she knew nothing beyond the certainty of herself on the way.

❖   ❖

They had come out of the rugged hills. Diony looked at the trees and the growth in the new world into which she had entered. They were of a familiar kind, many of the shapes already known to her, but here of a great size. Evan Muir told her the names of many kinds, riding near her to call out the names as he pointed. He pointed out the sweet-gum, grown here to a height above a hundred feet. Its bark was brown and gray and was marked with vertical lines, a beauty in the forest. It flowed with a balsam gum inside, he said. It was a mark of dignity wherever it was passed. Diony would ride with dignity under the boughs, her back straight and her thought high.

There were white birches gathered among the clumps and tangled masses, the leaves shining brightly green and quivering in the air. Squirrels

ran about over the limbs of the tall ash trees and
quivered and leaped among the lightly shaken and
lightly shadowed leaves. Among the trees grew the
witch hazel, a low tree of wide leaves, hung now with
the empty seed pods of last year's flowering. It gave
a balm which was useful in the healing of wounds,
Muir said, and he told of other witch trees and
named the witch wand by the power of which water
is discovered flowing underground, of great service
in finding where to dig a well.

Through the dark of the forest bright streaks of
color swept quickly or glided softly about—the birds.
They were red, yellow, blue, gray, brown, gold-and-
green, black washed over with bronze and lit with
fire. They were living jewels in the dark of the great
trees. They went continually from the path and
darted about in the undergrowth, or swept lightly
away to the upper boughs. Their calls and cries
made a continual song and a language that spread
through the trees and receded to the outlying forests.

The way had eased down out of the hills. They
walked through orchards of crab trees where the
crab apples hung. At Rock Castle River the trail
divided to make two, Boone's Path and Logan's. A
part of their company bade them farewell here and
took the path toward Boonesborough. The Perry
family, the Lucas family, and Scruggs went toward

the right, toward Boone's Fort. Moving forward in a smaller company they were passing now through the last of the Wilderness Road, nearing the forts. The path emerged from the hills and came out onto the great fertile plateau where the rolling forests lay as a giant mantle over the earth. Then Gowdy and Jack went toward the left to search out the land there, but they would come later to Harrod's Fort, they said. Thus Berk's party was now reduced to six persons, four carrying guns.

Berk smiled easily, casting backward toward her a bright look. They went plodding down under noble trees, their limbs crooked to the weariness of going and their sinews strained, their gaunt frames beating forward. Diony could not now remember what lay far behind. Over her thought flowed continually a freshness as if the world were new-born. While she rode through a low-lying valley approaching a ford, riding ahead of Elvira and behind Muir, a parrakeet flew over the trail, flying low, but it went into a tangle of dogwood boughs that interlocked with the coffee tree. There was bright yellow shading to orange over its head and neck and its body was bright green. It clambered among the boughs as she walked the last of the long trail, its beak of a pale clear yellow.

Around them stretched the delirium of a fine land,

level expanses delicately tilted to fine curves, here and there cane patches of rich fat growth, here and there noble trees. At a camp by a stream they cautiously made ready to rest, the last night in the open. Sitting a moment on her little mare, the pack animals huddled about to have their loads lifted and the people stirring cautiously from the trail, she said to Berk:

"What do we want here? What did we come for?" She was shaken with delight and wonder.

"We want a fine high house, out in the rich cane. We want a farm to tend . . . fields . . ."

She had a sudden overwhelming sense of this place as of a place she had known before. Feeling that she had been here before, that these events were the duplicate of some former happening, she left her little mare to graze by the trail and walked cautiously into a meadow.

These are of those who lived in Fort Harrod, who built the stockade, who manned the walls and sallied out to meet the enemy. With some of them were their wives and children. Some were present at one time and others at another, and some were dead before the late summer of 1777, but the dead lived in the report of the living.

They were James Harrod and his wife, founder of Harrodstown, Harrod a man of great strength and sympathy.

John Floyd, who was like Harrod in the goodness of his heart.

They were James Berry, Whitley, Francis McConnell, Manifee, Mogohon, John Gass, Nathaniel Randolph, Joseph Lindsay, James McDaniel, John Hays, and Hugh Wilson, who was the father of Harold Wilson, the first child born there.

They were John Lythe, a preacher, and James Cowan, Richard Hogan, Hugh McGarry, Thomas Denton, Levi Todd, and John Sovereigns with his sister Hannah and their mother. Mistress Sovereigns and Hannah had been for six years captive among the Shawnees. Mistress Sovereigns had been mutilated by her captors, her tongue having been cut so that she could not speak thereafter.

174

They were William Coomes and his wife, Mistress
Coomes, who taught the first school at the forted town, she
having no book from which to teach but an arithmetic which
she herself transcribed by hand.

Major George Rogers Clark, military leader, in command until he left for his great campaign in the Northwest.

Of military men, in and out from time to time, were John
Bowman, Anthony Bledsoe, Edward Worthington, and the
great Boone and Logan, with others . . . were Joseph
Bowman, Leonard Helm, and William Harrod, who led
companies in Clark's army and took part in the fall of the
Illinois country; were Silas Harlan, Isaac Bowman,
Robert Todd, Simon Kenton, John Todd, Abraham
Chapline . . .

Barney Stagner, an old man who cared for the spring
within the fort, who kept it clean, who admonished the
children if they played near it and guarded it from pollution.
He would wander into the woods and if he were warned of
danger he would say, "The Indians won't kill an old man
like me." He went up the stream to its source, a half mile,
and he was found dead there, his head cut off and carried
away.

William Ray and James Ray, boys in their teens. William
was killed in the spring of seventy-seven. With James and
two others he was out on Shawnee Run, five miles from the
fort, to clear a piece of land. Thirty or forty Indians came
and William was killed, the others hiding. James ran to

the fort, and his speed was so great that the Indians were amazed. Blackfish, the chief, said afterward that there was a man among the Long Knives in the caneland who could outrun all his warriors. James Ray was one of the night hunters, one of those who went out by stealth at night when an enemy was known to be at hand, to find meat for the people of the fort.

William Pogue and Anne Pogue. William was a handy-craftsman in the working of wood. He made chairs and vessels and farming tools, until he was killed in the summer of seventy-eight. Their children were Robert, Joseph, Martha, Mary and Anne. Anne Pogue, the mother, brought the first spinning wheel and the first poultry. She devised ways to make cloth, having neither wool nor flax, using the wild growth of the forest.

V

In the middle of an afternoon they rode into Harrod's Fort. Tandy and Muir had gone forward to announce the approach and a throng of men, women and children stood about the gate cheering.

"Four guns more!" The men and boys cheered and shouted and flung out gay profane words to see these armed men come into the fort. The arrival was strange, surrounded by joy that quivered on the faces of strange people, by strange voices saying intimate words of affection and welcome. Strange hands caught at Diony's arms and passed down her sides, feeling at her flesh, and the women carried her away to a cabin to ease her.

Cabins and high stockade walls made the fort, the lives of two hundred people enclosed within the fortified place. There was a stir of people about the stockade, a lively movement about the gates. The men went out each day to their clearings, taking their axes and their rifles. Some were fearful of invasion, remembering the attacks of the earlier season of the year, but others were unafraid, saying that the crisis of the war was passed.

When Berk and Diony had rested three days as visitors in cabins here and there, a man who owned one of the fort cabins offered to sell his claim together with his garden patch outside, and Berk, having money in his belt, bought a temporary claim to these holdings. In their own house within the stockade then, Diony and Elvira spread the utensils from their pack saddles and began to make life in the wilderness. The house was built, as were the other houses of the fort, of round logs fitted neatly at the corners. The roof sloped inward toward the enclosed square of the fort. Within the cabin a ladder was built against the outer wall, at the top of it a small hole or chink. In time of invasion one might climb the ladder and look out to see what the enemy did. The chimney was made of carefully laid logs and was lined with mud, and the floor was of beaten earth. The cabin was new, smelling of fresh green wood.

Diony learned quickly how things are done in the wilderness. A woman of the fort, Anne Pogue, taught her how to make a broom by shredding a hickory pole, grain by grain, until the brush fell in a fluff about the lower end, to be bound then with hickory splints. When she had learned the art of a broom she swept the earthen floor of her cabin, knowing that she swept the new earth of Kentuck. At Anne Pogue's advice she laid her shoes away during the summer, saving them for winter use, and she made herself moccasins. Thus she went lightly over the ground on soft-shod feet. She cooked the game meats over the fireplace or baked the corn-pones there. She had one iron vessel and one pewter spoon, having lost the other utensils Polly had given her, but there were a few vessels in Elvira's collection.

"It was that triflen little mare lost me my spoons," Diony said, unable now to remember the whole terror and weariness of the long passage. "She brushed the spoons offen the load, along with the books, into some creek."

Life was reduced now to a few simple things. One could count the things of existence and find them a few. Bearskins piled in the corners of the cabin were used for beds. Elvira seemed tall and strong, direct and simple, as she moved about in the stockade, unhurried, attending to her wants with a firm, light step. When Berk had viewed the country for a week, hunting here and there, he chose a rich acreage some miles to the south of the fort, land grown in cane and forest. He paid for the land with money from the money belt, and he began at once to build a strong house on his acres.

He would stand his rifle and his axe in the corner by the fireplace and sit relaxed on the skins while Diony placed the food on the rude board, a rived log that was fastened to the logs of the wall. Elvira would carry the water from the spring and pound the corn in the mortar out in the quadrangle. She made a vat for the tanning of leather and a hopper for the leaching of ashes to make lye. Sometimes Diony sang over the making of the food, feeling that she was moving through an adventure which was at once difficult and unrealized. She had grown a greater strength, but she felt small and light before the greatness of Elvira, who moved at once among the strong women of the fort. She could not discover all that Berk was contriving. One evening while he sat on the skins, his head against the chinked wall, she realized his slow smile which came, outrunning fatigue and despair. His beauty was allied then to his unfathomed wishes. "How did I come to be here?" she thought then, running swiftly back to Albemarle, to the morning in the cow-pen.

The fort stood on a hill above the creek, the land falling away from its walls on every side but on the south where it rolled out on a rolling upland. There was a great gate at the north and there were smaller gates at the other sides. The wall stood sharp and stiff, high above any man's leap or climb, and from without it seemed unyielding and secure. At each corner stood a high block-house to guard the walls, and this house had an upper story that projected from the lower part so that rifles might sweep the entire wall. The great wooden gates would swing back easily in spite of their rude bulk. There was always a man or a woman near the gates to open for any who had gone out. Inside the wall there was a hum of people who came and went, a walled town being a busy place. In the central square there was a smith's shop where tools and guns were mended, and near by was a hominy block, the property of all, where corn was pounded free of the husk.

Diony's cabin stood in the north wall to the west of the gate. From the sunny doorway she looked out on the quadrangle, the cabins far across the enclosure, and behind these the trees of the forest.

❖   ❖

The Indian attacks of the early part of the year were the recurring talk of the fort, the stealthy nearness of the enemy being a continual menace. Women lingering in the open court would tell the newcomers of the fights. "I was out to gather yarbs," one woman said, beginning a tale of terror. "I happened to be at the hole in Harrod's cabin to look out and I was surprised to see a stir in the brush." They told swift stories of heroism and death, or they turned back to their labors. Their linsey jackets and skirts were soiled, were patched and torn. Diony and Elvira would join them at the block where the hominy was pounded or they would wait with them beside the spring while one in turn dipped water into her piggin. Their voices continued from one recital to another.

"I was at Logan's enduren the siege," one said. "I saw Burr Harrison fall to the ground, shot through, and I saw Logan make ready to run outside the stockade, Harrison's wife beside herself with grief. I saw Logan run out where the bullets came like hail, and he pulled Burr Harrison to his shoulder and ran back, bullets over him like rain. . . ."

"We lived out on Caney Run a short spell last year and into the spring. One night came a tap at the door and a voice in whispers told us to come to the fort. The woods full of redskins, he said. Walked nine miles to warn us in the dark of a night and helped carry the little boys when they gave out and couldn't go further. Harrod, it was. A big man that never tires, and a heart in him like pure gold."

"And Logan is of a great size too, a giant."

"A big heart inside his breast."

"Logan, his body made big to hold his big heart."

"And Boone is a wonder amongst men. Not even the redmen are of such a cunning in the woods. In each fort, all three, is a man you could take for a pattern to make men by."

Their voices were familiar as known now to differ one from another, and Diony had learned their names. She learned the ways the women used. She whittled a spoon out of dishwood, working day after day, and when the first was done she began another. The garden place Berk had acquired lay toward the north beyond the creek. Once when the woods were known to be free of savages she went there with Berk and Elvira. There was a low temporary cabin on this ground, a mean hut which no one occupied since the enemy made life outside the fort insecure. Berk viewed this humble shed with contempt.

"I want a fine high house, the roof high up off my head," he said, turning back to the stockade. "Room for a man to lift up his head in."

She saw, as in a shadow, the great high house he had begun on Deer Creek, eight miles away in a country she had not yet entered, a country that kept continually beyond her. Looking into Berk's report she could dimly see the creek there and see the cabin arising on the bank to the right. A half mile from the cabin, up the creek, was the Lick, the place where the animals had come for many years to lick the salty stones about a mineral well. The trampled space covered two acres, and here the ground was bare of tall growth and trodden to a hard stony crust. There were deep furrows and licked-out gullies where the animals had worn away the soil and the rock with their tongues through ages. The animals hunted one another at the Lick. Kind preyed upon kind and there were blanching bones strewn thick over the ground as the trails drew near the salt. One walked there on the skulls of beasts. Knowing of the Lick, Diony felt the presence of the animals beyond the fort wall, panthers creeping, the swift wildcats, the wolf at night, buffaloes, elks, bears running clumsily, deer going swiftly.

❖   ❖

One day while Diony stood within the north gate looking toward the creek and the rolling field opposite, a man came out of the forest toward the east. He came singing to make his presence known. He stood on the opposite bank and looked up toward the fort as if he watched it with pleasure and curiosity. His face was clear-cut, his eyes bright and his nose slightly beaked. When he came near the gate Diony opened it for him, and he began at once to talk about the fort and to praise the block-houses. He said that one of the cabins outside the wall belonged to him. He had helped to build the town in seventy-four.

"You are a strange man at Harrod's," she said. "What mought be your name?"

"Boone is my name," he said, "Dan'l Boone. Harrod would know me."

He stood in the gateway to talk with Diony. All the animals of the Lick were powerful about him then, felt and realized as he stood near, but he arose from among the beasts and his eye was more clear and more cunning than theirs and his courage more cool, his daring greater. He stood without hate above the beasts and above savage men. He smiled as he talked, and he lingered at the gate as if he would talk with her for a little, and she felt her heart leap and flutter within to know with whom she was speaking.

"Like all the balance I walked to Kentuck, or rode my nag, over your road," she said, "marched here over the trace you made out for us. I'm obliged to you for a road, right obliged and beholden."

"You're right welcome to it," Boone said. "If I marked out the way, you had to go it with your two feet, and so the road's yours too for the trouble you took to walk it. And the danger was yours whilst you went the way."

"A right perilous journey," she said.

"An Indian says to me, at Watauga when Colonel Henderson made his treaty, says he, 'Brother, we give you a fine land, but I believe you'll have a trouble to settle it. Trouble,' says he."

"A fine country though. I reckon I have been ahearen about Kentuck or Caintuck, by whatever name you please to call it, ever since I was that high, and report always said a fine land. And a heap of unexplored corners there must be. Places a body could get lost in and never find himself again."

"Parts you could explore, yes, boundaries of land not yet spied out, I reckon," Boone said. "Yes, I could find new ways to go and creeks to travel, falls to spy out, caves and wonders to see. But I don't reckon I'd get lost in e'er one. Not to say lost. I never was lost. I was bewildered right bad once for as much as a week, but not lost. I never felt lost the whole enduren time."

"You always felt at home in the world," Diony said. "You felt at home with what way the sun rises and how it stands overhead at noon, at home with the ways rivers run and the ways hills are. It's a gift you have, to be natured that way."

"Elbow room is what a man wants," he said.

Men in the cabins of the south wall had discovered Boone's presence at the gate and there was shouting, and a salute was fired. Diony saw him go toward the inner square and she saw the men there give him a great welcome. She turned back toward the gate and stood with her hand on the rough latch, searching into Boone's words as they remained now in her memory. He had said that he was never lost. She felt the presence of his voice as still speaking after he was gone, and felt the breadth of the out-reaching land as she had had report of it from one and another, as if it had been there beside her at the gate, as if it had come in the flesh to breathe and smile, to speak to her. "Never lost, not once the whole enduren time," she said, smiling. "It's curious." She walked three steps beyond the gate and looked at the four parts of the sky to try to place herself rightly under it, to set the winds to rights and to feel secure above the green of the earth. "I'm not the Boone kind," she said. "I never was. . . . I'd be more at home somewheres else . . . I don't know where. . . ."

The early August sun came down warm over the gate. Outside lay the beginnings of fields and a rolling land that was rich in wild growth. She stood apart from the trampled turf and apart from the hewn logs that were still half green, as one looking from without upon the turnip field beyond the flow of the creek, belonging in no sort to the passive herbs, but allied in some way to the distant crying of wild turkeys toward the cane brakes.

It was the first dawn of morning. Sleeping on her bed of skins within her cabin, Diony heard a great flapping of wings that beat rhythmically on the air, slowly and full of power, the cock preparing himself for his early morning cry. The great pulse of preparation throbbed through the fort and then the fowl rolled out his challenge, the first crowing of the dawn. Wondering at the power in the cock's wings, Diony lay waking. A vague menace followed the crowing, and the dogs were stilled, but there was an uneasiness among the cattle. They lowed in sudden bleats as if they had lost the security of the herd, and they walked about the stockade enclosure and shifted from the higher ground. The slow light was breaking. Then a great stir began in the fort, as if all the sleepers had awakened at once, the men running from the doors and the women calling. Men climbed the lookout places. There was an enemy in the woods without. Clark assembled his fighting men quickly and quietly. Berk took his rifle and his powder horn and went out to join the fighting squads.

Then Clark sent a man into the turnip field north of the fort to dig there as if no suspicion of an enemy troubled the garrison. With his men he stole out the south gate and made a swift march to the rear of the Indians and fell upon them there. When the fight was done, the enemy destroyed or routed, fifteen bundles were picked up, the plunder of the Indians. This battle was known as the fight of the Turnip Patch.

❖   ❖

Each thing she had brought with her from Albemarle was precious now and each was carefully saved
and spent in its best use. From the cut of linsey she
made Berk a hunting shirt. She cooked for their food
the green new corn, mashed to a pulp or left whole,
or she boiled the wild meat in the iron pot over the
fire of her hearth. The stockade was crowded when
the militiamen were at hand. She sat within the
cabin stitching the linsey cloth. The commander,
George Rogers Clark, came and went about the
stockade. He was a tall young man with clear eyes
and a tight mouth. Men carried forward the work of
soldiery, and the large strong women who could blow
the great wooden trumpet, the warning horn that
called the men home from the outside if there were
danger about the fort, assisted the men, sometimes
standing as guard at the gates. Diony moved then
among the minute things of the cabins. She took the
milk from the cow, and there was thus a little butter
to sweeten the corn hoe-cake. Women who had been
at hand during the spring had a dark rich sugar
which they had made from the water of the sugar
tree, and with these Diony traded to get a bit of the
sweet for her table. She would barter with a bit of
turnip seed, or once she bought a piggin of the sugar
with one needle from her needle book.

"You can come now, all," she would say when she

had set the evening meal on the table. Berk would come to the board, taking his knife from his belt as he came, ready to cut the flesh that lay steaming on the platter.

Berk worked all day at the beginnings of his fields and his house, or he would hunt in the regions beyond these. The land about the fort was drained by the upper waters of a stream the men called Pigeon River. Diony knew from Muir's careful report of it that this river crooked about through a wide expanse of land, gathering up many streams and flowing at last into the Ohio below the falls. A few miles away from the fort, toward the north, lay the great river of which many accounts had been made, the river of which the hunters had been telling throughout the years, the Chenoa, the Millewakane, the Ken-tuck-ee. Men who had hunted there told of it with smiles of delight. It ran between high cliffs, winding mile after mile, and the growth made color and shadows on the walls of tall white stones. She knew that she would not see the river until peace came.

Her pleasure of a river could wait. She knew herself to be the beginning of a new world. All about her were beginnings. The beginnings of fields took form as the trees were cleared away and the canelands plowed, and the beginnings of roads appeared where a man made a trace by walking to a stream, another following and another, and added to these the foot-marks of dogs and horses. She learned to fashion garments of buckskin for a man, working softness into the stiff hide and sewing the seams together with a leather strip of elkskin. Often there was dancing in the stockade. A fiddler would fling out a reel or a jig and the young women would gather in the dusk. Then the fiddler would call for dancers and the men would come, not caring whether they did or not, but dancing nevertheless. Then there were gay ironic curses, compounded of danger and scarcity and the need a man has for revel.

"We have a good time," a girl, Betsy Dodd, said, tucking her ragged jacket together so that it would continue to cover her. "We have a good time, no matter."

Diony looked at Betsy Dodd as she spoke, seeing her in some relation to Betty, for they were of the same age. A vague hostility to this girl clouded Diony's mind as she looked upon her, as if the girl of the fort would force her rags upon Betty. Looking at the strange girl while she danced, Diony saw then a vast likeness to Betty appear behind their external difference. The new girl was more easily led and more given to play. They were both small and slen-der, the substance out of which women would be

made. Betsy Dodd lived with her aunt, having no
parents, but into her insecure life she brought security, as if she were enough within herself. Diony felt
a pity and a tenderness for her as she stepped lightly
about the floor and made laughter with the men.
She went lightly into the dance, tucking her little
ragged waist-garment about her more securely.
There was dancing every night while the fiddler
stayed there.

The next week a preacher came, one who had
visited the fort at Boonesborough and preached there.
He seized upon the rhythm that swayed the fort in
dancing and turned it to the uses of religion and he
called for repentance, saying that wickedness was
rife there. Then there was singing where there had
been dancing, and there was a hearty flowing of
tears, Betsy Dodd being one of the first to sway with
the preacher and cry out for grace. Then Alex
Harmon married Molly Anne West, who had been
widowed by some battle early in the year. The week
was filled with subdued happiness and put-by mirth,
but the wedding was let have full sway, incidental
to evangelism. There was great merriment.

"A poor make-out way to get married, though,"
a woman said.

"Molly Anne and Alex can call it married, just
about, preachen and prayen no matter. But they

better make it legal against the law comes to Kentuck."

"There's law a-plenty. A new day come now."

"Court is in session now, Harrod's full of judges from all the forts, five men, and she says there's a lack in the law."

Kentucke was a county now. The Court of Quarter Sessions was meeting in the fort. Some of the women disputed in favor of "Transylvania" for a name for the country, but others disputed for the old name, "Kentuck." Frequently there was a quarrel as to which law was the right law, and the rights of the proprietors and of Henderson were denied or defended.

"Henderson, he bought off all the south Indians. Whatever Indians come now come always from the north," the dispute continuing.

"But you can't buy a nation. . . . The days of lord proprietors are forever over. . . ."

Diony was startled at these sudden ghosts from Albemarle that walked now in the cane country. She had been in the fort for a month now and the ways the women used were well known to her. She made clothing from the cuts of linen and woolsey she had brought, for the garments she and Berk had worn on the march were now well spent with hard use. She knew what passed about for gossip and dispute. And she knew that the children and some of the negro retainers were afraid to go near the spring at night, fearing to meet the headless ghost of old Barney Stagner there.

✦   ✦

In September the corn was brought in under guard. There was a small battle at one of the cribs on Harrod's Run five miles to the northeast of the fort and three died during the fight or later. The militiamen were shifting about. Major Clark, with twenty-two men from Harrod's Fort and fifty-five from Logan's, started for Virginia, but Captain Montgomery arrived at Logan's with thirty-eight men, and Captain Holder arrived in Boonesborough with forty-eight. These small armies were moving about in the cane. The country seemed more at ease as autumn came, but the corn crop was scanty and the game about the fort was less abundant.

Diony and Elvira cooked pumpkin in their iron vessel and thus they had a dainty sauce to eat with the bear meat. There were a few turnips saved and Berk bought corn from those who could spare him a few measures, for he had arrived too late to plant a field. He worked all day at Deer Creek now, buying help in the lifting of the great logs that made his house.

A cold season came in November when the wind blew in a gale all day. It lashed the last of the leaves from the trees and flung the dry twigs and withered berries about. The scouts reported that no signs of Indians were to be found in the woods.

"No Indian would make fight on such a day," Elvira said. "He'd hide in a warm gulley and wait on a better season." She tied her shawl over her head and went out of the house, and Diony wrapped herself well and followed after.

They went through the gate and out into the open, their garments blown back in the northwest gale, their bodies leaned forward to push against the windy flood. Elvira carried a basket and Diony knew that she had in mind to go to the nut tree at the garden patch across the creek.

When they came to the tree they found the nuts thickly fallen. "They make fine victuals," Elvira said, and the wind tore her words apart and made of them a hissing breath, "Fine victuals, fine victuals," turned into a withered, toneless cry. She stooped over the nuts, gathering, while her words were severed from her breath and flung outward without meaning. Diony, having struggled too long with the wind, had a weariness come over her, and she went inside the hut to ease herself from the power of the gale. Inside, the floor of old trampled earth was clean and dry and the logs kept the force of the wind without. She sat leaning against the wall, resting on the earth, and she fell into a brief sleep, and waked, remembering much of what Polly had told her and hearing the words of admonition and advice that flowed under the throaty kindness of her mother's voice. She dreamed then a brief picture of the nuts falling through the windy air and arriving in her basket, unassisted by her hands.

Suddenly a low unearthly wind seemed to be blowing through the hut and through her own body, striking the walls apart and dividing the quiet inner warmth of her being from the cold that leaped to the surface of her skin. Then she knew that she was hearing the low whoop of a savage and that the dark shadow that covered the doorway and then moved away was an Indian. The man had gone from the door but his shadow lay faintly dark in the opening.

She had screamed two sharp cries, sitting stiff with terror against the wall of the hut. Then she arose slowly and leaped to the door, and she tried to force the door shut, but strong hands pushed her back. While she struggled with the door Elvira came. She lashed at the man with a rail, working outside, and she tried to beat him away from the door, but Diony saw that he was eager to have her life before he would turn to face Elvira. There was a confusion of blows and arms, and Elvira, beating about with the rail, forced a way into the hut and stood beside her, panting for breath.

Another came. Two dark men looked in at the door which Elvira was trying to force shut, their bodies beneath their faces painted in stripes. Their large mouths were spread in cries that were subdued to whispers and their chins were thrown back. One called out an oath learned of the white men. Diony set her whole strength beside Elvira's strength to try to push the door, and they leaned together, plunging forward. The Indians cursed again and flung their strength, all together, calling the epithet they had learned to say, heartening themselves with the white man's oath. Elvira was straining with renewed power and Diony leaped back and thrust with her whole reserve against the door, flinging the entire spasm of life itself against it, but the Indians strengthened themselves again with another oath and thrust, both together, and the door moved back, opened wide. Two strong young men stood fixed before them, two men opposite two women. Elvira stood slightly above the rest. Two opposite two, they hung fixed in space.

Then one of the two men moved slightly and his arm shot forward. His hatchet crashed on Elvira's face and beat upon her, and as she fell forward hands pushed her back. Then Diony saw the hatchet that leaped over her own head, and a great blow fell as a stiffness that tightened through her being and shut pain out. She felt the faint jar of her fall as if it were a tremor passing over a remote world, and oblivion spread over her. She dreamed of her home in Virginia, of sitting beside Betty in the half-light under the high window, drawing threads of linen off the distaff to the whirr of the great wheel. A sweet, sinister presence, Betty, continued beside her, saying, "You stayed with me. You didn't go there." There was sweetness and security in the dark room, a great rain falling outside and crashing over the dog alley. Then she waked a little out of the pain that throbbed over her and stiffened her head to a tight sheaf that crushed her thought. She saw Elvira's body lying still and she saw that the scalp from her head was gone. She tried to move, but she slipped back into her oblivion, making one last effort to hold the present where it demanded service of her. It was clear that she must close the door. This demand became a light down that floated in the substance of forgetting.

A voice deeply within her forgetting part began to say, speaking with swift syllables, "Since you cannot deny that the great Mover and Author of Nature continually explaineth Himself to the eyes of men by arbitrary signs . . . all those bodies that compose the mighty frame of the world have not any substance without a mind. They take being through being perceived or known. . . . When not actually perceived by me they subsist in the mind of some Eternal Spirit . . ." A light down floated over the dark of her understanding and blew without consequence across a great dark space, and she caught at the first fleck of it which signified that she must close the door. A second lighter thistledown drifted across the dark where the voice still discoursed of signs that continually explain deity, a lighter flake of unrelated substance, which informed her that Elvira was dead, that she lay scalped on the floor. She heard a horn blowing, great swift cries calling alarm to all scattered people, and she tried once again to close her will about the necessity to live, to arise and close the door, but she was enveloped in greater darkness and her pain turned back upon some inner and mightier frame, which had been as yet untouched and untested, and asked it again for some kindlier sign, some final explanation.

❖   ❖

She lay on the bearskins in her fort cabin. Berk was helping her back to life and a strong draught burned in her throat, her heart beating swiftly. She lay in a long semi-sleep, reviewing what had happened in the hut, knowing that Elvira had given her life for her. Elvira forcing a way into the hut, coming to her assistance when she might have hidden in the brush or run to the fort, this design became a firm pattern that lay under all her thought and all her sense of Berk coming and going about her. She had talked with him of this; they were agreed in it; Elvira had died for her. She lay in a long torpor, but whenever she awoke much had happened during the interval. She was given savory drinks and her wound was treated with bruised herbs of medicinal power.

Two men, one a joiner by trade, had made Elvira a coffin. Under guard Berk and Jack made her a grave in the woods on the hill beside the fort. Diony knew of these matters while she lay in a half-sleep, the women beside her fire to talk and to tend her.

All night the rain fell, beating against the clapboards of the roof with a steady flow. It would wash away the blood from the earth-floor of the hut. It fell steadily over the whole caneland and washed over the walls of the cabin. Three women sat beside the fire. Now and then they would put the cup of savory drink to Diony's lips, and then they would go back to their whisperings over the hearth.

"Oh, hear it," she whispered, rising stiffly to her elbow to speak. "Hear the rain."

"Blessed are the dead the rain falls on," a woman replied, an old saying, a comforting chant. It mingled thereafter with the beating of the wet on the boards and the wash of water down the fort wall. "Blessed are the dead the rain falls on."

Morning, and she was awake to the world again, the storm being over. Four days had passed. The world was fresh made and the sun mild and bright, and all the trees were still. A square of the sun lay in the open doorway of the cabin. A sudden knowledge ran over her that the trees, the clearings, the doorways, the beasts, the children running in the open court, the women and the men passing about, were having morning. Morning had not been destroyed. Morning had not been broken. She arose from her bed and walked a little way into the quadrangle. The sunlight fell, tender and cool over her shoulders. It was difficult to make real now the bitter cold of the day when she had gone with Elvira to get nuts in the garden.

❖   ❖

Berk fastened two deer horns over the fire and rested his gun there when it was not abroad with him. At the back of the room the garments they were not wearing hung on a few wooden pegs, and overhead the bear bacon and deer quarters were hung to dry. Gyp lay outstretched beside her door. The cow wandered into the woods to graze but she was brought home at evening and enclosed within the stockade wall. Elvira lay in the ground at the burying place on the hill beside the fort. Jack lived in a corner block-house, a barracks place. Elvira had died for her. This was Diony's life now in the wilderness; thus was she placed and related. Berk went continually to the clearing on Deer Creek. He was indifferent of the life in the fort cabins and he gave the arrangements there little thought. In December he made Diony a bed, conceding this comfort to her necessity. While he pinned the poplar frame to the wall she looked to search his face half fearfully, knowing that he conceded that Elvira had given her life for her. Then the acute point of life within herself, the I, Diony, withdrew from him and she watched him drive home the pegs to make their bed and wondered if her power were enough to meet whatever he would expect of her now.

Women came to speak to her at the door of the hut. They were the same that she had known in Albemarle or on the way, now wearing different names and faces. Molly Anne was a bright chatterer.

"I wish my fleas would take their nap of sleep whilst I take mine," she said. "It's wearisome to have your fleas want to run and play over your skin when times come to rest."

"Call hit fleas," another voice. "Molly Anne Harmon ever was one to put on a brave show-off front. I'm a plain home-made woman myself and I'd as lief call every kind by hits right name."

"Whatever kind 'tis you've got, all is, I wish mine had the good manners to sleep when bedtime comes."

Thus they spoke, seeing the new bed prepared. The timbers that made the frame seemed large, as if they filled the cabin, the bed growing in bulk now that it was raised from the floor, and making a new stress for itself.

There came to her a rush of matured thought, such as she had never known before, and an assurance that she might bring all these happenings into relation with what she knew from her father's books, and on the instant she felt a nearness to Thomas Hall, as if she had grown in size to comprehend the whole of his thought. Elvira had died for her; it was once said she was not married to Berk Jarvis; the Author of Nature, the great Mover of the Universe, continually explained himself by signs that appear in the mind. A new idea ran swiftly over her. Elvira had died for her. That married her to Berk Jarvis if Coley Linkhorn's words were not of sufficient power. The Author of Nature had surely made a sign here, by the way of Elvira's superhuman goodness. The illusion of knowing passed and she was left again in insecurity, and she glanced at Berk's grim face.

When he had finished the frame he began to fill

it with fresh wild hay, and Diony spread this over smoothly. He then brought skins and spread these over the hay, and Diony laid them out in a smooth order, and she brought her blankets and the coverlet, the Whig Rose she had woven in Albemarle.

"It minds me, how we make this bed, of how these-here little wrenny birds and redbreasts make a nest. You see it in the spring-o'-the-year," she said, wanting to save them from remembering sorrow. "First he carries up a straw and then she carries up a stick or a straw, and then he takes his turn and comes up with a straw in his mouth."

"But I don't aim to bring in the straw, one blade at a time, in my mouth," he said, lending himself to her pleasure. "Iffen you want to be a wrenny bird you have to be one without my help."

Diony knew what lay back in his mind while they made pleasant retorts about the task of the bed. An escaped prisoner, returned from the Shawnees in Ohio, Andrew Lawrence his name, had brought news of what the Indians did. Lawrence had been a captive three months and he had learned the Indian's speech. He said that a band of young Indians had returned from the south at the time of the late harvest. They told of marauding among the forts in the white settlements in the canelands. Some of their comrades had been killed, but one of the returned men carried Elvira's scalp at his belt, being proud of it because it was marked curiously with one bright gray lock. The man who boasted of the scalp and carried it was named Blackfox among his people. Sitting among the Indians at Chillicothe, Lawrence had heard a brave story of an attack on a cabin where two white squaws were surprised, in sight of the fort town the Long Knives had built in the cane. The story called the large woman the fighting squaw and it was said she had a strength fit to kill a buffalo in the power of her arms.

Thus Diony heard report of herself by the mouth of Lawrence. Two white squaws, herself one of them, were named over and over. She was a white squaw among the Long Knives, then. She saw herself from the distance, a long dim vista reaching down from Ohio. She saw a white squaw, a strong young woman with rich life in her, a faint red under her sunburnt cheeks, her linsey dress casting a dull shadow in the dim cabin. She, the white squaw, walked over the earth floor and went into the deeper shadows beside the fireplace.

❖   ❖

When her wound was healed, Diony took thought of how she would prepare deer hides for clothing. The vat Elvira had used was at hand, a locust-tree trunk hollowed out. She spread layers of skins in the vat with hardwood ashes to serve for lime. She took Elvira's place at the grinding of the corn. She would lift the pestle by pulling of the sapling pole that hung from the scantling frame above and watch it fall into the great hollowed log called the barrel, where the corn had been poured, and as she used her strength thus she would feel the presence of Elvira. The winter settled over the fort and the corn became scarce. The turnips and pumpkins were used before January, and often the scarcity of game drove a man to kill one of his milk cows. She saw Joe Tandy give Betsy Dodd small presents of corn, a handful of corn passing between them while he looked at her smiling face. A gift came to the fort from the Virginia Legislature. It was a great boiling kettle for salt-making. This present had been brought over the long Trace on pack horses.

Moving about within her cabin, Diony made food ready for Berk, who worked steadily at his clearing all through the winter, building there the house of which he talked but little. Report said of it that it was the beginning of a great house. She sewed him a shirt of buckskin, pushing a thorn through the tough hide and lacing the parts together with strips of leather. Elvira's wheel hung from the rafters overhead, out of the way, for there was nothing to spin. The women of the fort brought her soothing drinks and gave her advice, reciting stories of their bearings. The wound in her head had healed now and the pain was almost forgotten, but in her sight Elvira walked with the great and strong women of the fort. Her large firm feet bare, she, Elvira, would pass toward the hand-mill to grind the corn, or she would be seen momentarily passing at the gates. Then Diony would sink into a web of pain and gratitude, and in the tangle at last some inner spark or motion would arise which wanted to be free of the web and wanted to be of some unity or account in its own right.

She would sit in the cabin at twilight, resting on a stiff little chair she had bought from a woodworkman of the fort. The supper waited on the hearth, ready baked before the fire, and her few wooden vessels were ready to contain it. She would prolong her reverie until it fell into a clearly defined desire.

This was a new world, the beginning before the beginning. Sitting thus alone in the cabin, while Berk looked for the cow on the snowy creekside and brought her safely to the fort, while he, with the other men of the stockade, dragged fodder inside the wall, getting the wood, closing the gates—sitting thus she would see a vision of fields turned up by the plow. A moist loam rolls up to take the seeds and the rain into itself. Over the field some birds would go swiftly, darting here and there, calling now one and now all together, plovers tossing over a made field to go to the creekside beyond a low rising shoulder of turned loam. A field! This would be a great happiness.

Or again: A vision of sheep sprinkled over a pasture or turned in on a hillside to crop the stubble and glean a fine rich eatage for themselves. On their backs would grow round fat fleeces of fine wool to be sheared away in the spring, to be spun into yarn and woven. The sheep stand in a strange stillness, each one bent to the earth, or they lift their heads and look off toward the south, all looking together. Their small thin faces are pointed toward some invisible which they discern as if they examined it carefully, their small feet sunk into the low herbs, the wool put over their backs in a soft round coat. The odor of wool floats lightly about them as a more subtle coat they wear over their fleeces. To make them run forward to obey some command the farmer would cry out a musical "hou-ee," and "sheep-ah, sheep-ah!" It was a vision. She saw thus in the embers in her cabin within Fort Harrod in the cold season of the early year, 1778, wolves howling on the hill beyond the burying place.

A vision of stone walls and rail fences setting bounds to the land, making contentment and limitations for the mind to ease itself upon. The wearying infinitives of the wilderness come to an end. The land stands now, in vision, as owned, this man's farm beside that man's, all contained now, bounded, divided, and shared, and one sinks into the security and lies down to rest himself. Through the farms run lanes and well pounded roads, making a further happiness, ways to go to meet a neighbor at his own house.

A vision of neighbors, a man living to the right, a man to the left, each in his own land, their children meeting together to walk down the road to a schoolhouse or a church. Or the women learn of one another, each one using the best of her skill to make the food or the clothing a little better than they were before, each one wishing to do as well as the others, and some, those with skillful hands, excelling the rest.

A vision of places to sell the growth of the farms, there being farms now, a vision of some market place off in some town beyond the fields, where iron and glass could be had for the surplus of the harvest, where could be had books and journals and tools, clocks and vessels of earthenware, pewter spoons and vessels of brass, steel knives and smooth shoes for their feet, needles for their fingers . . . It was a happiness to think of.

Berk delayed coming and she knew that the cows must be lost. The little children in the next cabin were crying for milk, being unable to eat the harsh corn-pones and the jerked meats. She heard bobcats screaming in the stony places toward the west, and Gyp, her dog, whined at the door, wanting to be let in. Men at Harrod's cabin fired a rifle, a signal to those outside. There were more than a hundred men in the fort now, and some of them being wary hunters, there was always wild meat enough, but the turnips and pumpkins were gone. The children would gather into the mother's cabin at nightfall, and the sounds of the fort were then subdued under cabin rafters. Tears gathered through her entire being to hear the little children cry for their supper, wanting milk.

A vision of bridges over streams so that their horses or oxen need not be imperiled in flood waters and their goods lost, so that they might cross easily over and take no thought of the matter, so that they need not lash logs together to make a raft. The road runs smoothly down through settled fields and comes at last to a river where it runs lightly over a structure of smooth logs neatly trimmed and jointed, placed on stone pillars that stand well out of the flood. It was a wonder to dream on in the mind.

A vision of fine cattle in the pastures giving a rich yield of milk and cream, well chosen beasts that stand secure in good barns, not the wiry little scrub sort that run on the open range and live in constant fear of wild creatures and savages. In the pastures too are good horses, graceful riding beasts, easy in hand, smooth carriers, strong and sound.

Bees, then, in hives set in neat rows near a dwelling. They gather sweet from the wild growth in the un-cleared places and from the pollen of the corn, from the white clover. It would be a civil picture, the hives cut out of well sawed logs and left to their own devices until the honey made a rich, sweet fatness within. Then a man, Berk Jarvis perhaps, goes among the hives and robs the bees of their harvest, and a woman, herself, Diony, stores the honey in earthen jars of which there would be a plenty.

A dream of letters written between one and an-other, of messages sent freely through long miles of travel. A courier waits at the door, his horse pawing the earth, ready to go hence. One folds the pages together and writes a name on the outer page, writing "Mister Thomas Hall," writing "Mistress Polly Hall," writing "Mistress Betty Hall." . . . The courier takes the letter into his hand and goes swiftly, carrying the letter to the one named. The vision grew dim because of the long, scarcely broken tangles of trees and stones that reared themselves in the way, but it cleared itself and was renewed to become a vision of messages received, of word sent to her. A letter comes to her hands that are now folded in her lap. She feels the crisp edges of the paper and reads eagerly what is inscribed within, messages from a man, Thomas Hall, telling her how all fared in Albemarle. It was a vision: there were no letters; no word had ever come to her.

A dream of knowledge, of wisdom brought under beautiful or awful sayings and remembered, kept stored among written pages and brought together then as books. Books stand in a row on a shelf where a narrow beam of light falls through a high casement over a desk where one might rest a volume, where one might sit for an hour and search the terrible pages, looking for beauty, looking for some final true way of life. In them, the books, Man walks slowly down through the centuries, walking on the stairs of the years. . . .

Berk came at last, white with new-fallen frost. The children had become quiet, their cries now soft and full of content. Her vision went with the flare of a fresh stick among the embers. She set the supper on the board and their hungers were satisfied.

❖   ❖

During the cold of midwinter word came from Boone's Fort of disaster there, disaster touching all the forts of the canelands. Boone, with those who had gone to make salt at a lick in the upper region of the country, had been killed or carried away to the Shawnee country to a probable torture. There was terror in the land. Many started back along the Wilderness Road. Report said that Rebecca Boone mourned Daniel as dead. She had loaded her goods and her small children to pack horses and had gone back to her relatives in Carolina, for a woman needed a hunter and a fighter in this country.

Diony contemplated Boone's loss to the forts and remembered his own saying, "Never lost, you might say, the whole enduren time. I never felt lost." He would not be lost among the Shawnees.

She herself was of some other kind. She was a beginning before the beginning. The gaunt woods were swept by winter and the new fields were bare under the rain. There was little to eat but corn and but little of that, the old season being near an end. The women at work at the mortar would carefully guard each grain of corn that not one might fall to the ground and be lost, the children standing hungrily by, their eyes making food of it.

Berk was going with five others to a place toward the west to make salt and to get whatever game could be found. He had loaded three horses with the kettle and the axes and powder. She knew that when he came back there would be a child in their cabin, and she took a sharp farewell of his blue eyes as he stood beside the door of the house tying the last axe to the pack beast.

The frozen earth offered him little promise of the frozen west toward which he was going. With two strong men he lifted the great iron kettle into place on the pack animal, taking the greater part of the lift but making no show of his great strength.

"You're a strong man, Berk Jarvis," she said. "But one strength you have not got." She stood, large and full, beside the door.

"A woman's work is a woman's work," he said. He smiled then, and the beauty of his delayed smile went swiftly to some hidden part of her and made life beat more swiftly there.

"What manner of child do you want me to get borned for you, Berk Jarvis? While you go west to make salt?"

"I want a strong boy-child. Name his name Tom. It's a good kind to get borned in a fort."

"I'll tell him about his man-parent as soon as he gets borned, and tell him what way you went and what-for you stay away. I'll tell him you are off to do your work at the salt-maken."

"Tell him you did your work whilst I did mine. Tell him his mammy is a strong woman and not afeared of him, borned or unborned. Tell him she's in no way frighted to have him come here."

"I'll tell him his granny, Elvira Jarvis her name was, died whilst she tried to save him and whilst she tried to save life in me. I'll tell him this while he is in a way to get borned."

"And tell him the scalp is all gone off Elvira's head, the white lock gone offen her, and it's said a redskin, Blackfox, carries it on his belt beyond the Ohio."

"And I'll tell him what manner of woman Elvira Jarvis was, hearty and strong and kind, and I'll say to him, whe'r he ever grows to be a man or not he's to set out forthwith to be the kind fitten to walk the earth she walked over."

"Say more. Tell him when his pappy, Berk Jarvis, comes back from where he's gone to make the salt needed in the fort, he'll never rest content in his bed or get borned another until he goes beyond the Ohio and kills Blackfox, so help me God, or kills men enough of his kind."

"That's a heap to tell him," Diony whispered, spent with a sudden fear. "I couldn't tell him so much as that. I couldn't."

"Tell him like I say. I want a strong man beside me on the earth. Get me a strong boy borned against I come back with the salt. So help me God, it'll be

like I say, like I told you. I'll not get borned another
. . . I'll bring back salt and skins this time when I
come, but I'll go another time. It'll be like I say."

He kissed her once for parting and stood with her a
moment, speaking without words. Then he went,
walking beside the pack animals, going to the fore
to lead the brown mare that carried the kettle.

VI

THE spring delayed, the earth frozen and the mornings white with frost. The trees stood stiffly reaching for something they could not contrive, and the rolling earth reached away beneath a mantle of old leaves. About her spread a gaunt world. She kept the fire on the hearth and half listened while the women who waited with her gave counsel.

"Bearen, it's a woman's work," one said.

"You wouldn't want a man-person about then."

"Men are good enough creatures, but somehow they forget."

"In one ear and out t'other, that's a man's way."

"Aaron, my husband, he has to set down how old each child is and when this one and that was borned, write it down with a quill."

"And see iffen you would ever forget?"

"And can't remember, off-hand, whether this one or that was borned in a summer season or cold weather, wet season or dry."

"Men are a forgetful race. I could name what we had to eat the day Mark was borned and what cover we had on the bed and what way the candle looked whilst it burned."

"Or if it's death, it's the same. As apt as not they won't remember the season."

"But I recollect for six I had, four alive and two dead."

"The year I had Mark, before and after, in the Shenandoah Valley country, I recall a fine corn crop that year and how big the turnips grew, some so big around they would scarcely go inside a cup of a half-gallon content, and I recall a neighbor came by and said there was war in Boston, the King's soldiers in a ruction with the people there, but quiet came after, and I recollect how the toads sang in the grass about the house that summer and Wallace brought one inside the house in his little hand. I recollect the smell of the toad when he put it against my face. I recall I wove a blanket outen the left-over wool and dyed blue for the border, and Aaron cleared a new field all enduren the summer and we made sauce with the fruit of the crab tree that grew against the far hillside. A man came by down the valley and he said a band of forty men, Boone amongst them, had gone on a long hunt into Kentuck to bring back a hundred horse-loads of skins. The man had a twitchet beside his mouth and his two eyes not exactly alike in color, and I recollect a leathern poke he carried that nobody was let see the inside of. The next day Aaron caught a bear in a trap and that was a rare sight, for the bears were nearly all cleared outen that country then. I recollect the next day thereafter Aaron bought the ox wagon and paid the miller with five hundred pounds and over of tobacco, but Aaron would have to look where he's got all set down in figures before he'd know when he did this. That was October, seventy, and Mark was borned in December after three weeks of uncommon cold weather. Then it turned off fair and we had a pretty January."

"A woman remembers as much as a man forgets."

"Hit's a part of a woman's work to remember. I remember for all the men in the house."

While the women talked thus beside her fire, Diony knew that the hour had come for her to do her greater work. The child was born at the end of a wet night, in the dawn of a fair day. It was, as Berk desired, a boy-child, and his name was Tom.

After three days Diony laid Tom in a cradle that was made of a hollowed block of wood, a cradle that was like a wooden shield, resting him on a cushion of soft pelts. She saw Betty in the round of his small face, and saw Polly in the flesh about his eyes, and thus he was a messenger from Albemarle. She would look at him swiftly, turning to him with wonder, looking for more communications from the distant.

Turning to him thus, searching swiftly for Berk, she saw Elvira in the hard curves of the child's mouth when he cried with pain.

The salt-makers were yet away. Diony sat with Tom in her arms on a great buffalo fleece before the fire, which Harrod himself often tended for her. He would bring in the huge back-log with a great kindly clatter. About her stretched the brown of the hut, the walls of logs and the earth floor lit with the changing flames in the fireplace. She remembered all that Berk had said, his parting words being written into her memory of the hours before the birth. Now she delighted in the living being that was in her arms or in the cradle beside her on the buffalo hide. Threats and pledges became vague beyond the pleasure she had in the sight of his small body and in his quivering helpless flesh lying on her two out-stretched palms or held against her breast. Sitting on the great black fleece she crooned to him, making a song to sing over him, singing:

> Pappy's gone to get a skin
> To wrap the little baby in.
>
> It couldn't be a mite of harm
> To keep the little baby warm.
>
> Shoot a fox or shoot a bear
> To keep the little baby here.

A faint new green began to tint the brown of the

hills as a veil lying lightly against the ground, and a woman said, "There'll soon be greens for sauce." One day Betsy Dodd came with a basketful of wild mustard and purslane she had cut on the sunny bank of the creek where she had searched carefully over a wide space to get enough of the tender new growth to make a sauce. Diony cooked the greenery with a cut of venison and a little salt, making a dainty feast.

"As I came past the gate," Betsy said, "I took it in my head to wonder was the moon of a similar kind to the stars, and Joe Tandy, he happened by then, and he said I better keep my eyes on the ground a little spell longer, or anyhow until Kentuck is safe for astronomicals."

"Is Joe still out by the gate?" Diony asked. "You could go and fetch him to come eat the sauce and the venison with you."

Betsy went outside and she called Joe from the doorway. They were gay over the supper. Diony saw Betty in her cabin, a Betty Hall who had tempered her idolatrous love for a sister with the favor of a young man. The illusion that this girl was one with Betty followed her when her back was turned and she was in a trance of delight to see what it would be for Betty to accept the compliments of a young man. She thought of Betsy's fate as identical with Betty's and they were one to her. Betsy's pleasure in the baby was such as Betty's would be, and the two girls, as one, crooned over it as it lay asleep on the pelts.

❖   ❖

The trees made as if they would come into leaf and Diony looked out from the fort onto the first spring. Anne Pogue's hens laid enough eggs for a setting, and there were colts among the half-wild horses that were turned to graze in the woods. The people were restless, wanting to go out to their clearings and begin a civil life. Then Berk came back with a great leather sack of the salt and two horse-loads of dried venison. On the night of his coming there was noise and laughter in the cabin. Many came to see Berk in his pleasure with the child and to witness what it would be to have a child born while a man went away to hunt wild meat and to make salt. The first hours of his return lay entirely in an illusion of safety and plenty. There was enough of everything.

"He's borned now to his man-parent," Diony said to those who came in. "It's like the first day he came."

It was the first day again. Diony and Berk would sit together over the cradle, a shield of smooth wood lined with pelts and a bit of a blanket, and they would look at the infant and at each other, and smile. "I didn't know you would think it was such a wonder of the earth," she said, "this baby I got whilst you went to make salt." Day after day his pleasure lasted, and Diony hoped that he had made newer promises within himself and that he had forgotten his oath.

"What person does he look like?" she asked. "What person does he favor?" Her pleasure waited fearfully on what he might see when he searched Tom to make his reply.

"He favors Betty," Berk said, "but he has a look of Mistress Polly in his cheeks. He favors these women now, but by and by he'll grow into the shape of a strong man."

The birds had come back from wherever they had been and their morning twitter and clatter, their shrill cries and whistled notes, their pure flute-calls, were blended and severed to flow apart and mingle together through all the early hours of the day. The crab-apple trees against the hill beyond the creek tossed about in the wind and flung out pink and white flowers that spread white in the sun, or, blown all together away from the wind, they turned over and about and were obscured to burst again into wide blooming when the wind eased and gave them a brief calm. The hawthorns, the wild haw trees, had put white flowers out beyond their brittle thorns and they made a sweet scent that blew with the wind that came up from the west by the way that the creek ran. New spring winds swept over the fort and over the forest, and they beat Diony's skirt in a quick rhythm when she went without and tossed the ends of her shawl where they were frayed, bathing all her flesh with a quick desire for more life and a delight in all that she had.

Oh, it was a new day in a new world. Molly Anne was small and dark-haired, with freckled hands and withering skin that had been burnt by the sun and the rain and the winds of nine summers in a wilderness. She was gay with her talk, believing that all women loved all men, as in their inner hearts they do, and she was ready to make surmises and to laugh at any serious matter. Betsy Dodd was little and quick, her legs like two wiry brambles that tossed about in any wind and danced as easily as the water rippled over the stones in the creek. Her mouth fell easily into smiles and her eyes caught the eyes of any child or woman or man and danced over them to the core of their liking. She was everywhere, in the quadrangle, out on the creekside, in the school cabin, in Diony's cabin with little Tom on the buffalo fleece to prattle and croon a small speech she had devised there.

Harrod was large and hearty-handsome, his eyes black like his hair, a great man who went continually among his people, busy in the fort, in the smith-shop, in the cleared places outside, captain of the militia and one of the night hunters along with James Ray. He was big, and generous of his great strength, ready to help any man, even the lowliest.

Anne Pogue was a wonder among the women. The year before, soon after Diony had made her journey over the Trace, when the Shawnees had scarcely gone from the woods, she had, with the children to help, made a sally out into the open and gathered a quantity of the wild nettle to bury it in the water of the creek, weighted down with stones. Thus she had rotted the outer stalk away from the fiber, and later, while Diony healed of her wound, during the early winter, she had hackled the nettle and used it as if it were flax. Now she took forward the process of making a nettle cloth, weaving all day at her loom and making a frail smooth fabric, scanty and precious, and Diony bought a cut of it to make herself a scant gown, and Berk paid for it with the last of the silver from the money belt.

James Ray would stop at Diony's door, James Ray, the night hunter, a youth who was as swift as the buck deer in his running. His bones were long and lightly formed, gracefully notched and fitted together to obey swiftly the command of his mind, the sovereign part of any man. His fingers were quick in their sense of any projection the earth might put forth, of the sort to play over wires and make music, to play over the winds in woody reeds, to handle chisels and pens and brushes. He outran all the warriors of Blackfish, and he and his kind were better deserving than they of a fine caneland.

Joe Tandy and Evan Muir set pails close under the sugar trees to catch the sweetened water that dripped from the openings they had made through the bark, and when they had drawn enough of this liquor they brought the vessels to the fort on a drag to boil it in the great fort kettle until it became a heavy syrup. Then they fetched this to Diony's cabin to boil it down again, and with Betsy Dodd to help in the stirring she made a fine crystal of it that was poured into wooden molds and broken into lumps that were sweet and good to taste.

Jack Jarvis came back from a long meander in the West where the water of Pigeon River flows in great rolling forks, then tawny with the new wet of the spring. He told of fine lands there, rich bottom places that would make abundant fields, and of high knobs where the game beasts were still hiding. He brought back dried meat from his long season of hunting, brought cured elk saddle and buffalo hump, bear bacon and buck haunch.

❖　　　　　❖

A bright cold morning, and Betsy Dodd came to the cabin door, speaking hurriedly. Her relatives were going to the Falls of the Ohio to stay in the fort there, she said. She was distressed to go, and she stood warming her hands before the fire, rubbing her hands uneasily together. Seven people were going out, three of them carrying guns, the departure already prepared and the people about to assemble. Diony saw then that Betsy was thinly dressed for the journey and she offered her foot-mantle, the large cloak that she had woven in Albemarle.

"I'll come that way next month," Joe Tandy said from the doorway. They laughed together then, and all partings were defeated. Betsy moved lightly through the cabin, making no marks on the earth floor.

"Iffen I couldn't find a way to send the foot-mantle back before Joe comes I know he'll engage to fetch it back to you," she said.

The foot-mantle took a part in their laughter as it was tried on and taken off again. Betsy Dodd seemed very like Betty Hall then, a Betty who had known hunger and cold. Diony saw her thin little winter-starved face beside Tom's face as she leaned low over the cradle, and Tom's likeness to Betty Hall came out clear and plain then, as if he supplied all that Betsy lacked in the likeness; but the child opened its eyes, and likeness to Berk passed over its forehead.

Then Diony took from her table-board a pone of bread and a fine slice of baked venison, and she gave these to Betsy to eat along the way. Betsy laughed again, and she was grateful to have the food that was wrapped now in a napkin of nettle cloth and pushed under the mantle. She went quickly toward the gate when her aunt called her, and the seven rode away then, their horses slopping through the spring freshet that swelled the creek.

"I lay Joe Tandy, he'll about marry Betsy," a woman said, a group of women gathered at the spring when the seven had gone beyond their view. "I look to hear report of a bride afore summer is done."

"Who'd do the marryen?" another asked. "Out here in these parts, who would? You could let a Baptist or a Methodist preach you outen hell, but you better let the priest of the English Church marry you iffen you want it legal."

"Married or single, I've got to go to my baby now," Diony said, and she pushed herself nearer the water out of her turn. "My breast tells me he's hungry when it aches to be free of its milk."

"A Methodist married me," a woman said. She dipped her keeler full of water and walked defiantly away. "Five youngones I've got to prove hit by," she called back as she went toward her cabin.

Diony went swiftly to her cabin and took Tom

into her arms to still his cries, and she felt the ache
go out of her breast as he drained it. Holding him,
she began to piece together the opinions of the women
and to study over some of the ways of the earth, thinking that a marriage might be legal and not rightly
placed in religion, or it might be religious and lack
the law. It was difficult to bring law and religion into
one use, for she remembered the ways of the Quakers
as her mother had told of them, and she remembered
the ways of the tidewater from her father's account.
There was a woman in the fort who was married
without religion and even without the law. Tom had
screamed loud angry cries because she had not come
when his hunger first appeared. His hunger would be
the same and his demand on her for milk would
come, even if she were not married to Berk in religion
or in the law, and a county government had been
fixed upon the wilderness of the caneland. Men
wanted law to live by, she reflected, remembering the
court, but the women gave their thought to other
things and followed a hidden law, and Tom followed
a hidden law now while he was little and in her arms,
but he would want another law after a while. Thus
her thought went forward until it made a center in
the small mouth that beat a rhythm on her breast
to draw food out of it.

❖   ❖

In the dark and the rain of the night there came a crying at the gate of the fort. Two women and a wounded man were there, begging to be let in. Men came out of the cabins and opened cautiously, and those outside came within. They were of the seven who had gone out during the morning, and they told a story of attack. Two had been killed and one, wounded, was hiding in the woods. Betsy Dodd had been carried away as a captive, and all the horses had been stolen.

Men went to the aid of the wounded man and brought him safely in, and the riflemen prepared to go out at daybreak. Betsy Dodd was acutely felt as not being inside the wall now. Diony sat by the fire with other women, retelling all that they knew of Betsy. The night was dark outside and the hour undetermined; one might still say "this morning" of Betsy, recounting of her, as "This morning she warmed her hands at my fire, and where is she now?" "This morning she sat beside me on the skin before the hearth . . . This morning she ate into her mouth a piece of the loaf-bread you see on the board there. . . ." A vague sweetness had been the most of her, a ready acquiescence, as if the whole of her were given freely to her circumstances. She had played with the children when they ran in the quadrangle, and she had sat in Mistress Coomes's school, but she had done a woman's work at the mortar and she had taken a woman's place in the dance. Joe Tandy and Evan Muir, with others of the young men, had made an incautious sally out into the dark. Women huddled near a fire in a cabin told fearful stories of captives.

"Made her walk every step of the way, and made her carry around her neck the bloody scalps of her own children, tied around her own throat," one ended a story of horror.

"They make a war in your own breast, those redmen."

"But they won't kill her. They won't kill Betsy."

"Unless she gives out of her strength and can't go further. In Detroit they pay as much again for one taken alive as they do for a scalp."

A woman sitting by the corner of the hearth spoke then. She had been a captive in Tennessee. Another had seen a fearful thing in the Kanawha country. They were Sallie Tollivers whose tongues were let go for a season, the first woman bearing a strange likeness to the Tolliver woman of Albemarle, the same tall spare frame, the same bleared eyes, the same abstracted gaze. Now she did not shrink into forgotten corners, her mouth dumb, but she sat with others of her kind. The woman lit her pipe with a coal of fire, picking the coal lightly out of the ashes with her bare hand. She told a story of plunder and rapine, her cabin burned, her children killed while they ran to hide. Then she dropped the pipe to the hearth out of her hand that had suddenly lost its strength, and she began to call each child by name and to tell of each one and to say why each had been lovely, her eyes closed now, streaming tears, her body shaking in spasm.

The young men of the fort were out at all times, scouring the region toward the Falls, a wide area of hilly land, scouring the region northward. Diony knew a continual grief and apprehension. Joe Tandy came and went and the young men were steadily contriving.

❖   ❖

Berk's house on Deer Creek was well advanced in the building, for with men to help he had hewn logs throughout the winter and fitted them into place. It was roofed securely now from the weather. In the mind's eye Diony saw the creek that ran down through their rolling lands, and she saw the great stack of hewn logs Berk had erected into the form of a house. Beyond the creek Evan Muir's house stood, a small cabin surrounded by a garden which was now well started, and beyond this Alex Harmon had built for himself and Molly Anne. The three houses stood together in the remote valley. Berk was plant-

ing his field of corn now. He would work all day on
Deer Creek and come at nightfall to the fort. At
evening beside the cabin door or before the hearth
he worked at fashioning an axe and he fitted a strong
handle to his hunting knife. It was as if he prepared
for a journey, and wishing to delay him Diony would
sometimes put little Tom into his arms, but he would
lay the child back on its cushions in the cradle and be
busy again with his tasks.

Whispers were busy about the fort. It was said that
Clark had gathered an army in the back-country of
Virginia and was preparing to march against the
Northwest to capture the forts along the Mississippi
and in the Illinois. "We have to defend here," was
said; "we can't go with his army. Our own are, you
might say, in the thick of danger." "I belong here,"
a man said. Diony stirred corn in her wooden bowl,
old corn mashed in the mortar, and she spread it in
cakes on the stone slab and set it near the fire to cook.
It was hard to know what mind to hold when necessities called two ways at one time. The mind of the
fort seemed broken, turning about in dissent and
confusion. Jack Jarvis had gone with Clark toward
the west. Whispers and confused opinions beat about.
Berk fitted a knife into a strong handle and he seemed
scarcely aware of Tom, who could turn his head
about now and follow the light with his eyes. The

whispers arose and fell about the name of Betsy Dodd.
She had been killed or had died on the way north.
Scouts from the region about the Great Lick brought
news of this, and brought convincing proof of it.
Diony's foot-mantle, torn by the beasts and faded by
the rains of the spring, was brought back.

Diony searched the foot-mantle when it was
brought to her, scarcely believing it to be the same,
but the signs of her own hand in the weaving were
there. Faded and blood-stained now, and beaten into
the mud in the upper country of Kentuck, she could
still see the black-and-brown plaid as she had woven
it, and she counted the threads in each plaid and
found them true to the mantle she had devised.

There was a deep inner pain when she realized
Betsy as broken and flung back into the earth, Betty
and Betsy being curiously identified in her thought
of them. She would not break her happiness with
Berk in the child, fearing to touch this with grief,
and for this she would not make any audible outcry
in the cabin. Hushing her grief under her great desire that Berk would continue to delight in their
child, she went about her tasks with a show of mere
pity and regret. She walked about the enclosure with
her infant in her arms, working at the vats where the
leather was tanned or at the kettle where the soap
was boiled. One day at sunset she went toward the

stockade wall where her gourd seeds were planted, to see how they did, and she found the tender shoots of them coming from the ground.

When she came back Berk was in the house, working at his short axe to make fast the handle. He talked about the house on Deer Creek and murmured a little of what he had done there. He had hewn boards for doors and for window shutters. The place would soon be in all ways secure, he said. There was a floor throughout the whole great room and the hearth was of one great stone. Diony wished for him to see her in the cabin, now, holding Tom to her bosom, putting Tom aside to tend the bread on the hearth. She was afraid of his concern about the axe and of his continual care of his weapons, as if they were not already strong and bright enough.

"Last week," she said, "I put my gourd seeds into the ground and now they're up in a fine way. By and by I'll have me a whole crop of sugar bins and home-made noggins and tankards and pitchers, all a-growen on a fence. If the turkeys or the buzzards set a bill into e'er one of my noggin crop I'll be plumb bereft. I got a place already for every last dish you'll see a-growen there."

He murmured a little of the house and of his work there among the doors and shutters. After he had planted the corn he had finished the chimney, carrying the stones from the creek bed. It was a great work, the chimney. Diony saw him, a large strong man, plodding up the low hill from the water, carrying stone after stone, his blue-eyed gaze fixed on the ground before each labored step. "Hit's a fool house," a man said once of it in her hearing. "Berk Jarvis builds a fool house on Deer Creek. A load beyond any man's heft to lift."

"It's a pity there's not some charm known to a man to move rocks and stones as fast as his wishes can go and his mind think stones moved and set in place," she said.

The sight of Berk plodding with dull rocks held in his stark hands, his back bent over dull stones, this vision stood opposite her present sight of him as he sat moving his hands deftly over the axe to fit the handle to the blade. His wish to have a better chimney than any other man, a taller roof and a finer sweep to the dimensions of his hall, a hearthstone of one great slab of rock, this filled her with a swift flow of pride so that she moved with dignity through the hut and stooped to the hearth with a graceful bending and drooping of limbs.

"We'll go to the house and live there as soon as you'll take me," she said, with a rush of delight. "Indians or not, we'll go there. Gyp is a good watch-dog for a night, and we'll watch ourselves of a day.

Oh, let's go there. It would pleasure me to be there beside you, to help carry the stones even."

His remote gaze was fixed on the axe and his pleasure was all in the neatness of the handle as it fitted into place. He followed it with slightly tilted head as he turned it about. Seeing through the intervening miles Diony could place their two fields, as he had told of them, and she could see the house, facing the east and the stream, surrounded by the rich encroachments of the high cane, the plowed parts marked evenly by the springing corn. Muir's field lay beyond the creek, and still seeing afar she could see his small cabin and Harmon's cabin beyond it. Muir often stayed at his cabin at night, to be ready for labor as soon as daylight broke, and Berk had stayed with him many times of late. Remembering this, she worked at the board to cut slices of the baked meat, making ready their food, and she felt a coldness as of a sudden chill spread through her to stiffen her bones and put minute bristling fine hairs of pain over her skin. Then her fear took form and was known to her mind: that Berk seemed intent on keeping his vow, the promise he had made to himself before he went to make the salt. Meanwhile he had taken the axe and had gone without on some mission unknown to her.

❖   ❖

Berk came later to the cabin, leaving Lawrence at the door. About him there was a satisfied turn or manner, as if he had just said, "You do thus . . . whilst I do that. . . ." He walked toward the fire-board and placed his rifle carefully there.

"Diony, bake me some journey cakes," he said.

"Oh, no, no. Not yet," she cried out. "You better rest at home a little spell. You better."

"I'm rested and eased a-plenty. Too long I've been here now. Journey cakes, Diony. Bake for me. I'm bound to go."

"The corn is planted and there's beans to sow and salt to make again after a little. And Tom, our baby, wants a pappy to carry him on his shoulder and to get borned another little calf so the old cow will give milk enduren next winter. It's been a while since you took notice how Tom can hold up his head and how pleased he is when you come."

"Bake the journey cakes, Diony. I'm pledged to go and you know for why. You and Tom will make out together. My own mammy is not all buried in a grave."

"You're too apt to carry revenge and to think back too often. Did I marry a man to carry revenge inside forever? Couldn't you think about your wife you married in Virginia and brought the long way over the Wilderness Trace, and my own mammy is dead

to me as well as yours? Have I had e'er word of her
since I left there or am I like to have one? You are a
selfish man, Berk Jarvis, and you want all the grief
and trouble for yourself."

"I'll go as I say and no word can hold me. Could
I lay me down at night to sleep whilst I know one of
those red devils carries my own mother's hair on his
belt for a wonder to show?"

"We live at the very inside of war, in the middle
and midst of hate and kill. There's blood on every
side of us. Every man I could name in the fort has
had one killed, a brother or a father or a child, a
sister or a wife carried away. Martin Wilson's wife,
up on the Kanawha, found her own way back home
after two years gone, came back with the Indian
baby she had two months later. You are a lucky
man, Berk. No youngones in the house but the one
you fathered for your own self."

"Iffen you can't see your way to bake my cakes
for me and sew my seam, I'll do for myself, all. I'll
parch myself some corn and carry it out in a dry
bladder. I'll go, like I said."

"You're a lucky man, more fortunate than a
dozen I could name that now stand inside a mile of
here. Your mammy died a whole death at one time,
a quick death, and if her scalp is still gone it's as
like as not thrown down before today and withered

to the dust where it would be in the end, no matter."

"You're a hard woman, Diony, and I'll not listen to your talk. If you're not of a mind to help me I'll go without help."

"And the Indian that carries it is dust, as good as dead and withered, and you mought as well forget what he carried or carries a little spell longer until he goes the way he's bound to go."

"I'm engaged in my own mind and no talk can turn me."

"And Martin Wilson can't go back to his home because he can't mend his hate for this little Indian child his wife, Lettie, has got in their cradle, her own baby that she pities and holds in her arms. He can't find his way in so much trouble, his hate torn in two. You've got a clean hate, Berk, all pointed one way, not one barb of it turned back to stick into your own side."

"I aim to leave here before sun-up, and iffen you're not of a mind to help I'll do all for myself. I'll go as I said afore."

"You've got a hate in your mind without reason and you want to kill. It pleases you to aim at a red body and see him fall down. It's like a joy in your heart, to see a redman fall down when your bullet goes into him. He throws up his arms and screams and his back crumples under him, and you have a great joy in your mind. . . . Your mother, Elvira, died to let me go on in life. If she had run to the fort his hatchet would 'a' cut me down and I would be the one in the grave now, my hair as like as not on some redman's belt beyond the Ohio. Myself, Diony. Would you go then on a hate journey, to get back my hair?"

"I'd go, it's likely, the same as I go now."

"Then Elvira's life is my life and I say for you not to go. I am still in life, and Mistress Elvira is inside me to say what I say. What Mistress Elvira meant when she came past the redman and stood beside me in the hut. That's what she's here to say now."

"You make a trick with your words to snare me, Diony. I'll go and no man can turn me back. I'll swear before God to go and get the scalp of the red devil or I'll get some of his tribe and kin. Go on away from around me and take your hands away now. I'm pledged to go and you'll not entice me back. I'll burn his town where he lives and I'll take back what he carries on his belt, if he carries it still. I know what part he lives in and Lawrence knows. I'll keep this pledge before I ease myself to live in my home again."

He mended the fire while he was speaking and the

glow fell over the darkened room now. He took up the leather shirt and began to pick at the seam to take away the broken parts of the thread, and as he leaned slightly forward, he was fixed in a posture that seemed eternal, and she remembered another moment of fixity when the redmen stood before the door of the hut. His blue eyes were turned upon the leather and they shone as if they were dim glass. His great frame sat, tall and strong above the chair that held him. His face was large and firm and delicately lined about the eyes. His hair was brightly brown where it faced the firelight, the club of it tied behind with a leather string. His being filled the house, the fort, the whole land as far as she could conjure it in mind. He arose from his posture and walked toward the fire, and he set a fresh log over the flames and put the vessels about. His strength was of such a measure that the logs and the vessels seemed as small toys in his hands, as if he subdued his power to bring it under the roof of the cabin. A rush of pity moved her then, as if strength itself were calling for compassion. She moved toward the table-board and began to busy herself there.

"I'll bake whatever cakes you need," she said, speaking slowly. "I couldn't say I'll bake e'er flavor of willingness into one, but I'll bake for you, Berk, the substance of all I promised when Coley Linkhorn joined us together. I'll get for you whatever you need and sew the seam. I'll bake the journey cakes tonight."

❖   ❖

Diony stirred water into the meal and prepared a rich shortening of bear fat to pour into the dough. While she worked at the board, Muir came to the cabin asking for Berk, who had gone now to the smithy, and presently Tandy came. They talked of the war roads north and of the ways to go to keep near the beaten path without following it too nearly, and they asked leave to bake their cakes by her fire. Andrew Lawrence came, the one who had told Berk of what Blackfox wore at his belt. Then Diony asked sharply what he intended, and she knew that they were a council of war come to meet Berk. She flung the soiled mantle into a corner and prepared to help set the cakes to bake on the boards. Joe Tandy sewed himself a strong pair of moccasins and Lawrence began to mold bullets. Then Lawrence drew a map in the ashes, showing the shapes of the rivers they would cross and showing the hunting ground in the Shawnee country where Blackfox went to find meat. Berk came bringing the finished knife, which he hung beside the horn old Bethel had etched for her.

> Berk Jarvis I am your powder horn
> I am your friend since you were born . . .

The words of the horn beat in her throat as she stooped over the corn mash and poured in the hissing fat. The men talked of their needs and of their weapons, or they disputed of the quantity of food they would carry. "We wouldn't want to stop to kill meat," Berk said. They talked without mirth.

"What I said when I went to make salt. You recollect what I said," Berk answered her inquiring look. He was standing beside her at the edge of the hearth. "You are my wife, Diony. It's time I kept my word . . ."

"Well?" she said, making a question.

"I'll bring back Elvira Jarvis's hair," he said, his face close to her face, stooping to make his words fall level with her ear. "I'll bring back what I promise. . . . I can't live longer withouten I keep my pledge."

"I came to Kentuck to get . . . What did I come here for? I came to get a fine farm in the cane," Diony whispered. "A fine high house, fields all about it."

"I'll never rest until I do what I promise myself to do," he said. He made a strong oath to surround all his promises and built up his determination to a self-pledge from which he could not escape. He shook with a mingled sob and an oath, and he kissed her with one deep kiss and pushed her away. His blue eyes were drawn under their bent lids and narrowed at the corners. "Oh, I'll do what I say. When I do I'll come back here quick as I can."

"A fine farm is a puppet could wait," Tandy said. "We're bound to go north whe'r we ever come back or not." His reasons seemed frail beside Berk's great reason.

Diony walked about among the men, getting this and that as each required, or she sewed the seam for Berk. They would leave at the rising of the moon and be gone far on the way before sunrise. McGarry was there, a bold fighter and an unforgiving man. He watched the young men as they made ready and his presence strengthened their hate in all that they did. Evan Muir labored with his short sword, making it shine in the light of the fire and bringing the blade to a fine edge, or he measured powder into his horn, and Gowdy, who had come, poured the bear grease into the molds for Lawrence.

Berk, walking the floor, his weapons now ready, each one trimmed to a fine edge, stopped beside the door and with a quick sweep of his arms upward and down, he struck the door post with a great blow and drove his battle-axe into the soft wood to try its edge. The blow made his oath anew and it left a great wound on the surface of the door log.

"It's a well put-up house," McGarry said, "to stand the strength put against it." His presence added a continual approval and a strength to the oaths that were taken and the silent pledges of Tandy and Muir. A perpetual anger burned under his way of saying a simple thing about the power of a door post.

Diony remembered Betsy Dodd then, whom she had in part identified with Betty, and she remembered that Elvira had given her life to save her own, and as she stooped to gather the foot-mantle from the floor of the hut, recovering it from complete loss, it came to her in the act of saving the bloody cloak that if Berk got scalps in the north she herself would be liberated from her supreme debt to Elvira. When she had spread the garment on two pegs she turned about, feeling a hardness within.

"I'll take care little Tom comes to no hurt," she said to Berk. "Tom, the boy I got borned for you after we came to the wilderness."

"I'll make this-here a safe place to get borned in. I've seen a baby's skulp on a pole . . ."

"No red white-trash could affright me," Gowdy said. "Sell you a horse today and steal it back tomorrow. Make war on women and children in a house, on the unborn even. I saw in Tennessee . . . It's known to all what I saw . . ."

Outside the early summer night waited, the east beginning to pale with the rising of the moon.

Beetles were coming out of the ground in a great swarm and they were beating the dark with their new wings, and the frogs were crying in the creek pools below the fort. Diony gave each man the things he required and she had filled each pouch with journey cakes of the pounded meal. She felt the hardness that stiffened the flesh about her eyes, and she had no tears now. She remembered her own past hurt and the wound she had received in the hut, the scar that lay still fresh across the back of her head. Her life was cut apart, Berk going, and into the rent poured anger. She let the men out at the gate of the stockade and stood at hand to close after them. "Don't forget what you go for," she said to Berk as he passed her by. Outside, the men went singly across the wide moonlit space and were lost in the rounding of the hills.

VII

THE clothing of those who had been in the fort for a year or more was falling into rags and there was nothing out of which to sew more garments for winter wear. The women took continual thought of how they would find clothing to save them from the cold and of how they would clothe their children. The nettle cloth was not sufficient.

"The men can wear buckskin. A man-person, seems, can make out with a buckskin suit," they said, one or another speaking the thought. "But I couldn't content myself to wear a buckskin petticoat."

There were no sheep to cut for wool. The women talked of this when they gathered in a cabin or at the vat where the skins were prepared. Diony would send a swift thought out over imagined pastures where sheep grazed, her hands knowing the whole process from shearing to weaving, her hands longing for their weaving knowledge to have a place. Then Anne Pogue began to try a quantity of buffalo wool to see what could be made of it, and she drew it into a silky yarn, the other women telling of what she did

248

with wonder and half-belief. She made a black yarn
of a fine brittle texture, and presently she wove a bit
of it on a warp of the nettle. All day Diony heard the
beating of her loom as the slay pounded the buffalo
wool into cloth.

The great scar Berk had made lay green across the
front of the door post. He continued away and her
hate went with his hate. Anger sank more deeply
into her mind and worked quietly there when she
remembered Elvira lying on the floor of the hut,
when she saw this picture clearly. It would fade to a
dimness as she went about her daily labors, but it
would return when she sat quiet to give Tom his
drink from her breast or when she lay down to sleep.
She would recall the cool security of the inside of the
hut, the warm sun outside, herself sitting lax and
secure, on the cool earth floor; then the coming of
the savages and their hushed war-cries, her terrified
knowledge that her end had come, that life would
now be cut off from her and she would be left alone
with whatever . . . then Elvira pushing a way into
the hut. Herself not dead then, but continuing.

She marked the days as they passed, making a sign
for each one on the door of her cabin. When Berk
had been gone twenty days by the count, Muir
walked into the fort one day when evening was falling. Bringing her cow through the gate, Diony met

him there, and a patter of quick questioning fell
from her lips. He had come back from the north with
a wound in his hand.

Diony tore strips of nettle cloth to bind up his hurt
after she had washed it clean. It was a bad wound, a
week old now. Between his groanings while she
tended it he told of all that had happened in the
north. With Lawrence as guide, Berk and his men
had made a stealthy foray into the Shawnee land,
into the river jungle where Blackfox habitually went.

"And on the next day, what?" she would ask.
"And then?"

It was a story of encampments on the river bank
high up in the Ohio Valley, of swift forays and
stealthy flights. Berk rested now on the bank of the
river, Muir said, but he would make another sally.
He had sent Diony three trophies, three tokens, Muir
said, and with one sound hand he stirred about
among the pile of things he had dropped beside the
door. Three dark scalps were the gift. They had been
stretched on a frame of bent withe and they were dry
now, three long black scalp-locks of a coarse hairy
substance, each like the tail of a horse.

"He got this on a Tuesday," Muir said. He told an
incident that made the Tuesday scalp stand apart
from the Thursday ones. He went away to the corner
house where he slept. Diony hung the tokens over

the fireboard, above the place where Berk's gun and powder horn rested when they were put by.

Scalps hung in other cabins and thus hers were no wonder to see, but those who came to ask after Berk would sit for a short while under the fireboard recounting.

"I dreamed last night three witches walked across the hill toward Logan's Fort," Molly Anne said, "and I took it in head, even in my dream, that they went for no good, that they went to carry bad omens. When I waked I looked to see was the moon set, and for a fact it was well towards low and red like blood."

"When you hear the dogs howl without cause you can look to hear a report of war," another voice. "Last week the dogs howled all the fore part of a night and next day the ravens croaked until the day broke away fair, towards noon."

"You wouldn't have to wait for ravens to bring you word. You'd know hit. There's war, ravens or not."

"Some men gather war around themselves, but some, it seems, gather peace."

"But the war, it's there, whe'r you gather it or not. Some men leave it be."

"Some men is natured to leave hit be. Seems."

"You can't leave it be."

These shapes, crooning of war, went from under

the fireboard, and Diony blew out the candle and
lay in her bed to rest. All about the fort, over the
whole caneland, the high pitch of summer had come.
The stars of summer were in the sky. There was no
money in the belt now. She thought of Berk's corn
in the field at Deer Creek and she began to contrive ways to have it plowed, thinking that she might
trade some trinket, as the empty money belt perhaps,
to Harmon for a plowing.

❖   ❖

The gourds were flowering on the stockade wall.
Five-petaled white clouds were flung out on the hewn
fence, each petal of a crumpled texture, an indetermined mist, as soft as fine linen that has been beauti-
fied by use. Some of the flowers were withering and
some were passing into the fruit, passing daintiness
by to become of a great hearty sort.

"Hit takes a fool to grow gourds, was always said."
Molly Anne made a joke of the fine growth of Diony's
gourd vines.

The cabin was as Berk had left, but for the scalps,
nothing being added. She had one pewter spoon and
two wooden spoons which she had cut out for herself.
In the iron pot she boiled the meat, if there was game
to be had, but the pot was often idle now that Berk
was away. There were three wooden platters from

which food was eaten. Berk had carried away the sharpest knife in his belt, but there was another that served her needs. Her tools and the bed on which she slept, her fire beyond the hearth—she knew all their ways as one would know the people of his house.

"Hit takes a fool to grow gourds, I've always heard said," Molly Anne called out to see Diony's pride in her fine noggin crop.

"There's a heap of gourds in the world, no matter," Diony called in answer. "Fort Harrod is full of gourds, some in every cabin, and it's a wonder how they got here, if it takes a fool to grow the gourd-kind."

She was a tall strong woman and a child clung to her breast. She passed her tools from hand to hand, lightly, knowing each one lightly, each one intimately sensed at the ends of her fingers and in the lifting parts of her arms and shoulders. For drink she had three pewter cups or flagons, two of them from Elvira's goods. She longed for a sieve through which to pass the meal to strain it of the husks, and she thought of the smooth fine loaf that was eaten in Albemarle. She helped Anne Pogue to make cloth of the buffalo wool or to make a thin cloth of the wild nettle fiber, or she tended her child to keep him free of the vermin. Remembering some phrase from

a book which was now more than half forgotten she
had a sudden sense of herself as eternal, as if all that
she did now were of a kind older than kings, older
than beliefs and governments.

Although the year was at July her bread-food was
still the old grain of the previous season pounded to
hominy or to meal. About her the children of the
fort watched eagerly for the growth of the corn,
measuring daily the height of the stalk, for they
wanted soft new food. The corn increased each day,
watched and measured by the eye, the mind following it into the wet of the rain and the heat of the sun
or into the dark of the night when it rested from
growth. The blades swung lightly in the wind and
the field was a field of great grass, allied to their
flesh by the needs of hunger until it became their
flesh held in abeyance by the slow processes of
growth. They waited upon the corn. The tassel came
first of the flowering, came as an infinitely tender
stem folded into the upper sheath but marked with
delicate carvings which increased in size and became
small buds, as yet sterile of power, holding only the
matrix of the pollen, the mother of the male princi-
ple, the green sappy stem of the corn. Diony looked
now for Berk's coming, herself appeased of hate. He
had killed enough. She wanted him with her in the
cabin.

Having no skins out of which to make moccasins
and her old ones being worn away, she left her feet
continually bare. Her skirt was made of the buffalo
wool woven on a warp of the nettle and her jacket
was of the cloth of the nettle, these garments woven
on Anne Pogue's loom and bought with her labor.
She tended Muir's wound with a medicinal salve
of slippery-elm bark pounded to a fine meal, and
when the angry flesh began to cool and to form a
scar she soothed it with bear grease. One day while
she leaned over his hand to lay on the elm poultice
he told her that he had planted a field of flax.

"Against spring comes you'll have flax to spin,"
he said. "It's a field of blue flowers now."

Elvira's wheel hung from the rafters, but hearing
of Muir's field of flax she saw the distant spring and
saw herself drawing a firm filament, a hair-like
thread, from the distaff, making ready for weaving.
It was a momentary desire, her first need reappear-
ing to overthrow it, Berk being yet away. Carrying
little Tom in her arms she went with the boys and
girls to the field near the fort to see the progress of
the corn. There were delicate shoots at the side of
the stalk growing out of the sappy stem, the female
element having come now, taking form on the surface of the everlasting mother, the corn itself. Within
the sheath were the delicate beginnings of husks, as

yet pale and green and tender, scarcely unlike the
buds prepared to hold the pollen above on the top
of the strand. Within the pale, tender, female husks
would flow the fine white milk of the corn which
would congeal to be their food.

❖   ❖

There was dancing in one of the cabins. A fiddler,
back from his wars, had been unwilling to go with
Clark into the Northwest. The people of the fort
shifted and new faces continually appeared, and thus
a new fiddler played, one who had no knowledge of
Betsy Dodd, but he played the same tunes that were
played formerly, and the forms and figures of the
dance were the same. The half-grown girls danced
first, and their ragged little half-length skirts hung
limply over their quick little thin legs. Then Molly
Anne would join, the first of the women to take a
part, and others would follow, the men and the
women stepping carelessly into the reels.

"There's no varmints in the woods today. Might
as well dance on't."

A man stood on the high ladder against the wall to
look out on the open spaces. There would be dancing,
a set flinging at a bit of a reel, but all would stop then
to listen or look upward to see that the man at the
loop-hole made no sign. Diony knew what troubled

the fort. No news had come from Boonesborough now for many days and the summer was at an end. Scouts had been sent to discover what caused the silence of the other fort.

Molly Anne always knew the news of the stockade; news gathered to her and was by her dispersed again. She was a ubiquitous woman, and there were three children in her cabin who had inherited ubiquity from their mother. News and opinions of her floated about in turn. It was said of her while she danced that if Alex Harmon were killed in a battle she would grieve heartily for a week and then brighten up to catch Muir.

"Molly Anne, she married in too big a hurry. She might better 'a' looked around a spell longer."

"Hit wasn't known to her what a fine-set-up widow-man had come down the Trace, when she tied up along with Harmon, she and Harmon already known to each other back east where they did live. And Muir, nobody a-knowen he was widowed . . ."

"She keeps her eye on Muir though, you notice."

"But not more'n she ought, I hope."

Comments thus accompanied the music of the fiddle and counter-opinions were passed about to touch the stillness that came out of Boone's Fort and make surmises of it, or flow back to Molly Anne's intentions or desires.

The morning brought business about the inner

quadrangle and business about the spring. Toward noon the scouts appeared before the gates and there was running hither and thither and Molly Anne was calling Diony from the door. Men gathered to the gates that were flung open, and by the time Diony arrived with Molly Anne to stand at the edge of the crowd and listen, the scouts were well into their story and were answering the questions and oaths of comment. Boonesborough had endured a heavy siege that had lasted nine days. They were a garrison of but sixty men and only forty of these were fit to carry arms. Three hundred had come from the north, Shawnees under Blackfish with white men from the King's army as officers. Twelve days they had camped around the fort, but three days were spent in parleying before the fire began. . . .

Here Diony ceased to listen, giving heed now to her own inner query. For if all the Shawnees had come under their Blackfish, had marched down from Ohio with guns in plenty, where then was Berk? How had he kept out of their way? She made no spoken comment, but these questions took form within her and changed the shape and aspect, the whole color and kind, of all the land as seen over the fort wall, of all the day as it shone out of a blue sky. The scouts were speaking, going forward with their telling, retelling now with more detail.

"Surrender was what they wanted, to carry off the whole of Boonesborough to sell in Detroit." The comments flew about and the story doubled back. "The Indians dug a mine, tried to dig a way under the fort wall, but the fort made a mine that threatened to meet it halfway. . . . Picked up, after it was all over, the Indians gone, a hundred and twenty-five pounds' weight of bullets near the fort . . . as many more bedded in the logs . . . Two killed and four hurt right bad, a fearful time . . . Three hundred outside, ranged around in full sight south of the fort, to cut off retreat this way . . . Only forty inside to hold guns . . . First-place Blackfish calls a parley with Boone, to meet outside the fort wall."

Boone had come back from captivity in the north, had escaped from his captors in the middle of the summer when he saw that they were preparing to invade the forts in the cane. Of the three forts, Harrod's alone had passed the summer without a siege. Diony loved Harrod's then with a rush of thankfulness, loving the security of the inner court, loving the women who came to pound at the mortar and to dip their vessels into the spring. Out of this passion of security for herself and Tom rushed her continual query: Where had Berk gone and where were Tandy and Gowdy? Why was there no news of them? An army had come down from the north,

walking over the way Berk had gone. War stood back
for a brief interval, giving place to questioning and
giving place again to safety and kindness in the fort.
The women who met at the spring spoke kindly together, giving way to her with acts of gentleness.
Boone had come back; where then was Berk?

Walking back from the spring a new query entered
her mind. The women had been kind to her because
they knew that an army of Shawnees had walked
over Berk's track, because they had made an answer
to the query. "Berk Jarvis never is lost neither," she
said. Boone had come back whole. The questions and
answers leaped up in her thought and lay down in
the middle of her confused anxiety. In the cabin she
took the scalps from their place above the fireboard
and set them in the heart of a great flame that burned
in the fireplace, having no longer any pride in them.

Indian summer came in the quiet hazy days in the
end of October. The hickories had turned yellow and
the oaks and maples were flaming red. The unex-
plained smoke of the forest and the stillness of the air
were a continual menace, and the women would
pause at their labors to listen. They were forever
listening. A woman walking beside the fort gate
would stop and turn her head to listen. Children at

play inside the stockade, little children running in
their games, would listen, stayed in their acts of play.
Men came from the cabins at dusk and sensed the
still air. It was the Indian summer, a strange un-
seasonable warmth moving lightly out of the south
and scarcely swaying the still leaves. This was the
favorite hunting time of the redmen and they were
known to be scattered through all the woods. The
cattle were restless when they stood together in the
fort enclosure, as if they heard some noiseless approach. Waiting and listening, Diony had these two,
to wait and to listen, etched into her sense of flaming
leaves and still hazy air.

Word came from Virginia in November. There
was much talk of what had come to pass. The Virginia Legislature had annulled the claim of the proprietors and had given Henderson large tracts of
land elsewhere toward the west. The forts and all the
canelands and forests and near-lying rivers, all,
would never be known as Transylvania, a pro-
prietary state. The disputes about the hominy block
and the spring were at an end. One law had played
over another law in the minds of men. Kentucke
County of the Colony of Virginia had been made
sure, and the new name and the new law settled
quickly to the fort.

Clark had gone into the Northwest country, men

said, and he had taken three forts there along the
Mississippi River. It seemed very far away, not
clearly known, not placed on the extended curve of
the earth. The autumn had increased in its power to
blight and had moved into the early days of the
winter. Other news came. Hamilton, the King's
general, had moved westward from Detroit to occupy
Vincennes on the Wabash River.

"He's the Hair-Buyer," Molly Anne said. "He
buys hair offen the redmen, skulps. He traffics in
skulps. He leaves his business in Detroit in good
hands, no doubt, whilst he goes out to set up a place
to buy in the Illinois."

He had been named the Hair-Buyer. The people
of the fort hated him and blamed him for their disasters. . . . The Hair-Buyer had moved west; this was
the report; and Clark was farther west, men from
Harrod's Fort being with him there.

The gourd vines had withered from the wall and
the gourds were plucked and laid by to ripen to a dry
hard woodenness. A drouth burned the land to a
strange brown after the growing season was done,
and a strange smoke lay among the trees of the
forest, as if the known earth were passing away. A
new way of being was required to meet the burnt-out
lifeless hills. Molly Anne came across to Diony's
cabin to borrow a thread to sew a rent in her under-

coat, and she said that one Joseph Lair was just
come within the stockade gate, back from the north
country, and that he had said that Berk Jarvis was
captured by Shawnees and carried to Detroit City
to be sold. Diony went out into the powdered air to
search out this man and to have from his own lips
all that he knew of the capture.

The man had the report from some other and
there was little more of it to tell. There was no report
of Tandy or Gowdy or Lawrence. There was whispering, and some of the listeners turned away as if
they had some other knowledge. "It is very well
known Berk Jarvis is dead," one of them muttered.

"How?" Diony asked sharply.

"Jonathan Stone went by today on his way to
Logan's, and he said it was very well known Berk
Jarvis was dead. Said he was killed at a ford up by
the Big Sandy Creek. Said July was the time."

Diony would not grieve. She set herself to combat
the news of this last disaster. She took thought of
what the winter would be, Berk gone, herself without
a hunter, but these considerations faded before the
pure loss of Berk. She contrived a surprise for the fort
in Berk's unexpected coming, his return whole from
the north, and she devised ways for this to take place,
mornings when he walked back through blinding
snows, noons when he appeared suddenly at the

door, evenings when he came hallooing from the forest—her inner part feeding forever on what it lacked.

❖   ❖

Over the fort a great star shone at evening, a bright token of loneliness and cold and danger. Wolves howled soon after nightfall in the hills toward the west where a low red light burned in the sky long after sunset. Her dog, Gyp, barked at the evening star, feeling loneliness, but fell to silence when the wolves bayed. Diony would bring her cow within the stockade when the other women and the boys fetched home their beasts. She would milk close beside her cabin door, turning the cow to wander again on the range when she had finished. Muir brought her some pulled fodder for her beast and this she stored in the loft of her dwelling. Cold settled nearer and the first snow came.

Muir had harvested the corn at Deer Creek and much of this he brought to Diony's cabin where it was secured for the winter in the loft, and he brought nuts from the hickory trees. A corn-shelling party, out with Colonel Bowman, was fired on from the canebrake. The much desired cane had become the most treacherous part, making ambush. Seven had been killed. A continual report of the siege of Boonesborough was passed about. The menace of Indians

moving in civilized armies was added to the old menace of lurking parties of the enemy in scouting
forays.

Diony and Molly Anne made soap for winter use.
They boiled the leached ashes in the great salt kettle
with a quantity of bear fat they had saved. Diony
stirred the great pot and the unsavory vapor that
arose spread about her. Molly Anne tended the
fire, chopping the wood and thrusting it under the
kettle.

"Man is a poor sort," Molly Anne said. "Seven
dead now."

"Seven new graves, and no time to mark which
lies first or last. Buried in a hurry."

The wind blew the flame this way and that, driving the smoke and rank vapor of the cooking grease
into their eyes. Men seemed of little account, measured by the breath of a throat which was lightly
taken and lightly quenched. Light breath huddled
within the stockade, desiring life, but when some
sudden crack-of-doom snuffed life out it went without protest.

"We live in war," Diony said. "There's peace inside the stockade, but that's as far as you can say
peace goes."

When the soap was made and poured into the
great gourds that were to contain it, she turned to

the task of making moccasins. Muir had brought her
a large deerskin, smoke-tanned, the hair gone from
it. She had a fine skill with the sewing of leather now.
She put her bare foot on a large piece of the wet
skin and tied the leather about her ankles. Then she
sat before the fire until the skin dried in the shape of
her foot. She sewed the heel seam with a thong as
high as the ankle and gathered the surplus of the
upper part to a plain side-piece. She lost herself in
the tedium of the work, bending hour after hour over
the careful stitching. When she had made the moccasins she began to stitch a buckskin hunting shirt
for Muir and to sew together pieces of buckskin to
make a pair of breech-garments, and as she sewed
she often thought with agony of Berk and wondered
what woman, if any, would be sewing buckskin for
him. Remembering his smile, she would think that
some redskin woman might be sewing leather for
him, and she would hope with a great, deep inrush
of vital breath that this might be true, not allowing
her picturing mind to hold images of alternatives—
Berk's body broken by the beasts, his bones lying out
now stiff and white in some northern woods.

Muir had retted his flax soon after the cold rains
had rotted the stalks. Often he remained in the fort
for many days together, unable to go to his clearing
because of the deep snow. On these days he worked

in the workshop making a loom, trimming the beams from stout hewn boards and fitting all together with well trimmed pegs. One dark day in midwinter a pack train came conveyed by armed men, brought from Virginia. Forty horse-loads of ammunition had come for the forts in the canelands. After this coming a sense of power settled over the fort.

Diony took Elvira's wheel down from the roof beam and made it ready for spinning. Seeing how the loom took form and knowing that the freezing of the winter had rotted the wood from the threads of the flax, she knew that the act of weaving was near at hand, the wheel being ready. A faint pleasure stirred her to meet the pleasure of making a smooth fair cloth. One day, leaning forward, as she stitched at a buckskin garment for Muir, she wrote in the hard earth of her cabin floor:

"Why will Berk Jarvis stay apart from me when we are wedded with a child I had here in the wilderness? He could break the thongs and straps that hold him. He could make himself a new strength."

Busy trampling feet obliterated the query. The tools for weaving were becoming, little by little, more exact, making ready for the threads, but a cloth would not be finished for many days yet. It would be a linen cloth for the summer. Her garments now were made from the scant cloth of the buffalo wool. When she went outside she wrapped herself in the foot-mantle which was stained with the death of Betsy Dodd, being glad for the warmth of this garment when she went from the cabin to milk the cow or to grind the corn. A woman said to her by way of consolation, "Hit's very well known Berk Jarvis is dead. There are widows enough, seems. . . ."

One day life seemed of one sort and another day it seemed of another. There was much sickness during the winter, but she remained well, and she tended those who were low, making medicines out of the barks and herbs of the woods. In a time of alarm she blew the horn at the gate to call men back from the clearings. Tom had learned to run about the cabin, teaching himself during the early winter while she sewed steadily at the skins. He had learned to keep himself clear of the fire, and if he ran headlong in one of his journeys across the floor he stopped short at the hearth. She would leave him to his own devices, in his own care, while she went to the cabins of the sick. She had become one of the strong women of the fort. Over her strong body, now and then, a sudden inquiry or an opinion would flow as a stiffness spreading down from some higher place.

"You were not married to him, nohow," a voice said within her. "It was said long ago, and many times, that you're not of a truth married."

"That's why he keeps away."

"Who keeps him?"

"God, maybe."

✧   ✧

The child's hair was more yellow than Berk's and it curled lightly above the temples in the way of her own hair, but his skull was from Elvira. When he laughed, Betty came into the cabin; but when he sat puzzling over some bit of thread, studying closely some mystery of bent or knotted leather strand lost from her needle, his mouth slipped in pretty curves and angles and was the gift of Polly Brook. When she sang to him in the quiet of the winter dusk, finding song after song in her memory and making songs out of the matters in her father's books, then sometimes the child lifted his head suddenly and looked upward into her face, and it was Thomas Hall who looked there, as if his hand had been lifted to say "harken." He had learned to eat the boiled hominy and to call it by some name of his own, and he would cry for it if it were not at hand when his hunger appeared. A woman said in her presence, "You might as well say Berk Jarvis is dead."

During the winter Diony made the child garments out of the last of the cloth that she had brought from Albemarle, but the loom stood ready for weaving, and in the early spring she began to spin a thread of flax, the genesis of cloth. She sat at Elvira's wheel before the fire, her feet on the pounded earthen floor, drawing out a fine filament from the purring wheel, and the child ran about her feet and learned to prattle and chatter above the music of the spinning. A man had said in her hearing, "Since Berk Jarvis went to his death . . ."

Now and then Muir would hang a quarter of venison or a bit of bear meat in her chimney to cure, or one of the other men of the fort would bring her a cut from their hunting. The winter was cold in the huts. Men brought wood and piled it beside her door and she chopped with her axe if the pieces were not of the size suited to her hearth. The child watched eagerly for the coming of Muir, who brought him bits of sugar from the sugar-making. A child called in her hearing, "The widow Jarvis gave me this thread, it's mine. . . ."

She taught her child to call Berk's name and to watch for him at the doorway. If she wept in the cabin he wept to see her, and thus she stopped all tears. The winter had been mild, men said, little snow and but little continual freezing. It had been hard in the cabins nevertheless. It slipped imperceptibly into the cold, raw spring. Muir spoke of the Deer Creek fields and he told her that he would plant some corn on her land and that they would share this crop on a half-and-half plan, the land being her own now. A woman said, coming from the spring with her filled piggin, "Eight widows in the fort, I said to Aaron awhile back . . ."

❖   ❖

She continually spun the flax, making thread. Seeing what was piled on the distaff she was haunted by flying strands of gray, clinging threads of fine gray yarn, haunted by flax and hair. She pushed the likeness from her mind and made the wheel draw the threads into a firm twist, but the power of the flax in its likeness to hair prevailed and arrived in her thought by some inner way so that all that she did with her hands mocked back at her as if it would say, "See, your mishap . . . Elvira . . . she came here . . . and thus . . . see." It was night, the spring well advanced. She recounted to Berk again and again the story of her disaster, of his loss. Grief talked to grief and protest addressed protest.

"He forgot me when the year was only half done," she said, addressing Berk, asking for redress. "He went off after revenge, to kill Indians to satisfy the death of his mother." She drew out the thread and wound it on the spindle, her presence turned toward Berk as if she would still recount to him all that con-

cerned herself. "He forgot our child I had here in the
wilderness." Berk was bade to witness Berk, to blame
and despise. She flung out one long sobbing cry for
this and another to follow it when she realized the
crookedness of her thought, wailing then without
reason, but the tears and the cries of the child stopped
her.

She arose and walked to the door, hushing the
child, and she looked out at the moon that shone over
the still fort. Beyond the wall reached the trees where
strange and fearful winds blew, lapping the leaves
about in the fresh cold air of the spring. The night
was full of spring and death, birth coming forth by
compulsion to meet death on the way.

When she had wrapped the foot-mantle about herself, folding Tom warmly beneath it, she went out
into the night. She began to think that Berk might be
dead. Having formerly rejected this idea of him,
whether it came to her as news or opinion, she now
approached it and examined it carefully. Berk was
undoubtedly dead, gone out of the earth forever, she
was thinking as she stepped through the soft, rain-
beaten floor of the fort enclosure. She remembered
his passion for her and she knew then that he had
gone out of the earth, for no length of distance and
no necessities of revenge would keep him from her
continually. The cabins were shut and still, the win-

dows dark, and as she accepted the lateness of the hour which this darkness signified she knew that Berk was gone forever out of life and knew that she had known this for many weeks and had secretly grieved for it already.

She went toward the north gate and, finding it opened, she went outside. The quiet speaking voices of two men came to her and she knew that two were walking beyond the creek to search for a straying calf. The wind blew in a cold way among the fresh leaves, tossing them without regard for their new life and sending gusts among the trees, rising and falling away. A moon shone in the zenith and it made intense shadows and bright patches of light among the trees. The new life in the earth leaped and quivered with the throbbing leaves and the swaying herbs. She heard small animal feet scampering off into the shadows, and a sudden warm breeze came bathing her over, followed by a colder waft that made her shiver with its strangeness. The land reached away beyond her knowledge and beyond her power to imagine it. The infinitives of life, beetles and owls and animals, leaves and throbbing trees, endlessly growing, oppressed her, and she was afraid, less of the wolf-cries toward the south than of the indefinite earth.

"Boone said he was never lost in a wild country,

not in his whole enduren life," she cried, walking aimlessly. "I'm a strong woman, but I'm not of the Boone kind. I'm of the other sort." She cried and wept, shuddering without tears.

She went back suddenly toward the wall of the fortification and rounded it to come to the gate, but the men had gone inside and the gate was closed. The stockade stood, straight and stark, as of little account in the night, but shut within itself, involuted to secure its way of being from what lay outside. She walked back into the region of the trees, making no choice of her way. Dead sticks and old leaves broke under her tread but the indetermined life that blew about in the spring air was nowhere broken. She walked unevenly toward the south, mounting low hills and turning away from any stream she could not cross, in and out of the moonlight. She became very tired from carrying the child, but it slept, wrapped warmly in the cloak.

She sat for some time on a log, the owls crying continually and the furtive steps of beasts crackling the twigs about her. She continually remembered on her side that the whole mighty frame of the world had no being without a mind to know it, but over this lay another way of knowing, and she saw clearly how little she could comprehend of those powers on the other side, beyond the growth of the herbs and the trees, and to sense the hostility of the forest life to her life, and to feel herself as a minute point, conscious, in a world that derived its being from some other sort. The indefiniteness of the outside earth, beyond herself, became a terror. The cry of the owl was known to her as something true or false, and she loaned her ear to it acutely to try to discover if this were the true sort or the other kind. A false owl cried far off among the trees, of the sort she had heard on the way from Albemarle, and another as false answered farther away toward the west. Her arms caught Tom close and made as if life were precious, as if they would preserve him.

The tree on which she sat was a fallen sycamore of a great size, its branches white in the moonlight. She walked aimlessly to the larger end of it and she saw that the trunk was hollowed to make a cavern where it lay, a space of it opened to the moonlight. She crept into this cavity without caution, but no animal disputed it with her, and she laid Tom down beside herself and fell asleep.

When she awoke the moon had set and the dawn was beginning to light the sky. A planet, performing like a small moon, made a crescent in the east. The birds began to arouse, and the cruel, restless dawn began in the trees, the long slow dawn when the birds were insatiable in their pronouncements. The

birds arose above the life of the herbs and declared
themselves superior, but their declarations needed
to be continual. Diony lay in the soft decaying log
and heard the clamor among the birds, feeling the
vegetable life awake with the sun, each kind standing
still in some lewd demand of the light. She came
cautiously out of the log and looked about to discover
what way she had come there.

The dawn was increasingly full of terror. There
was no curtain of dark hanging among the trees and
no charm such as met the terror of the moonlight
and dispersed it. There was no whimpering of false
owls, and she peered into each vista before she entered it. Feeling that all the hostile forces of the earth
pursued her she went quickly down among the trees,
in terror of the indefinite forest, as if she would run
home to God, being lost.

The walls of the fort appeared when she passed
over the hill. The cleared space about the stockade
was used for grazing ground for cattle, and over this
pasturage the milk cows were drifting, being let out
of the fort for the day. She brought her own cow back
to milk it, and driving it before her, she passed
through the gate. No one offered comment on her
passing and none knew what way she had been or
how far she had gone.

❖   ❖

Scouts came from the Falls of the Ohio bringing news of the Northwest. Clark had captured Vincennes and all the King's men that manned the fort there. A company of men was coming through Harrodstown, bringing the prisoners that had been taken, and among these was the King's lieutenant-general, Hamilton, whom the people of the forts had named the Hair-Buyer. There was a fever of excitement in the fort when it was known who was coming.

When they came there were twenty-six prisoners, brought by Captain William Harrod. They were kept in the fort for thirteen days, all resting from the long march and preparing to go to Virginia. Among them were officers of the King's army, captives now. The women of the fort gave Hamilton no courtesy.

"Goes the Hair-Buyer," one would say when he was taken past her door.

"Your Indians, they took my boy's scalp, and you bought it," another.

They gave him no rest. When the prisoners were gone along the Trace toward Virginia the spring was done.

VIII

AMONG the men of the fort were several handy men, craft's-masters with wood, who made chairs and baskets, pails and tubs for washing, noggins and piggins and keelers to hold drink, to hold the milk that was precious here, the cows being few. They made plows and harrows and cut out spoons and forks and beams for a loom. Of these had been William Pogue, but he was gone now since the late summer of seventy-eight. Evan Muir had learned of Pogue and he had put his learning to use. He fashioned a cup from a knot of wood and he shaped baskets from hickory splits and made vessels. He trimmed beams and set together the instruments for weaving.

Diony strung thread after thread on a warping frame, making ready a web for the loom while Muir trimmed the last beam and set up the instrument in a corner of the cabin, opposite the bed, where it filled six feet of space and made a dark shadow on the wall and on the floor. While she walked back and forth carrying the thread between her fingers and spreading it, line after line, on the warping pegs, Muir told her of a fine field of grass she had on Deer

Creek, and what good grazing the cattle would have there. In another year, he said, he hoped to have a few sheep, and then there would be a fine white wool to make into cloth.

When the flaxen threads were tied on the warping beam and threaded through the heddles and the slay, the warp was ready for the weft and the act of weaving was near at hand. Molly Anne and two others came to wonder at the smooth fine web and to say again and again that it would make a more firm cloth than the cloth of the wild nettle.

"A tame thing is ever better than a wild one for strength," Molly Anne said.

"Is that a true thing?" Diony asked.

They thought of it again and could not answer. Diony's skirt was then made of the wayward fiber of the wild nettle, but a tame cloth was in the making now on the loom. She herself was of the tame kind, she reflected. Muir whistled a tune and looked at what the women did with amused eyes, glad to see the approach of a sturdy cloth that would give good wear. He seemed broad and sturdy then, moving about the cabin and casting a great shadow when he stood in the sunny doorway. Beside the hearth, with Tom clinging to his knee, he would sing a stave of his song:

> There is a wild boar in these woods,
> Cut 'im down, cut 'im down.

He grinds our bones and drinks our blood,
Cut 'im down, cut 'im down.

Anne Pogue's geese cried out a high thin musical clamor over the noises of the fort, over Muir's song, and Diony began to shoot the shuttle through the warp and beat the thread to a firm cloth, building an inch of it while Muir made his great rude singing roll over little Tom's high sudden laughter. The thumping of the slay, pounding cloth, knocked with irregular rhythm upon Muir's song of the wild blood-drinker and bone-grinder, and the terror of the boar was known to Tom as a thing far beyond himself, and he flung up his head and laughed, catching Muir's knee in a spasm of delighted fright.

Molly Anne's small boys clung to Muir's shoulders or climbed over his knees and they laughed with the roar of the song. Diony kept at the cloth, watching closely what she did, but she heard the song and the laughter of the children over the comments of the women and took all together into an outer web that surrounded the web of her hands.

"Sing the wild-boar song again," a child's voice was calling, and another, "He grinds our bones. Sing hit again."

"I reckon he do drink our blood," a woman's voice.

They were clamoring and talking. "A many a good man has gone out to find this-here beast."

"And never came back, it's a pity."

A child called out "Injuns!" and little Tom crept close to Muir's knee and hid under his great leg, hiding his eyes.

"Fifteen months old, and look, he knows danger and where and what sort 'tis," Molly Anne whispered.

"Sing it again. He cut 'im down. Sing Bangum went to a wild boar's den." They were shouting and then Muir was singing:

> There is a wild boar in these woods,
> > Cut 'im down, cut 'im down.
> He grinds our bones and drinks our blood,
> > Cut 'im down, cut 'im down.
>
> How shall I that wild boar see?
> > Cut 'im down, cut 'im down.
> Just blow your horn and he'll come to thee,
> > Cut 'im down, cut 'im down.
>
> Bangum blew his horn a blast,
> > Cut 'im down, cut 'im down.
> And the boar came splitten oak and ash,
> > Cut 'im down, cut 'im down.
>
> Bangum drew his trusty knife,
> > Cut 'im down, cut 'im down.
> And he stabbed that wild boar outen his life,
> > Cut 'im down, cut 'im down.
>
> Bangum went to the wild boar's den,
> > Cut 'im down, cut 'im down.
> And he saw the bones of a thousand men,
> > Cut 'im down, cut 'im down.

The children recounted the story of Bangum, each one trying to tell above the rest, crying, "Bangum, he drew his big keen knife, said How shall I that wild boar see? said Blow your horn and he'll come on a run." To this recurring clamor and refrain Diony wove the cloth and her thought rode on the sweep and beat of her hands and the sway of her body rather than on the terror of the boar and the men lost in his pursuit, but these were known to her dimly.

It was night, the work of the loom put by and Muir and the others gone from the cabin. Diony wanted to be weaving, having a passion to make cloth, to get herself a fine strong dress and to make clothing for Tom, but the light of the bear-grease candle was dim and insufficient to guide her. There had been a stir in the fort all day, for the county business of entering land had drawn men from the outlying stations. A low fire burned in the open square where men were camped. She carried her keeler to the spring to fill it, waiting while two other women filled their vessels, and as she turned away, moving off through the half-dark, intimate voices surrounded her to say their minds, opinions coming out of the dark in scarcely distinguished identities. A voice saying:

"You might as well marry Muir. As well marry him as have him for a husband."

"Who might?"

"You. Diony Jarvis." The voice was near her shoulder, its breath on her cheek.

"Hit's what he wants, sakes bless us!" another speaker farther away.

"Hit's what he expects. What else? A woman-person takes a man's keep through a whole season."

"Food scarce, too, and hard to come by."

"It's said in the fort you'd as well marry. If a man fends for a woman, it's said, he has a right to expect, as his due."

Their voices drifted away into the dark, and the light in the open square lay over the mass of burnt logs. Men were sitting about the illumined ashes. The land, as filling with people, seemed now as of a sort slightly different from its former aspect, as if the distances from one place to another were less than formerly.

❖   ❖

A colony of hornets was building papery nests on the roof beams of Diony's cabin. The hornets flew about overhead, coming and going all day, but they made no disturbance beneath, and they were let be. They caught the house flies that came to the cabin and thus they kept the air drained of fly-pests. They made no offer to molest Tom as he played on the floor beneath them, but they came and went through an open chink high in the wall or they darted about in the bright sunlight of the upper doorway catching flies. Diony moved about beneath the hornets, boiling food at the fire, going out to grind the corn at the mortar, making moccasins, boiling soap at the kettle outside, carrying water, rebuilding the fire, tanning skins at the vats, grinding corn again. While she stirred the soap through a warm May afternoon she considered again and again the hornets on her wall and the owls that cried at dusk and hunted the birds for their food. The way of an owl is just, she reflected, and the way of a wolf is just to the wolves, and the ways of white men and redmen, each to his own sort. She thought this a curious idea that had come into her mind and she pressed more inwardly upon this thought to try to make it yield her some final saying or some true knowledge. In a moment of fine clarity she thrust more and more inwardly to try to find some rule or saying, some form by which to know complete justice. Her eyes were fixed on the bubbling fluid that mounted in globules and fell away, letting steam out. She could not find an inner and final point by which to be guided, but rather she saw a little harmony which men are able to make with one another or with a few kinds. The reflection passed beyond her power to know and seemed to float in the rising vapors of the soap.

It was late May. The men were out for war again, all the fighting men having been summoned to meet, as soon as they had planted the corn, at a rendezvous at the mouth of the Licking. They had gone on the march then, the high commander Bowman. Harrod commanded the men at Fort Nelson, Holder the men from Boonesborough, and the riflemen from Logan's Fort marched under Logan himself, and Bryant's Station under Todd. The men of Harrod's were commanded by Captain Harlan. . . . They were an army, the first and most formidable that had ever been levied in the canelands. The women were left to help guard the forts with the children and the disabled men. Muir prepared Diony a rifle and he left her sufficient powder and bullets. The army had marched to surprise the Shawnees at Chillicothe.

The fort kept careful guard, men or women always at the lookout places. Then the men were back, tired and torn from the long march, having lost nine men. They had burned a Shawnee town and had struck their blow to save their country from a threatened invasion.

❖ ❖

Weaving cloth throughout June and July, Diony had a continual delight in the loom, seeing the cloth

form under her fingers thread by thread, a firm tow
linen resulting from her pleasure. Muir brought her
beef from a steer he had grown for butchering, a rare
dainty. Many more people were reported to have
come into the country. It was said that there were
stations and forts scattered over the whole central
plain, as far away as the Falls of the Ohio. Men were
making farms out of the wilderness, and a better
security had come to the land. She could picture herself at Deer Creek, in the cabin Berk had built there,
and her mind contrived images of herself going about
there, making food over the wide hearth, making a
garden.

"It's a prime good cloth," Muir said, looking at
the work of the loom. "A fine quality."

The hornets flew about overhead, draining the air
of flies and gnats. "The hornets are on our side," she
said, looking upward. It was noon and the bright sun
came through the opened door. She knew that the
cloth was not a good cloth if it were compared with
the cloth she had made in Albemarle where there
had been more leisure for tooling the thread. She was
saddened a little that Muir should praise the cloth
with such fervor. "It's only middlen fair," she said.
It was better than the cloth of the nettle, she conceded. She wanted to talk of some other matter, not
of the cloth, and she spoke again of the hornets in the

air above, for the cloth seemed now as of an intimacy between herself and him, as if he praised it more than was its due. On the instant then his life-furthering goodness filled her being and she accepted his praise of the linen as a report that came from his inner part in some pure and simple way.

"I expect I won't be back here inside a week's time," he said, waiting then for her to speak. "I'll go on back to Deer Creek . . ."

She wondered at the pleasure the loom gave her and she saw herself as some strange woman, some other, outside her former knowledge, sitting happily in the great loom, before the web. Some other, not herself, arose from the weaving bench and went happily across the room to stir the pot that simmered over the flame where food was boiling. A tall, well grown woman, beyond herself, her hair pinned up with thorns, took a drink from the gourd, waiting one moment to spy out her image in the still, clear water of the piggin before she broke the mirror by dipping into it. The face under the water was hearty and smooth and the eyes were strange and large and clear.

"I wouldn't want to name e'er thing to you that wouldn't please you," he said, "but what would you say if I said I'd like to see us get married?"

Diony heard this as words already known, as a

desire well stated by many acts of goodness toward her. She stopped near the loom, her hand stayed in some act of preparation, and she looked across toward the child, as if she would ask his judgment before she made her plan. Muir was speaking again, saying, "We could go out to Deer Creek and live there. In my house or in your house, whichever you'd rather. . . ."

He went away, having left this unanswered, giving her time, he said, to answer it in mind before she replied by word of the mouth. The country seemed fair to her in midsummer as she contemplated it from the fastness of the stockade and from the fields near the wall, and she let her mind dart here and there about over the farther parts as she had report of it. Men said that there was a strong fort now at the Falls of the Ohio and that Clark was in and out of this with his army. A large fort had been built in the middle of the caneland, high up in the country. This was Bryant's Station, a place to shelter the people who were building a town, Lexington. The Deer Creek bottom would be green now with the corn Muir had planted, and this corn they would share. There would be a plentiful supply of water in the creek, water to be used in security and without stint. Molly Anne Harmon would live in the farther cabin, near enough that a loud shout might call her, but

far enough that the intimate sounds of life need not
continually pass.

"Would I go to Muir's house?" she asked herself,
testing her desire for Deer Creek and for the privacy of
her own place. She began to think of Muir then, letting
the enticements of the homestead pass. He had told
her that he had once been married, in the Shenandoah
country; that his wife had died and he had come away.

She let the weaving rest and played often with
Tom, running with him on the floor of the cabin,
laughing with him in a romp on the buffalo fleece
before the hearth. Ten days had passed when Muir
came. He had waited for the melons to ripen and he
brought a great sack of fruits from his gardens, together with berries from the wild briars.

❖   ❖

Molly Anne Harmon was in the cabin when he
came. She made a bright clatter over the vegetables
as they rolled out of the great sack and over the
melons in the basket.

"You're a lucky woman, Diony," she said. "You
get all the good outen a man and you don't have to
be wedded to him neither."

"What's wedded?" Diony asked. "What is it?"

"It means wash his dirty shirt in the creek. I never
see you wash e'er shirt for Muir."

There was dancing in one of the cabins, the fiddle flaring out over the summer dusk. Molly Anne left to go to the music, but she fingered to the last the great sack of plenty as it was poured out on the table.

"Kentuck grown, every last one," Muir said. It was a rich earth. The fiddle beat the essential notes of a dance tune, making the strong notes of the measures, as if it walked under the tune and lifted the heavy earthy parts on strong shoulders. Diony went about in her cabin, making a feast from the bursting sack on the board, and she cut a fine melon and put it on the platters. Muir was quiet, sitting beside the hearth, but he watched her as she passed about, and he seemed less willing than formerly to play with the child. He seemed troubled, as if, having spoken once, he would not speak again, but he smiled at the child when it brought some trifle and put it in his hand. He was a great presence, filling the room then. At the last, when he looked at her, saying some trivial thing about the melons, she knew a passion of such force that it would seem about to rock the earth, to shake the stones of the ground, to uproot the trees and disturb the rivers. When he had kissed her enough they planned what their wedding would be. They would marry the following day, Squire Boone being at hand in the fort, he said. When Tom fell

asleep they went from the cabin and entered the
place where the people were dancing, and presently
they had told that they would be married.

There was little with which to make readiness, but
the necessities of the morning kept Diony busy while
the early hours of the day lasted. She made her hut
neat, and she searched out her few garments and
found a white collar for her throat, the pin from the
Montfords holding it together. Molly Anne came and
one or two others, and they said she must be married
during the morning because Squire Boone had need
to go at noon. Men went about the enclosure with
rifles in their hands and there was a whisper of an
outward march. Muir came and then many crowded
into the cabin, and Boone was brought. The morning
seemed to follow its own design and to assume the
wedding to its own form, there being hazards in all
other forms. Her own pleasure diffused widely
through the strange day.

She stood with Muir in the center of her floor, and
Boone's voice was lifted above the hushed bodies of
the men and women gathered about. Men crowded
at the doorway, rifles in hand, some of them making
coarse bright sayings suggested by the nature of the
act begun by the preacher. Diony heard these sayings as if life were temporary, to be caught as it came
and used whatever way were permitted between the

two uncertainties that flanked it. Molly Anne held the child, Tom, she wanting to have some part in the occasion; but Tom cried and Muir took him into his arms and held him there while he completed his promises, and Tom was quiet thereafter.

When Boone had said "Man and wife," there was a stir among the people. Some of them called for dancing but it was morning and the fiddler was gone. Men called to Muir, making clear their wish, and he brought a bottle of black betty out of some hiding place and let them have it without competing for it. It ran freely among them and loosed their tongues, and there was a great clatter. All would come back to wish Diony good luck again and again, and she gave the melons from the sack for a feast. A man said to her, "Are you sure Berk Jarvis is dead?"

"It's late to mention that-there," one said.

"Hold peace. Hit's forever after now."

"Forever has come to pass now."

"Squire Boone said 'Man and wife.' Hit's outside of reason to name any other sort."

Diony gave them the ripe melons, putting aside the sinister speeches and taking those she desired into a relation with her pleasure. The women were kind, and they helped to pass the melons about, and they made a great wonder of the fine ripe fruit.

❖   ❖

They rode out through the woods and cleared spaces toward Deer Creek, Diony carrying Tom in her arms, past goldenrod and purple weeds, past tall grass and cane. Muir named the trees, calling them by their kinds, and he talked of his fields. Three pack horses carried Diony's things from the fort, the loom and the spinning wheel making the greatest bulk. The loom was taken apart and piled as beams on the back of a strong beast. Gyp ran under the feet of the horses and Diony's cow with its calf was driven before by a man from the fort who assisted in the removal. A great content settled into Diony's thought. She was glad to be free of the walls of the stockade and glad to be going to open land, her own place. At every moment she was aware of sadness and aware of Berk as the builder of the house, but over her sadness lay her delight in Muir, and as she rode she continually thought of her hand as about to rest upon his shoulder, but he rode a little before her, his rifle ready in his arms, and the caress was not possible. They went over low hills and through patches of cane and timber, through reaches of land already known to her by report, and they came at last to a stream that ran shallow in the August sunlight between green banks and tangles of growth, Deer Creek. Their horses walked through the water for a half mile and the cabin came into view.

The house stood on the right-hand bank on a low rise of ground under two beech trees. Beyond it along the creek lay the field that was now green with tall corn. The procession left the water and came under the beech trees, and the plovers cried with a high thin shout overhead, circling over the clearing, and the crows put off to the farther woods. Back of the house stood a bank of tall trees that made a green wall before the blue of the sky. Diony walked forward toward the house, having put Tom on the ground, and she looked at it, her house, Berk's house, an object of their desire. It stood higher than any cabin at the fort. The walls were made of logs of an even size and each one was trimmed to fit its fellows neatly at the corners. The windows were fitted with board shutters and the doors, front and back, were of hewn boards neatly put together. There was as step rock before the door.

She walked to the end of the house and looked at the stone chimney that stood outside the wall. It was built of the creek stones broken evenly, carried from the creek bed below. It was a monument to a man's power and persistence and skill. Muir came to stand beside her then, and her pleasure in being there, in having him beside her as a warm hearty presence, yet living, as a readiness to contrive ways to live and be, flowed over her mind, and she took his arm and walked with him into the house, passing the strong hewn door.

Inside, the walls seemed high overhead. The loft was enclosed with boards above, but the great roof beams ran straight the length of the house, each one a hewn tree of the forest outside. In one corner an open space in the enclosure overhead marked where a stairway should be. The long sweep of the empty spaces that reached back from the hearth was a pleasure to the eye, and the hearth rock was of one great stone. The chimney, the walls, the great hearth-stone, the fine proportions, these were the most of the house. It was bare of all else. It began somewhere outside of life and met life with dignity, making no compromises. Diony and Muir brought their things inside and began their occupation of it. Diony set her vessels on the hearth or hung some of them on the pothooks. The hollow emptiness of the wide room spoke back to all that she did, making comment, but the warm flow of her blood within her own flesh made comment and reply. She was glad to be there. Outside, Muir placed the calf in a pen he had made and he turned the cow to wander along the creek. He brought utensils from his small cabin and the furniture he had made to serve him there.

❖   ❖

Muir labored all day in his fields to make ready against the coming of autumn. He would sit for a little while at the fireside after he had eaten. Sometimes he seemed vaguely servile before the greatness of the house and humble beside the large hearthstone. When he laughed the sound came with a ripple of deeply breathed breath, as if the laugh had place somewhere within his broad back. The flesh of his face was deeply seamed with pleasure and pain that had been endured, that had passed over him. He seemed solid and heavy as he moved about, unwieldy and gentle. He would come slowly up from the creek field and place his axe and his rifle in the corner beyond the door. When he slept he often cried out a troubled angry oath that hacked and drove, that pitched and thrust through his groaning voice, as if he were fighting again in some old battle, but if Diony spoke to him in his sleep or passed her hands over him, he would wake and laugh a part of his deep laughter. By the time of the harvest she had ceased to feel a shock at these outcries of his sleep or a shock to remember that she had not even yet passed out of the reach of war.

In autumn the passenger pigeons came as a great cover over the firmament, flying high as the wild geese fly. They settled in the trees and their coming was a roar of continual thunder. On the ground they ate the fallen acorns and they would brush the old leaves aside with their wings to free the nuts. After four days they arose with renewed thunder and, blacking the sky with their wings, they set forth for the south, free wings going in a great company toward some magnificent purpose in which all shared. When the pigeons were gone the days became steadily more cold.

Muir built a strong solid fence about the pen for the cattle, and he built out-houses to shelter the beasts, the cow and the calf and the horses. He brought hens and cockerels and made them secure in a barnyard. Diony, calling hogs in from the woods, calling the cow, calling the horse, trying to tame the beasts to use the shelters provided, moved freely through the clearings and had a great joy in the autumn fields as seen from the door of the house. Molly Anne came with her boys to live in the cabin Harmon had built, and thereafter the old familiarities of the fort dropped away before a better discipline. She would come as a guest, knocking on Diony's door, and she would wait politely on the step rock until she was opened for and invited over the threshold.

Within the house, Diony moved through the large room and there was a quietness and a security continually over her thought. Three paces, and she had

scarcely stepped the length of the great hearthstone.
Muir made her chairs and tables, cupboards and
wooden dishes and tools. The loom stood to the right
of the fireplace under a window of tight, greased skin.
Muir would sing to Tom with a great roar, shuffling
his feet beside the hearth:

> There is a wild boar in these woods,
>   Dillom dom dillom.
> He eats our flesh and drinks our blood,
>   Tum-a qui quiddle quo quum . . .

"Sing it again," Tom would cry out over the rolling plucked music of the refrain. Or another:

> Come hither, come hither, my youngest fair,
>   The blowth is on the tree.
> Go dress yourself in silk and gold,
>   For a pretty prince comes courten thee. . . .

❖   ❖

Making moccasins for their feet, the autumn cold
growing each morning more of a threat of winter,
Diony sat in her doorway stitching the bits of skin
together. The sun was bright over the clearing and
far out along the creek some man was making a
steady crash with his axe. Two men were staying at
Muir's cabin now and beyond this Harmon lived, so
that Deer Creek seemed well manned and secure.
Tom could run about outside now and he could

save himself from falling into the creek or from running too near the feet of the horses, and he knew which dogs of the clearing were gentle and which would snarl and snap at a child. Diony stitched the moccasins, knowing that Muir hunted all day in the hilly country to the west.

She could see, as she stitched with the leather strand, the hills of the west where the caneland gave out and the rugged part began, and she could see Evan Muir and his companions there hidden in the forest. They had dispersed in pairs, but they would all come home together at evening. Muir is a hunter today, forgetting that ever he was a farmer or an axeman. She is aware of the long patient wait at the stream where the deer will come to drink, the wind blowing the scent away from the shrewd beast. Perhaps he, the beast, has been seen on the upland passing into a tangled part; he will come here; they are patient; she is patient, stitching with a slow thread. She can see Muir there, practising a sharp cunning to outwit the beast. He bleats the cry of a doe, the cry of the lonely female. The tawny hide is seen once, briefly glimpsed, but it goes into the brush. It is a game of hide and wait and wariness. She dreams herself into the picture as invisible, but there. Berk is a silent man and she can see the firm thin line of his mouth as he plots death for the beast.

The deer is cautious, half aware of some enemy, and he keep himself in the brush. Berk lets a long while pass and the morning seems opened and spread apart to make time for the wary delay. Woods-fowls come to the stream to drink and they splash and murmur their cries of contentment, but Berk lets them go their way. Finally the deer comes down through the glade and Berk lets go from his rifle, and the beast falls to his knees, beginning his death posture. A slow smile dents the thin lips of Berk's mouth and a hooked ripple of cunning and pleasure runs outward toward his cheeks. . . .

She waked a little from her reverie and found herself another strand for sewing, and she knew that fancies had come over her and that the hunter would be Evan Muir, not Berk Jarvis, and she knew then that the two were not the same. Dividing them she rearranged her fancy, seeing Muir in the woody hills of the west and restoring the buck to life in order to enact the real picture. Woods-fowls come to the stream to drink and they splash there, murmuring whatever cries are natural to their throats. Then Muir makes a swift cry by the way of his rifle and there is a sharp breath of smoke to float up, outward spread. The buck sinks to his knees and Muir smiles a slow smile of satisfaction, or if the wait has been long, he laughs deeply under his chest bones and sends up a heavy breath to carry his laughter.

When the animal has fallen the sport is ended and the labor is begun, a part well suited to Muir's talents. He will wait impatiently for the beast to die, saying, "Hurry, old man." Then he will skin the deer on the spot, as soon as breath has left him. The beast gives up his soft pliable hide, his limbs become stiff, and Muir's sharp knife is in his vitals, separating his limbs, cutting out the muscular parts. The skin and the best of the flesh are brought home then, the flesh to be smoked and dried, the skin to be salted for curing.

The winter came with a great fury, but life moved securely in the cabin. Storm after storm came, and the snow piled in high drifts. The coldest winter ever known in the caneland, men said. Alex Harmon came on snowshoes across the frozen creek and over the white field. Often the storm raged about the cabin for days together and the air outside was dense with snow. The beasts of the woods died of the cold and for this there was no hunting.

"It's a perilous time," Harmon said.

"The air is swinged with cold."

The air was indeed burnt with the cold. Muir had butchered swine in the autumn, and the cured meat was put by. There was sufficient food and sufficient warmth from the firewood that was well stored behind the house. Often it was a hardship to visit the beasts in their barn and to get them their food. Diony wove often at the linen cloth she was preparing. Spring broke then, coming slowly, and Molly Anne could come across from beyond the creek to tell how she had fared, to tell of the hard winter.

Summer and winter and spring, these ran over the cane country in irregular regularity, and Muir had cleared more space for a field. When he was obliged to go out with the militia he would take Diony and Tom to the fort, where they would stay in some cabin there until he came back. Vague news of the war in the east came now and then to alter their knowledge of it. The armies were fighting now in the south, in the Carolina country. Deer Creek seemed far removed from the uncertainties of war. But for Muir's troubled dreams and outcries when he enacted a battle, plunging and tearing at the covering of the bed, Diony could forget the uses of war and dangers. All day she moved in a secure way. A spring, 1781, and Muir fashioned a new cradle, one that stood on a frame and was thus lifted above the floor to a convenient height. Diony bore the child in May on a day when Muir had brought sheep to pasture on their half-cleared hillside. With the first cries of the child she heard the crying of the sheep.

She asked Muir to name the child as best pleased him and he named it Michael.

The child was a Muir child, having taken little from Albemarle, being no messenger from beyond the wilderness. Lying alone in the great room Berk had built, while Muir went at nightfall, taking Tom beside him, to make the sheep secure in the barn, Diony heard the bleating of the beasts. She looked at the new child then and saw that its face was marked with a likeness to herself blended with a likeness to Muir, the two likenesses dissolving into one thing at every point. The security of the room and the crying of the sheep outside came upon her as a pleasure, and through all this present happiness ran a vague design as of the temporary nature of it. "It's a Muir name, from a long way back," he had said when he gave it. The fixity of the name, as lasting from a long time back of themselves, played over and under her sense of all transient moments.

IX

THE evening meal was done and the vessels put aside, the wooden spoons and platters laid in order on the shelves. Rain had fallen since noon and the outside was soaked with wet. Diony put Tom in his bed and she hushed Michael in his cradle and covered him softly with his blanket. The wet outside was a weariness to the mind, and because of it she felt a lightness over her thought and over all her opinions, as if some inner motion or purpose were aroused to resist the dreary exterior, the dripping September trees and the sodden cane. Muir sat beside the fire, contented, weary in limbs but satisfied. Diony laid sticks together over the embers and made a more complete fire, and she swept the great hearth clean, making it pleasant. She moved pleasantly about the room, enjoying the acts of motion, as if beauty within her were spreading outward to make her flesh tingle and glow and to make her eyes bright, to make her gestures smooth and graceful. The bright blaze lit the room to the farthest roof beams and Muir stirred happily in his seat and began to speak.

"I'm of a mind to start some orchard in the older

field," he said. "Amos Reed has got a whole clump of little trees started, rooted and ready to plant out. Apples and peaches and cherry trees. What would you say to a piece of orchard down against the hill? Buy the trees offen Reed and pay with the filly colt."

She thought happily of the orchard and reckoned the years that would pass before the fruits would be ready there. She saw the trees set in rows, all in flower in some spring morning. She smiled to make known her pleasure in all these contrivances that made order come into the forest and gave themselves dependable foods that would come in their seasons, which could be predicted and devised after their own needs. She began to talk of the ducks and to tell of the old drake that fought Harmon's flock away from the water holes.

While she spoke of the ducks a vague longing came over her mind and she remembered that there were feathers in plenty and no lack to her by the way of the water-fowls. Her beauty flowed outward then again and hushed away her faint lack, and she lit two candles for the fireboard, not caring now that their making was a slow task and that tallow was not always plentiful. She spoke again of the ducks as she settled to her chair, and she made a plan for their better handling. While she was speaking thus, a man's voice called from the side of the creek, crying "Hello," crying "Ho, there," calling again and again.

Muir had put the bar across the door at sundown, a matter of habitual caution. He went quickly to the closed door and Diony followed to stand beside him.

"Who lives here now?" the voice called out.

"Evan Muir." The call and the reply were twice given.

Then Diony took away the bar quickly and opened the door, Muir still calling "Who's there?" beside her. In the light from the fire that fell in a broad shaft beyond the door, the rain was slowly dropping. Then Berk walked into the shaft of light and stood before them in the wet grass beyond the step rock. He came quickly through the door and caught her into his embrace, and he took Muir's hand.

Diony laughed and cried out with joy, and she put her arms about Berk in a swift, delighted frenzy, being unable to say any word but his name. Then delight and terror passed swiftly over her in turns and mingled together to tear at her mind and beat in her body, and she was scarcely able to stand, but she drew apart and went to the end of the room farthest from the fireplace and sat there in the chair beside the cradle.

"Did you come here by the way of Fort Harrod?" Muir asked this in a strained voice.

"No," Berk said. "I met a man on the way from the Falls. He said she'd gone outen the fort. He made off whilst I stood by to ask. He wouldn't talk after he said Deer Creek was the place where she was now. I came here."

Then Diony saw that his face was scarred with long marks that were bitten into the skin and the flesh, and that one of his eyelids drooped a little from its slant. He stood above the hearth, erect and thin under his dirty and torn leather clothing. He looked about at the walls he had built and at the hearth rock and the chimney. Muir moved back toward the left of the fireplace partly in the shadow and Berk continued to stand warming his wet body and looking quietly about. He stood before the fire in his own house as if he had come home to it.

"What went with Tandy and Gowdy after I left you on the Ohio in seventy-eight?" Muir asked, speaking quickly as if he would put the query between some gap in the major happening now being enacted. "What went with Tandy?"

"I never knew what. The Shawnees didn't take e'er one but me. I was surrounded by Blackfish and his men on the way as they went back from Boone's Fort. I always surmised Tandy and Gowdy came back, or maybe went to the Northwest."

Diony sat in her farther place, and she trembled with an inner chill, unable to see the right of what surrounded her, unable now to give feeling toward any creature. Swept of all, she sat in bodily pain. Then the least child cried out, a thin high wail, and she moved swiftly to bend over the cradle.

"Is Tom awake?" Berk asked. He came three steps toward the cradle as if he would come eagerly to see his child, saying, "Is Tom there?"

"No," Diony said. "It's Michael." She stood a moment over the cradle, making what she had said clear by her act. "Tom, he's past three years old now. He would cry a different cry from that. This one's Michael." And then she added, lifting herself from the cradle and standing erect, "It's Michael Muir."

She had hushed the child with her hand and she did not lift it from its place. She turned about then and stood beside the small bed that was built against the wall. "You could see Tom if you come here," she whispered. "He's here."

Berk had settled to a chair, and he sat for a space, looking toward the fire, seeming not to have heard what she said. But presently he arose as if he were in great pain, and he walked across the floor to the bed and stood there. He touched the sleeping child with his hand, putting his finger lightly on its yellow hair. He bowed his head then and went back to his seat and sat bent forward as if he would fall.

When they had sat thus for some time, each in the place he had taken, Diony arose and went to her board at the left far beyond the fire, and she arranged food on a platter. Then she drew a table near to Berk's chair, and she placed the dish beside him and brought him a large measure of rich milk. As he took the milk from her hand he glanced once gratefully upward toward her face, and he smiled in a troubled way. He seemed very large and thin as he sat over the table, and he ate hungrily of the foods she brought. When he had eaten he pushed the table away to the right. He sat quietly for a long space, and then he spoke.

"They staked me out at night, tied so I couldn't move hand or foot, tied between two posts. They tied me to a wild horse, both my hands tied behind me so I couldn't save my face from the briars. Twice they tied me up to burn me, but I broke away free. Whilst you run the gauntlet their drummer stands at the end and beats the drum, and the council-house is down beyond the long line of the clubs. Once they got me down on the ground . . . halfway down the line, my head so numb with the blows I thought a hailstorm had come up. But I flung two off and dodged past the clubs and broke free. Then they said I was a wonder to show to the towns, to show what a lasty strength I had. Then they took me to Detroit to sell me, and I was in a house there till my wounds healed over. . . ."

Diony thought then that she would not try to answer any of the questions of the world, but that she would let all remain as she found them. She swayed, uncommitted to any way, wanting to see right set apart from evil, but she could see only two rights of equal value, and she began to weep softly, keeping herself within the shadow. Muir mended the fire, bringing wood from the shed outside. Berk was speaking.

"I came home a long way, around through the land of the Ojibways and down the west side of the farther lake. I went up beside the Lake of the Hurons, to keep free of the Shawnees. I wanted to go the long way around and come into the Illinois. They told me Clark was there. But first-place I must have a weapon. I was stripped, not so much as a knife. A man, Ko-kosh, traded in Detroit. He told me what way I could go to round the lake and come into the farther land of the Ojibways. Then I engaged to go with him, Ko-kosh. That was the first part."

"A heap of changes can come over a country, and

over a man and a woman in three years," Muir said. He spoke in a hard way, as if he would put blame somewhere but could not name whom to blame. He had brought Berk a gourd of water from the piggin in the farther corner.

"I see the war, it's moved toward the north in the cane country. Martin's Station, high up in the cane . . . and Ruddle's, destroyed last year."

"Three years you've been gone, and a heap of changes can come over a country in three years' time," Muir said after a long spell of quiet. "And over a man and a woman."

"Seventy-eight, I went," Berk said. "And I was tied to a post in a Shawnee town, and I ran under the clubs twice. Then I went north and farther."

"If a man stays away from his home three years he can look to see a heap of changes."

"Oh, God knows he can."

"Why didn't you, three years ago and over, why didn't you break the thongs that bound you fast?" Diony asked. "Iffen you could come here now why couldn't you come then? Did you grow a greater strength in seventeen hundred and eighty-one, three years after you went?"

"I tried to break every night I was tied, but my strength was less than the straps that held me. I never eased myself from tryen."

"They told me you died in the Shawnee country," she cried out.

"I didn't die. Many times I felt pain to cut a man down to death. My face gashed to the bone, my arm torn, the flesh to hang down at the joints like strings. I didn't die. I reckon you married Evan Muir, Diony. I wouldn't question the right of it or put blame against you. I reckon you did."

Diony did not answer, hearing these words through a numbness that had settled over her. Muir replied after a little, answering:

"Squire Boone married us in the summer two years back. We married in the fort and came here to live thereafter."

"How could I live in a wilderness without a man to hunt the game for me and make the fields? A woman alone in a wilderness is a curious thing," Diony said. "Could I clear a field and plant for bread, and fell trees for firewood? Could I forget Evan Muir or put him outen my thought?"

"I put no blame on e'er a one. I put no blame," Berk said.

"The first winter was the pinchen time, even if the next was the season of such a cold as no man ever knew on the earth before, but the second was easier because I had Muir to fend for me outside."

They were still then for a long space, so still that it

was as if they all slept. Diony's gaze seemed fixed upon a dim circle that was made from her own vision, the quantity of sight given her being bounded by the line of what she now looked upon as she sat faced forward. The curtain of all she did not see surrounded the picture before her, a round picture. In the center lay the great hearth, flatly spread as if it were painted, and to the right of it Berk sat bowed forward, to the left Muir who was so still that she thought he had fallen asleep. Then Berk began to speak, scarcely lifting his voice from a whisper.

"One night, Diony, whilst I waited in the lodge of the woman, Shaub-cum-e-quay, where Dah-sing lived, the man I hunted with in the north, six months back and over, whilst I waited for the ice to break free before I started south, I saw down into this country as clear as if sight went without hindrance, six hundred miles or so, and I saw you walk across the floor in the house, this house here, Tom in your arms. That was six months or seven back, I reckon."

"Six months back or seven, that was early spring," Diony said, "and Michael not yet come to birth, but near at hand. I wove the linen to make his clothes, I recollect, at the loom all day, Evan Muir in my thoughts whilst I wove the linen."

Muir stirred in his chair then, as if he had waked from sleep to hear this speech. He stood up and when he had walked a few steps, forward and back, he seemed to be enraged, as if he burned now with a great anger and a great power. He spoke quickly, turning about to face Berk.

"You come back too late," he cried out, making an oath. "Iffen a man keeps away so long he can scarcely hope to find what he left when he went out. My work of two years is here, and surely that is a thing a man can't give over in a day. My own child is here as well as yours."

"I built the house," Berk said, "and I bought the land with my warrants. I married Diony first and the first claim is mine. You had your season. Now you can go."

"I'll not go so quick. My claim now is as good as ever yours was."

They were standing together in the floor. Berk's arm was stiff as if he were ready to thrust outward and Muir pushed his chair back from beneath his stride and stiffened himself, moving forward. "I'll measure the length of your eye-strings," he said. "You come here too late."

"I'll fight you with swords or with bare fists, whichever you'd rather. Cudgels or bare fists or swords. You can take your choice," Berk said. "I'll not give up my own . . ."

"I'll not give over so quick. It's all one to me what

weapons you handle. Whe'r it's clubs or swords, it's all one. I'll hold my own in my property now. Boone married me to Diony and you're dead in the north. You can go back where you stayed so long and keep yourself scarce from here now. . . ."

They made oaths and threats, crying out angry words, both speaking. While they spoke thus there was a hallooing outside and steps came near the door, voices calling. As the master of the house Muir went to the door, and when he had listened to those without he opened to let Molly Anne and Alex come in. Molly Anne was speaking:

"We saw your light burn late and we thought a body might be sick here. Alex, he says to me, 'We'd better go. There's a bright light in Muir's house yet. . . .'" She quit her speaking and cried out at the sight of Berk. When she had satisfied herself with crying her surprise and when she had shaken his hand, she sat beside Alex in a chair near the door. Muir had turned to his seat, and he set his chair to rights and rested himself in it, and Berk sat again in his place. Molly Anne was hushed out of her usual chattering, and presently she and Alex had joined the picture that lay before Diony's eyes, as if they were watchers to the scene that was fixed to move or lie still without her power to change it.

"What will we do?" Muir asked. After he had

spoken there was a long season of quiet. Then Molly Anne began to speak:

"When a man is gone from his wife and his home, when he's kept away by war or iffen he's lost in distant forests for such a length of time that she marries again to another, it's the custom, iffen he comes back again, for the woman to choose which man she will have thereafter, for her to take whichever is best in her eyes or the one she most desires. Time after time I've known this to be the case." She spoke out of her usual voice, speaking softly. "In Tennessee I had knowledge of such a kind . . ."

Alex Harmon was speaking: "I knew a man came back after five years in the Indian country, his wife married and settled with another. Then the people said let her choose, and let the other go away in peace and never show his face here again to darken their door whilst life lasts. It's the right and law in the wilderness."

"It's the law in a new country."

"Where judges are scarce and places far apart and hard to get to."

"Let the other go and never darken the door again. Go in a peaceable way, no hard words said."

Their voices were falling, one over the other. They sat together near the door.

"It's the law in far places."

"Let the woman choose which she most desires . . ."

"And let the other go in peace."

"Amen, amen."

"It's the law in wilderness places."

After they had spoken thus for some length they joined the general stillness and were fixed at the side of the picture as Diony held it in the circle of her sight. Then they arose quietly and went tipping softly out at the door which they closed after themselves.

❖   ❖

The rain had ceased. Diony knew this after Alex and Molly Anne had gone for she remembered three stars clearly seen above Molly Anne's head as she passed through the door frame, but the closing of the door put the stars from her thought. Gyp was barking and running about outside as if she were disturbed by the lights that burned late in the house. Diony saw her whole past, as if it stood still now to wait for some other, as if it were done, as if it were laid out in a design, a rise and a fall, a pattern. Molly Anne's soft report of the law in the wilderness and the answering report of another voice, Alex speaking, made, both together, a gentle moaning, and this she now remembered rather than the words they had said. The moaning sound recurred, rising and falling in her thought, lifting with the rise and fall of the blaze now that the fire had burned down to one flaming ember. There would be a choice; this fact lay as beyond her, lying outside the recurring roll of spoken phrases that chanted some final truth. Berk began to speak.

His words did not come freely, but were told forth with halting, but when they were let come free of his mouth they made strong pictures that did not fade out if one attended to what he said. He sat leaned slightly forward, his hands knotted together. The house seemed of a right size since he sat within it, the walls as if they were placed in a right distance over his head. The voices that were gone from the house continued in a soft murmuring that arose when there was quiet or fell if a present voice spoke. Berk's voice came clear of the blended sounds and patterns. He was retelling:

"My flesh torn and my sores festered. I didn't die. I was fevered for a right long spell. I stayed in a shed beyond Detroit and a woman kept me and tended my wounds. The British fed me. I was a prisoner, but I stayed in a man's house and a woman got me herbs for my sores. Spring broke then. I was withouten a weapon, not even a knife. I knew a trader named Ko-kosh, and that means a hog. He was out of the Ottawa nation, but he was in a manner French. He lived amongst his kin on the west side of the Lake of the Hurons, but he traded with the farther Ojibways at the top of the lake. He engaged to get me a knife and a gun and I would pay with my labor. I couldn't venture back through the land of the Shawnees. Iffen they caught me again they would be bound to sell my scalp. The British in Detroit are a sharp kind, Ko-kosh said. The Shawnees couldn't sell a man there twice.

"I could come the long way around through the Chippewas, the Ojibway nations, and through the Illinois. But first-place I must have a weapon. I went north with Ko-kosh in a boat with a sail. He had rum to trade to the Ojibways and we caught fish in the lake. Ko-kosh was treachersome but I could outwit his kind. I kept a close watch. He stole back my knife but I got it again. I wanted a gun. I couldn't come south without I had a gun and I couldn't hunt my food. We went north on the Lake of the Hurons. This was the first summer after the winter in Detroit. . . ."

The story fitted together and flowed apart, being caught up by his voice, which at one time seemed unwilling to go forward or at another time eager to relate. He had left Ko-kosh the Hog somewhere far in the north toward the head of the Lake of the Hurons.

He seemed thin and scarred as he told now, seemed wounded with a hundred sores that were now dry to a hardness. He sat erect to tell, his hands knotted together on his thighs. He had met somewhere another, Ba-be-dah-sing, and this name means "A sailboat approaching." A man, meaning "A sailboat approaching," had come to him with a great shout when Ko-kosh had stopped at a place to trade with the Ojibways. He was half drunk on the rum and he made a great noise. Then he had persuaded Berk to go apart with him. He traded with Ko-kosh continually and they spoke the same speech. He said that Ko-kosh was a bad man, that he would cheat. He said that he had dreamed a dream, that a man from the south would bring him a fine good luck. He made Berk welcome. Like all the rest of the redmen he lived by draining the wild things out of the earth. He and all his people, the men and the women and the children, had come to the part that is north of the Lake of the Hurons, where this lake and another come together in a rush of roaring water. They had come there to gather blueberries and to spear fish. The story was too long to tell, Berk said, and he fell into a silence. Dah-sing had given him the best he had. Back at their winter homes and all the redmen had met in a great festival when autumn came, to make ready for the hunt. It was too long to tell, Berk

said, and he seemed weary, but there was nothing
else to give ease. His voice went forward then. The
Ojibways were skilled fishermen and they caught
the whitefish and the salmon, standing up in their
swift little boats in the midst of the roaring cascades
that run between the two great lakes. The women
and the children were gathering blueberries. Then
they went north to the place where they live, when
they were through with fishing, and at their homes
there were patches of corn now ready for harvest.
Dah-sing lived in the hut of his woman, Shaub-cum-
e-quay, which means "Woman who likes milk." She
had been among those who gathered the berries, but
she became a part of the story now, a woman who
was dark and strange and quiet, one who murmurs
low answers to a spoken word. She would sit on a
rush mat beside the fire and bind skins together to
make garments. Once she told a story of the making
of the world by the way of a rabbit.

The redmen became creatures then, eating food
into their mouths and caring for their children.
There were pieces of dried squash tied on a string or
taken down and put away in leather bags. These
people are vain of their fine hair and they work over
it to make it stand about or lie down in the way that
pleases them, but hair on their faces is plucked out.
Diony had not thought of them as caring for them-

selves, as putting dried berries by for winter, as painting their faces with colors, as telling long stories, as boasting, giving gifts. Berk's voice was going steadily forward now, halting over a part of the telling, but continuing after the delay. Autumn had come into the story, he being now far above the lake. Dah-sing said that they could buy guns at Sault Sainte Marie, but first they would go on a great hunt to get skins to trade. They would fulfil his dream. He was glad he had met a man from the south. He called him Shaw-a-non.

"It's a long story, too long to tell now," Berk said. He shifted wearily in his chair and looked about at the walls of the house, at herself, Diony, sitting far back in the shadow. There was nothing else to be told then, and he continued.

There was a great ceremony to make ready for the hunt. Berk had been taken by Dah-sing as a brother. He was given great honor. Diony cast back into her memory to discover what events were befalling her while Berk enacted these dangers. She recalled the second autumn of his stay in the north. She was married to Muir then and had come to Deer Creek. She had made the house ready for winter, fastening the tight, greased skins over the window openings.

Berk's voice, telling the tale now without ardor, as if he were sending his thought elsewhere, had come to the account of the habitual homes of the Ojibways, north of the Lake of the Hurons and westward. There was a great ceremony to take him into the tribe and to prepare for the hunt. Then the redmen said that he must have a part of his hair plucked out and that the women would do this. It was the custom. Hair is not right, they said. It is not decent. It is not brave.

"I said in my inner mind, 'I'll not do this. I'll not let this woman, Shaub, and the other women pluck at my hair.' But when I studied it over whilst I went to sleep that night I thought it mought be best. Dah-sing was my friend. I studied it over. I thought I'd best keep his law for a spell."

The feast came then. Dah-sing killed his pet dog and had it cooked for a feast, and there was other dog meat. It was a ceremony. He sang a long song to some spirit, and he told again of his dream. Dah-sing and his brothers and his uncles made a feast of all the food they had. They made a big show and cooked all. They left nothing back for winter. Dah-sing had dreamed a dream of a pile of skins so great that he and his brothers and all his uncles were rich there-after. He wanted every part of the hunt to be rightly begun.

It was now early autumn, Diony remembered, placing herself in time with difficulty, placing herself in the matters of the earth. Outside reached the running fields and pastures of the clearing and beyond these the trees. Clearings were scattered over the whole of the caneland now and danger had moved farther to the north among the forts there, where Lexington was being built. Berk's voice applied itself again to the telling and another wave of the story rolled over the hearthside. He looked steadily toward the fire, speaking now:

"Then we went out, eight or ten men at one time or another, and we trapped beavers, as I said afore. We set our snares with twigs from a tree they call the 'tremblen tree,' a twig well liked by the beavers. Only a part of the Indians had guns. We drained the creeks and set snares. We got a great immense quantity. Dah-sing shared with me all I got, and we hid the skins under a pile of rocks until we could go back and rest ourselves and wait for the rivers to freeze across. Then we could drag the skins down on sledges, over the frozen water."

He told of the coming of winter in the north, when the cold became each day more of a blight and the snow began to fall. November, and the snow began. He had made a stronger lodge for this Indian woman, one larger and better, sufficient to hold Dah-sing and the three children and the woman, and to hold himself. It was set against a hill bluff in such a way that the snow would not pile over it. Then Dah-sing said again that the man from the south brought good luck.

"Did it ever come into your head, all the time you stayed there, that I mought be married to another?" Diony asked then, speaking suddenly out of the shadow.

"No, it never so came to me. I said to her a many is the time, 'I've got a woman of my own in the caneland of Kentuck.'"

"Well?"

" 'I've got a woman of my own among the Long Knives,' I said."

"And what then?"

"I said, 'My squaw can sew leather and make skins into moccasins equal to the best. My squaw can weave a fine cloth.' She said, 'What is the white squaw's name?' and I said, 'Diony.' I recollect it was after a spell she came back to me and she said, 'What does it mean, the name of the squaw? What does it tell?'"

"Well?"

"I said I mought have to study to answer, and I waited. . . . To find enough for it to mean, to satisfy the name."

The candles had burned down to their ends and they fell away altogether. It seemed a long while since she had lit them while Muir told about the orchard, as if many years had passed.

The voice was speaking, flinging toward her another wave of sound: "We made a bargain then, to go on another hunt, to get a quantity of bears. Some of Dah-sing's uncles had guns but mostly they had arrows and stone axes and sharp knives for weapons. We went northward above the Sault Sainte Marie, and that is a great meeting place for the tribes, they say. Then the great cold came."

"Oh, yes, the great cold. Where did you stay then?" she asked.

"I was far in the north. There was ne'er a thing alive to be found. Snow covered the whole enduren earth and the beasts were gone. They were dead under the snow, or in the swamps, frozen. We came back along a creek and we lived on the fish we caught through the holes we cut in the ice. We fought our way back through snow the like of which never fell on earth before, or seldom."

They sat still for a time then, and Diony remembered the cold and thought what it would be far in the north where, as report told of it, any winter is of a colder nature than that of a more southern place. Berk sat erect then to tell, and Muir sat erect to listen. All the air about the hearth seemed to move quickly, as if it were alive, as if it were awake. Berk had been through a cold of such a power that it snapped in the face like a whip. It bound all the rivers in a solid and flung great peaks and cliffs of spray up from the lake to stand in a yellow range of ragged icy mountains along the margins of the lashing water. He had hunted food through small holes he had cut in the rivers, but each night the holes were frozen and each day the fish beneath were more scarce and hard to find. Back of the crackling fact of the cold lay a soft moaning of voices, calling for a choice. One, the woman, would choose. Above this lay the power of the cold as it leaped and throbbed in the telling. There were days when all were hungry, but Berk and the Indian fished and kept life in the lodge. The woman had come back to ask the meaning of the name, saying, 'What does it tell of her?' Diony had a renewed sense of Betty, as if Betty were not far away, as if the sounds of her voice and the motions of her body were not far from these happenings. She remembered a day when she, with Betty to help, had dug potatoes in the garden patch, and Betty's voice flared up then, asking for a little bench under two buttonwood trees. Meanwhile there were five dark people in a lodge on the edge of the great frost. They receded with the cold, going more completely into it. There were three little boys in the lodge, under the skins that were spread on the floor. They would come out sometimes to climb and laugh together.

Diony wanted then to make them clothing out of the cloth of her loom and to give the woman gifts. She had become as if she were allied to all the persons of the lodge as their common mother, as if she were the one who would make them more safe and more warm, who would give them food and rest. Then she arose from her place and she lit more candles and set them over the fireplace, and she laid another stick on the fire. All Dah-sing's brothers and his uncles came into the edge of her affection and she pitied them and wanted to make all more secure. They were strange dark men, far in the north, in the density of the cold. All the feeble and the old died there of the famine.

He told of days when the wind came of such a force that the house quivered and swayed, and the men and the woman, with the children, were huddled under the skins to save life in themselves until the storm should ease away and more firewood could be brought. Strange, small syllables were mouthed now in the quick air before the fire, the speech of

Shaub-cum-e-quay and Dah-sing. Diony began to
feel a pity for Muir and to think of his nights of evil
dreams, and to hope that some other would now
soothe him back to happy sleep, as if war had passed
from her now and she were out of the way of battles.
These strange dark people in the north moved about
in the hard solid of the cold. Berk was quiet now,
resting from his telling. Her thought played back
over what he had told; one child had died and Dah-
sing and his brothers were seen making a small
funeral, laying out the child on a high scaffold among
some trees. But one day another child was born to
the woman, and thus there were again three children
in the hut.

Berk told again, having waited for a while, as if
he applied himself again to the act of telling, to
bring himself again into her thought. Then Dah-
sing's uncles and all his brothers said the stranger
had best be eaten because he was a strong man and
they had need of his strength while the cold lasted.
The cold stayed, they said, because they did not perform their duty and eat the man from the south.

" 'We will put the man from the south inside our
kettle,' they said. They met together to talk and to
smoke their pipe. Then I said to Dah-sing, 'The cold
comes from the north,' and he said he knew that to
be the truth. I made it clear I did not bring the

cold there. But the brothers and the uncles listened
to their own talk and they made mischief in the
council-house. They told of old customs and of the
law that had been kept in former times. No cold of
such a nature had ever come there before. It was a
spell, they said. It was a sign. They had lost the power
of their fathers. They wanted to go back to the ways
of the ancients. Dah-sing would come in to me to
tell all of a day, whilst the light lasted. . . ."

Diony stood erect in her place, her act a protest
against these dark men in the council-hut. She said
nothing, for her tongue was stiff in her mouth and
her words were dull and powerless in her throat. She
stood leaned slightly forward, looking across the well
lit floor, ready to hear of this new peril. Berk spoke
again then:

"I asked Shaub if it was a common custom there
to eat the flesh of men and she said not in her memory, but in the memory of her grandmother it had
been done. There was a great immense kettle that was
never brought indoors. It was this pot was used for
it . . ."

Diony cried a dull cry then, and she shifted in her
place, moving a step forward, seeing too clearly into
the north and seeing these dark men in the council-
house passing their opinions up and down, hunger
driving them to make a ceremony to fit their slaugh-

ter. She looked toward Berk then in silence and he began to speak again, addressing all that he said now only to her.

"I set out forthwith to outwit Dah-sing with a new dream, to keep my flesh and my bones outside of the kettle. I stayed in the lodge where Shaub kept and I would not go out into their sight whilst they were of this evil mind towards me. Three came to me there and I stood up before the three. I stood always as much as my head and shoulders above all that race. I stood up in the lodge over their heads."

He stood up in the floor now, before the hearth, facing Diony, but the wide space of the floor was between. "I said to them, my hand in their faces like this, my finger out, said, 'You will not put me in your kettle, you brown son-of-the-devil. I belong,' I said, 'to the Long Knives. Iffen you never heard it said what kind they are, you better go find out. You put me in your kettle and you'll not eat one bite of my strength. You'll eat ne'er a thing but my weak part and you'll breed weakness in your bones. Iffen you don't learn better ways to make strength,' I says, 'you are all doomed and you'll all go in the kettle of some better kind. You leave me be,' I says. 'I'm not afeared of any white trash the like of you. The Shawnees couldn't put me in their pot,' I says, 'and the Shawnees are better men. When life goes outen me,' I says, 'the strong part goes too, and I take it wherever I go when I go from here. You couldn't eat one least bite of my strong part and you are all a dunce race if you think once you can.' "

Diony moved back to her place then, but she knew that while he had spoken the last she had cried out with joy and that she had half lifted her hands to him as if she would run to meet him in the air. He continued speaking, his hand lifted again:

"I says, 'When life goes outen me the strong part goes too. You couldn't eat ne'er a bit of it. Whe'r I go to heaven or whe'r I go to hell or whe'r I go no place at all, whenever I go from here my strength goes along with me. I take my strong part and you'll never get it inside your kettle and you couldn't eat it into your mouth. God,' I says, 'what a dunce race it is here, to think it could eat strength the like of that.' "

It was known now to all of them what way Diony had chosen. Berk sat still now, as if there were no need to tell more, as if he had told his way back into his home again. He mended the fire on his own account and Muir moved slightly, moving back from the hearth to let the master of the house attend to his own.

"Has the rain eased?" Muir asked, looking toward the door, listening.

"It broke away fair awhile back," Berk said. "I look for frost any night now."

"Did these people in the north, did they make e'er other move to get you inside their kettle?" Muir asked.

"No, ne'er another. I didn't represent myself as a prophet or any learned kind. But I says, 'Winter is near over. Plain sense will tell you the cold will ease away now soon. And for a fact it eased away that very night and a wind came up from the south to make you know the ice would soon rot away. I set forth to outwit Dah-sing to make him dream again. I talked a dream whilst we sat before the fire and I said again the cold would ease away. And that night, for a fact, he dreamed again."

Diony sat in her place now. The story floated far from her, or returned to her in unconnected sayings. The cold had spent its force in the north and Berk had known by the way the sun stood in the sky that spring was at hand. All were weak from the long season of little food. Spring came, and they could find the tender shoots of herbs. The melted snow made a marsh over the place where the skins were buried and they were never found. He had planted a small field of corn, for he knew that they must have grain. "To dig is a squaw's work," they said, but he said to them, "We have to eat bread until the beasts grow back into the woods."

With the first cold of the autumn, when the pelts were of a fine, firm texture, the hair rich and soft on the backs of the beasts, he had hunted again far in the north. It was a long hunt. His leaving came. He had sold the skins at Sault Sainte Marie, the trading place, and he had found there the things for his journey south. These people, Dah-sing and his woman, brought gifts to him at the moment of his going. He took these gifts now from the leather pouch at the front of his shirt. There was a turkey-call made of a deer horn. The woman had given him a few carved bones to make a game like dice.

Diony went above by the stairs Muir had built in the house, and she brought blankets and skins down and laid them beside the door on the chairs Molly Anne and Alex Harmon had used. When she had placed them there neatly folded she went back to her place and she said:

"I couldn't have any man here with me tonight, or for a long while to come maybe. I couldn't. But a long while from now, after we are eased from this night, and after Evan Muir is gone to some other place and taken all his property . . ."

She wept here, remembering Michael and knowing that he would be in part Muir's property, and knowing that she could not let him go. But she continued speaking:

"And after he is settled somewheres and is content again, then Berk would be my husband, and that is the way I would choose, as Molly Anne and Alex said the woman would choose."

The men accepted these words quietly, as words already well known to them. After a long season of stillness, Muir spoke, half whispering, "It will be as Diony would choose. Let it be."

"I will teach Michael," she said, "to know his own name and teach him to know well who his father was, and to bear respect there. And I will never be ashamed when people ask, 'How comes it you've got one named Muir in your house?' Now Evan could go to his own house on the far side of the creek where there's room a-plenty. And Berk, he could go to Molly Anne's house and ask to be let in, to sleep there. There's room there, too, up in the loft where the boys stay, and here's skins and covers enough for both."

"It's past midnight. We mought better go now," Berk said. He stood before the hearth rock. "We'd best go. Best house ourselves the way Diony has said."

Muir arose stiffly and made ready to go. "It's said the war in the tidewater is moved to the region around the York," he said. "Men that came along the Trace this week said it was well known now George Washington had got the King's army in a pocket at Yorktown."

"Where I crossed a creek today at the place where the buffalo road meets the main trace, I met a man and he said what you tell now, said General Washington had got Cornwallis shut up in the York Valley and peace would come now to the tidewater, but we couldn't look for a whole peace yet here in the west," Berk speaking.

"The King, he won't give up the part this-side the mountains . . ." Muir took his rifle from the place behind the door, and he found his supply of powder and lead.

"It's my belief the King will hurl a new strength against us and send the Indians after us again, many times more," Berk said. "It's the King's generals that send the Indians down, and you'd hardly believe what a hard time they have sometimes to make the Indians go down to war. It's curious . . . It's late now. We'd best go."

They were standing in the floor making ready to go out. Muir took one or two of the skins from those Diony had brought, and Berk took likewise.

"It's a very good house," Berk said, looking about. "But it's not the whole house I set out to build here. I'll make another part equal to this and a fine wide passage between. Another chimney . . . Room enough fitten to entertain a friend or a traveler."

They had taken their rifles and a few of the coverings and they went out at the door. Berk, walking last, looked back toward her, but in respect to Muir he said nothing and he made no sign. Their steps went off through the wet grass toward the creek and they talked as they went together.

"I look for another year of mischief," Muir said. "The forts high up toward the Ohio will likely feel the danger and strain."

"Estil's and Bryant's, up toward the north . . ." Muir speaking now.

"Up high in the cane country. But we came here to stay . . ." Berk's voice arising above the damp night, saying some further thing, asking something about the forts and their strength. Their voices were lost into an indetermined murmur and their moccasined feet were slopping in the water of the creek.

Diony put the bar across the door and made the house ready for the night. But she sat in the dim light of the last candle, sitting beside the table, leaned forward on the board. For a little while she felt that the end of an age had come to the world, a new order dawning out of the chaos that had beat through the house during the early part of the night. Her thought strove to put all in order before she lay down to sleep. She felt the power of reason over the wild life of the earth. Berk had divided the thinking part of a man from the part the Ojibways would have put into their kettle and into their mouths. The least child cried, wanting its midnight feeding, and she took it into her arms, continuing her brooding. Boone said that he was never lost, she reflected. Boone moved securely among the chaotic things of the woods and the rivers. Beyond her picture of Boone, unlost, moving among the trees, she saw Berk standing before the redmen far in the north in the dense power of the famine and the cold, crying in their faces, "You will not put me into your pot . . . Whe'r I go to heaven or whe'r I go to hell or whe'r I go nowhere at all, I take my strong part with me. . . ." The whole mighty frame of the world stood about her then, all the furniture of the earth and the sky, she a minute point, conscious, soothing the hunger of a child. Boone, she contrived, was a messenger to the chaotic part, a herald, an envoy there, to prepare it for civil men.

The last candle guttered, wasting its strength and running down into an undetermined pool of dull fat, leaving the faintly lit wick to glow. The wick stood free of the grease, erect and unsupported, making momentarily a more brilliant light before it expired. She laid the child in its cradle and rested herself on the bed, trusting herself now to the extinction of sleep.

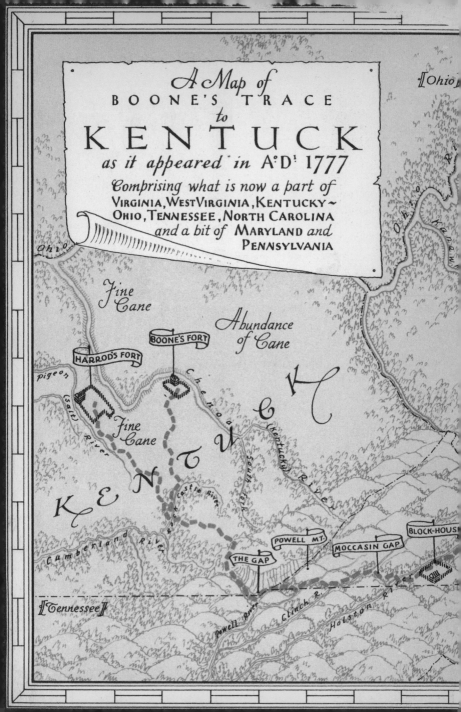